# Out of This World

## QUEER SPECULATIVE FICTION STORIES

# CATHERINE LUNDOFF

Out of This World: Queer Speculative
Fiction Stories
Catherine Lundoff
Queen of Swords Press LLC
Minneapolis, MN USA
www.queenofswordpress.com

This book is a work of fiction. Names, characters, places and incidents are products of the author's imagination. Any resemblance to real people or current events is purely coincidental.

Cover Design By: Kanaxa Design
Interior Formatting and Design by Terry Roy

ISBN 13: 978-0-9981082-3-0
Published in the United States of America

"Great Reckonings, Little Rooms" reprinted from *Time Well Bent: Queer Alternate History*. Lethe Press, 2009. Connie Wilkins, editor.

"Medium Méchanique" reprinted from *Ghosts in Gaslight, Monsters in Steam*. Minor Arcana Press/Gay Cities, 2013. Vincent Kovar and Evan J. Peterson, editors.

"The Egyptian Cat" reprinted from *Tales of the Unanticipated*. Vol. 30, 2010, Eric Heideman, editor.

"At the Roots of the World Tree" reprinted from in *Kenoma: Speculative Fiction and Myth*, edited b H.F. Gibbard. *Kenoma*, 2005.

"A Scent of Roses" reprinted from *So Fey: Queer Fairy Fiction*. Lethe Press, 2009. Steve Berman, editor.

"At Mother Laurie's House of Bliss" reprinted from *Ladies of Trade Town*. Harphaven Books, 2011. Lee Martindale, editor.

"Spell, Book and Candle" reprinted from *Khimairal Ink*, January 2008. Carrie Tierney, editor.

"Beauty" reprinted from *Zowie! It's Yaoi!*. Running Press, 2006. Marilyn Jaye Lewis, editor.

"Red Scare" reprinted from *Simulacrum*, Vol. 1 (2). January 2004. Lynne Jamneck, editor.

"A Day at the Inn, A Night at the Palace" reprinted from *A Day at the Inn, A Night at the Palace and Other Stories*. Lethe Press, 2011.

"Vadija" reprinted from *Such a Pretty Face: Tales of Power and Abundance*. Meisha Merlin, 2000. Lee Martindale, editor.

## Eleven tales of the queer fantastic by award-winning author Catherine Lundoff

Journey to distant planets, encounter angry ghosts, go on a quest for the Norns and meet Shakespeare's sister, Judith on your way to finding joy. Vampires, swordswomen, witches, the Queen of the Fay and even the occasional gentleman of the evening populate stories rich and strange.

## What reviewers are saying

"There is everything from steampunk horror to hard-boiled alien invasion to magical police procedural, each story both drawing lovingly from its literary inspirations and turning them upside down."

**~Heather Rose Jones, *Alpennia***

"Among my favorites in this collection are the Gaylactic Spectrum Award finalist 'At the Roots of the World Tree,' about an inept, socially awkward clerk at a living bookstore who is forced to forestall Ragnorök, and the collection opener, 'Great Reckonings, Little Rooms.' Riffing on Virginia Woolf's famous quote about 'Shakespeare's sister' Judith, this story reads like one of Shakespeare's own plays with intrigue, crossdressing 'identical' fraternal twins, and swordplay; best of all, it finally answers the question as to who actually wrote Shakespeare's works."

**~Keith John Glaeske, *Out in Print***

"Out of This World suggests entering other worlds. The worlds Lundoff transported me to were well worth visiting, and the distinctive voices of the characters drew me into their stories.

**~Sacchi Green**

# Introduction

OUT OF THIS WORLD ENCOMPASSES a decade plus of my fantastical work, everything from a steampunk ghost story to an alternate history to a fantastical mystery to a bit of yaoi with vampires. I included a couple of stories from my out of print collection, A Day at the Inn, A Night at the Palace and Other Stories, but everything else is from other publications, some of which have been unavailable for a number of years. Why did I pick what I picked? By and large, I chose my own favorite stories that featured lesbian, bi, gay or queer protagonists. I also included several stories that were fan favorites and a couple that were both. Unlike my earlier book, my historical stories are not featured here since those will be collected along with some new stories in a later volume.

Why "queer" speculative fiction? I've always enjoyed exploring fantastic worlds in a variety of genres. At the same time, writing protagonists who are lesbian, bisexual, gay or somehow queer-identified is very important to me, as a bi/queer-identified writer. We need to be able to see ourselves as heroes and villains, gods and monsters, knights and wizards and fair ladies and dragons and all the points in between.

I began writing at a time when LGBTQ protagonists were in decline, when it was harder to find our voices and perspectives in speculative fiction. The small presses and independent, feminist and/or LGBTQ bookstores and distributors were far more receptive, in general, than the larger publishers and chains to including queer voices and queer protagonists in their line up. While that changes from time to time, depending on cultural trends, it's challenging for many older queer writers who are not already published by large presses to break in or to break back in after a career hiatus. It's even harder now as larger publishers consolidate and merge and smaller indie and queer specialty publishers and bookstores close. The same is true for new voices, less well known writers looking to find their places and voices in the field.

So that is why I decided to take a leap of faith into the fabulous world of small press publishing. I am grateful for the opportunity to publish sfnal work that I want to read, my own as well as other voices in the future. Out of This World is the first book from Queen of Swords Press, a project that has been several years in gestation while I wrangled my way through the planning stages to get to the point of actually producing books. For now, those books will be my own, but I look forward to publishing books by other authors, more books, new books, new stories, reprinting old favorites and most important of all, entertaining readers. I hope that this will be the first of many volumes from Queen of Swords Press that you will be inclined to pick up and read. Thank you.

**Catherine Lundoff**

# Contents

# Great Reckonings, Little Rooms

## Act 1, Scene 1

THE YOUNG MAN RUBBED THE sparse curling hairs on his chin as if their bristles pained him somewhat and sighed as he put his quill back in the ink. The page before him was no less blank than it had been before the sigh so the sound brought him nothing more than the not unwelcome attention of his companion.

She rose from the bed where she reclined and walked toward him, her stride sinuous and seductive under her layers of skirts and bodice. As the light from the window fell on her face, she was not beautiful as beauty is commonly reckoned. No fair English rose here, pale of skin and blonde of hair. Instead she was dark, her complexion the deep olive of the Mediterranean ports, her hair the thick coarse black curls of an Italian peasant. Her lips were full, thick even, and her nose suggested a trace of Jewish blood.

Yet she was beautiful if one had the wit to see it. Her eyes were large and dark and luminous with intelligence, her teeth good and her figure fulsome and promising a glorious bounty to any lover who might strike her fancy. She reached his side before he had time to admire her further and leaned over to wrap her arms around his shoulders.

He closed his eyes and smiled as her lips caressed his neck lightly. His smile widened as her hand slipped down the front of his tunic but he stopped it before it could go further. She pouted at his gesture and snatched a book from the pile on the edge of the table, whirling away laughing.

A step on the stair cut short some of her merriment until a familiar knock sounded at the door. "It's Kit, come to lift your spirits, love!" The dark beauty smiled again as she swept the door open to admit their visitor.

The young man's frown was gone an instant before the man in the doorway might have seen it but somehow, he seemed to know it had been there. Christopher Marlowe swept into the room, a smile that barely reached his eyes twisting his lips. "Not pleased to see me, friend? But then," he caught the volume from the woman's hand, "you're hard at work on your Plautus, I see." He dropped into the chair in front of the table, his sharp gaze missing neither the pile of books or the blank page.

"Come to spy on my progress, eh Kit?" The young man gave his friend a rueful smile that took the edge from his words.

"I had hoped to find you at work on another play. Another play writ anonymously that might catch Henslowe's eye perhaps. Some light fair like your 'Comedy of Errors.' We are all a bit hungrier from the plague." Marlowe's lips twisted in a grimace. "And I myself have little touch for comedy."

"Ah, but your tragedies are for the ages, are they not? And we may all be a bit hungrier but you and Kyd and my brother, you mean. Would that I had the Lord Chamberlain's men speaking my words on stage for a fortnight!" The young man smiled up at the dark temptress at his side and kissed her hand.

The door swung open again, causing them all to start as another young man entered without knocking. This one's countenance was alike to the first's as two peas but for the ferocious scowl he wore and a more fulsome beard. "Hello, Will," murmured the young man at the table.

Kit's smile turned darker, something malicious in it now. "The one and only Shake-scene himself," he murmured.

The scowling man's frown deepened and he responded with a string of oaths that made the playwright laugh. The young woman in contrast, slipped behind the young man's chair. Will gave her a look of pure, frustrated longing before turning his furious glare on the others. "Still playing at being the man, Judith?" He snarled, his gaze locking with that of the seated young man.

The victim of his attack arched an eyebrow and stood with a graceful, catlike stretch. "Would you have me play whore to your poet instead, brother? Or mere muse? These are not roles that I desire."

Once the young man stood, the light caught his face. The contrast picked out the slight delicacy of his features but nothing more suggested femininity. At least not before the other stepped forward so their faces were closer. "Must it be whore then, sister? Surely you might have stayed at home and married a butcher or an innkeeper. Being in foal would look well on you." Will smiled cruelly as the blank page caught his eye. He glanced up to meet Judith's eyes, knowing how his words would sting, how unlikely it was that any man in Stratford-on-Avon would have her even if she wanted them.

"Careful brother, or you'll turn out to be all that Master Chettle had to say of you, the foul as well as the fair." Judith's lips twisted as her gaze challenged his. How had they come to this, they who had once been as close friends as brother and sister could be? She forced the thought from her face. He must never know how his blows struck home.

Will turned away a moment, shoulders stiff. Then he turned back a breath or two later, stance switching from combatant to orator. Years of acting smoothed away all but the calmest and most pleasant of his expressions. He bowed as if entering the room for the first time, "I shall begin again. Good day, Master Marlowe, Mistress Emilia, sister. I came not to dispense strife, though it comes on my heels, but rather to invite you, one and all to see my poor self appear in a new play of my own devising some days hence."

Kit raised an eyebrow and smiled. "Harlequin and Columbine, perhaps?"

Will gave a genuine laugh, hearty and deep. "It would please you to hear that, wouldn't it, Kit-cat? But no, I must disappoint here as elsewhere." His glance caught Emilia's for a moment. "I am to appear in a fine tragedy, that of *Titus Andronicus*. And it would please me if you were to attend, that afterward we might raise an ale to my new work. That is, if you can do so without being poisoned by jealousy." He favored his sister and Marlowe with an ironic smile.

"I…cannot, Will. But I hope that it may bring you glory." Emilia smiled, only her hands twisting together behind Judith's chair to suggest her agitation. She caught up her cloak and made for the door, but not before Will stepped in front of her and laid his hand on her arm.

"Though your eyes are nothing like the sun, Mistress, yet I would have them look on me kindly. In friendship for better times to come, at least, if the past is not enough." Emilia flinched as Judith surged to her feet and leapt forward only to be stayed by Marlowe's tight grip. Her eyes looked everywhere except at Will for a moment. Then she gave him a tremulous smile and the slightest of nods. A tear shone on her cheek. With a deft twist of her wrist, she broke free and vanished from the room.

Marlowe watched her leave, a strange look crossing his face. He whispered, "Was this the face that launched a thousand ships?" as the door closed but the other two paid no attention to him.

Will stared at the closing door as Judith relaxed in Kit's grip. She spat her words. "Ill done, brother. She loves where her heart goes and you cannot force it elsewhere."

"Put the pretty words to verse, sister and we'll publish it abroad for a shilling or two in my own name. But for now say you will come to my play and see how it is done." He smiled mockingly, then taking their silence for assent, turned on his heel and left without a word of farewell.

Judith slammed her open palm against the chair and bit off an oath before it could leave her lips. Would that she'd been born the man, not Will! The thought rankled her as it had since they were children.

Still, before there was Emilia, Will had been her friend for all that. They had sat together inventing tales and speaking lines for characters of their own invention since Will had taught her to read and write. Each had written poetry of their own but their first plays they had written together. Two minds as one. So of course, when they loved, they must needs love alike.

"I'd say give the girl up, but it's too late for that, isn't it?" Marlowe asked the question in an indifferent tone. He shrugged when she said nothing and gestured at the page. "Can you compose without your brother as muse? Or might another do as well?"

Judith bit her lip and was silent, wondering if Kit was suggesting himself as a replacement. The idea was very nearly too overwhelming to contemplate; the author of *Tamburlaine* offering his patronage to her! Or did he mean something else? No matter, she needed his help, in whatever guise it came. After a long moment, she nodded hesitantly, hoping with all her heart that she did not lie. With that fear uppermost, she pulled a page from beneath the pile of books and handed it to Kit.

He walked under the window and read it, frowning. Then he nodded once and handed it back. "We'll make a writer of you yet, little Jude. Only but finish it, and you'll hear the Chamberlain's Men speak your words as well as any other."

Judith let out a breath she hadn't known she was holding. Marlowe did not give compliments lightly; the work was good. Perhaps she might succeed without Will's help as long as she could play the man.

Kit continued, "Now, I'm off to Deptford to meet with some that I know. A small errand for my other master, the one who is no muse.

Come with me and we will raise a mug, there or in better company. You shall be Will as well as any other, at least for today. Nay, better for you are not an angry man in love but a happy lad. Of a sort." Kit smiled, his eyes warming, his charm more than any mortal heart could withstand.

She hesitated, still wondering what Kit really wanted. He kept her secrets and praised her work, even stood her meals from time to time in the months since she had come to London but asked little in return. Perhaps it was nothing more than a desire to be a thorn in Will's side, perhaps only the novelty of tricking the world around them. But if she did not trust him, she had no one else to play the part of brother, not as long as Emilia loved her and not Will. Whatever he wanted from her, she needed him.

Dismissing her misgivings, Judith smiled back as the playacting aspects of such an expedition began to appeal to her. Why should she not be Will for a few hours? She could imitate him so well as to be his shadow; she had done it enough since they were striplings, she should have no trouble doing it now. "Gentle Kit, I would not decline such an invitation were there twenty brothers betwixt us. Let us away to Deptford and the Moor's net." She caught up her belt with its sheathed dagger and fastened it around her doublet. Marlowe bowed, his expression sardonic, as he ushered her out.

# Act 1, Scene 2

Lincoln's Inn at Deptford was as like to any other house of its nature as might be: neither fish nor fowl, it was at once neither a public house nor yet merely a home. The innkeeper, one Mrs. Bull, let rooms to some who asked and served ale to many, yet she picked and chose her guests as carefully as she chose her ale and those who drank there often served several masters.

The Queen's spymaster, Sir Francis Walsingham, called "The Moor" for his dark complexion, had known many of the men who drank Mrs. Bull's ale. His ghostly hand lay heavy on the place, for all that he had been dead these three years past. The men who had served him as well as those who came after him worked in both light and shadow, their eyes missing little and their hands at once bloodstained and light-fingered.

This, then was the company that young Judith Shakespeare encountered when she came to Deptford with her friend Kit Marlowe. But she was not as concerned with the men who watched her as she was with walking as Will would walk, meeting their stares as he would. A sharp-eyed well dressed fellow hailed Kit from a corner table when they entered. "Marcade! Come here!"

"Mercury?" The nickname as well as the command made Judith raise an eyebrow despite her best intentions to keep her features still and impassive. But the fellow was handsome, near blindingly so and Kit had an eye for handsome lads.  She stifled a shrug as she trailed after him.

The seated man pulled the playwright down for a hearty kiss on the cheek before his cold, clear gaze fell on her. His expression shifted to something tigerish. "Did you bring your catamite here to parade him before me? Do you plan to govern me through my baser lusts, little Kit-cat?" The words were said softly but with an undertone of menace that sent a chill up her spine.

Kit laughed, the sound cutting through the dark layers in the other's tone. He laid a hand on the man's shoulder and grinned back at Judith. "Nay, sweet Tom! I am not such a simpleton as that, though who loves not boys and tobacco is a fool, as I have said before. Yet I know what I have. I give you not my catamite but my rival, Will Shakespeare, whose words are all the talk of London."

"I thought Shakespeare to be older, more manly." The seated man, who Judith realized could be no other than Tom Walsingham, Marlowe's patron and lover and the Moor's own nephew, raked her with a sharp glance. "Not a stripling like this one. He seems as real as your Dutch coin, Kit."

"One man may play many parts on the stage as in the world, my lord," Judith stepped forward with a graceful gesture. "And be as real in one as in any of the others." She gave him one of Will's most charming smiles, the one he wore to calm powerful men who might do him more harm than good.

Walsingham gave her another sharp glance, then nodded. "Well, he has a way with his words, like enough to the one you say he is. Here, make room for my friend Kit and his friend Will." This last command was delivered to the others at the table, one of whom gave Judith an evil look but moved aside nonetheless.

There was something in the fellow's ill-favored countenance, particularly the way he looked at Kit, which had her hand hovering above the dagger on her belt for a breath or two. His pockmarked face nearly burned green in jealous rage whenever Tom looked kindly upon the playwright. She wondered how Kit could bear it.

Yet the moment passed and soon she sat and spoke with Tom and Kit, raising a mug or two of ale until her spirits grew higher than they had in the last fortnight. But Tom's other companions, Poley and Frizer as they were called, cast a pall upon her spirits with their sidelong glances of ill will directed at Kit and soon, at her as well.

Kit plainly thought little of them, the proof in his disdainful manner and after a time, Judith took her cue from him. At first, she mocked them lightly, teasing them about their scowls and their graces. But the atmosphere of ill will did not shift. Finally, the ale loosened her tongue more than she had intended and she met Frizer's eyes with a fierce glare of her own. "Fellow, your looks are foul enough to sour good ale. Your manners mark you as churlish a cur as I have ever met. Have you fair wit or words to balance them?"

Tom laughed and Kit's lips curled in an amused grimace, though his frown sent her a quick warning. By then, it was too late. Frizer lurched to his feet, hand on his knife, and Poley caught his arm. He shook Poley off as he hissed, "Codpiece sniffing sodomite! Are you a heretic as well?" He jerked his chin at Kit. "Don't be in such a hurry to welcome your master below." With that, he turned on his heel and left.

This time it was Kit who laughed. "Am I heretic now? Such is the price of loyal service!" He glanced at Tom, his expression angry and wary all at once yet Tom was silent. His expression told Judith nothing but Kit must have found some comfort in his face because his posture relaxed somewhat.

Poley stood and announced that he must leave for other errands. He slipped away so quietly the others scarcely noticed his departure. Judith gave Kit a worried frown. A charge of sodomy was ill enough; to add heresy to it meant a trip to the executioner's block if it were proven. Or if you had no protection. She wondered if Tom would stand by him if the worst happened.

But no more was said. They drank more ale, debating the best of the new plays until Kit and Tom began to discuss philosophy and Judith fell silent. Her education had been slipshod, gleaned from the pickings of her brother's learning since their father saw no need for a girl to know such things. Still, it was fascinating and she absorbed all she could, Frizer and Poley forgotten in the flow of words until it was time for them to return to their rooms.

# ACT 2, SCENE 1

JUDITH DIDN'T SEE THE BILL posted on the church wall until three days after her night in Deptford. She was coming from the printer's office where she had pled her case for the publishing of a new play, not yet finished, when it caught her eye. The first few lines were a spiteful piece of venom accusing the Dutch of treachery and cowardice in their war with Spain, causing brave English soldiers to die in their stead. She might have ignored it but for the signature: Tamburlaine.

That was enough to make her stop and read it through. The play had been Kit's masterwork, the one that her brother and Kyd and all the other playwrights sought to emulate. It could be no accident that the name appeared on this document.

But had Kit written it himself? She scanned the verses; it seemed too clumsy for his hand, despite the touches that suggested his skill. And what had he to do with the Dutch? There was no connection as far as she knew, save what Tom had said of "Dutch coin." But she could make no sense of that so perhaps it was nothing, the words some private jest between the two. She turned away, trying to convince herself of that.

The words nagged at her though, filling her thoughts until she found herself at Kit's rooms some hours later. He should know of this, even if it had naught to do with him. At least he might be on his guard if something more lay beyond the verses than simple malice.

But he was not to be found at his room and the landlord sent her on to Tom Walsingham's lodgings. They too were deserted. A servant there said that his master had gone to the country and that Master Marlowe might have gone with him. He would say no more and Judith had no coin with which to press her case. She turned reluctantly from the house and walked home.

Emilia was waiting for her there, having stolen a few hours from her husband's side. She forgot the poem and Kit and even her brother in her lover's body.

The next few days passed quickly. She wrote and read what she had written to Emilia. She saw Will's new play and found the words to praise it. He glowed a bit, almost as he had before Emilia came between them. She wondered if he would find that glow of goodwill sufficient to read her new play, but she decided to wait. She would show it to Kit first. Whenever he reappeared.

# ACT 2, SCENE 2

WHEN TWO MORE DAYS PASSED without word, she could stand it no longer. She left her room that afternoon to walk to Deptford. It took some time to make the journey, which gave her ample time for thought.

She could not have said why she went now, except that there were rumors about the flyers that she'd seen, rumors that mentioned Kit. And Thomas Kyd had been arrested and charged with heresy, or so the whispers said. True, Kyd was no friend of hers and she liked his stiff prose little enough. But he was a friend of Kit's and if the charge fell on one, it might well fall on another. The thought chilled her

For this expedition, she had added more hair to her chin with an actor's art, forcing her face into a near mirror of Will's. It might give her extra protection on the street or in the inn if she appeared older, fiercer. She remembered Frizer's rage and shivered with no ale to warm her against it. Still, she must know what had happened to Kit; surely he could not have moved permanently to the country. It would prove too dull for such as he.

The inn was where she remembered it and the men at the tables were much the same. But this time she entered cautiously, searching for Mrs. Bull and whatever information she could provide and meeting few men's eyes. The common room was near to empty in any case so there were few enough to see her. She crept to the kitchen, then waited while the kitchen boy fetched the landlady.

When she finally appeared, her sharp black eyes studied Judith as if she was some new specimen, an exotic creature wafted in from far off lands. Judith stammered her questions and Mrs. Bull merely looked at her for a few moments. When at last she spoke, her voice was thick with unvoiced amusement. "One of Master Marlowe's friends, are you? Odd that he'd not have told you where he might be going if he was leaving London."

That lent steel to Judith's backbone. "I'm merely here to deliver a message and his landlord said I might find him here. It's all the same to me whether he drinks your ale or another's." She drew herself up and gave the other woman her haughtiest look.

Mrs. Bull made a dry sound like bones rattling that might have been a chuckle. "I'll not be telling tales of Master Marlowe but if he's to come here, it will be with Master Walsingham after sunset. Spend your coin here or elsewhere until then." The innkeeper shrugged and turned back to the kitchen, leaving Judith in the doorway.

She accepted her dismissal reluctantly, turning away to peer out the window at the murky sky outside. It was hard to tell when darkness would fall but it could not much longer, surely. She groped in her pouch for coin and found a scant few shillings. Just enough to buy her ale and a bowl of stew, even here.

Taking a deep breath, Judith slipped onto an empty bench in a dark corner and beckoned a servant. Food and drink arrived soon after and Judith bent her head to the task of eating, only looking up when the door swung open for those entering and leaving. It seemed like an eternity though the food was good. Men came and went but none were Kit or Walsingham.

At last she was done eating and drinking and had no more coin to allow her to linger. She stood slowly and made her way to the door in time for it to swing open, leaving her face to face with Frizer. He recognized her instantly, despite the extra beard she had carefully applied. The scent of beer hung over him like a cloud. "It's another sodomite heretic! 'Tis our lucky day, Poley. The Privy Council will pay well for this one too, I think." He herded Judith back into the room with an evil smile.

Poley and another man followed at his heels, the former giving her a glance of pure contempt. There would be little help from that quarter, she realized. Her brain spun with ideas for escape at the same time that she wrestled with his words. The Privy Council? Was Kit in the Tower?

Frizer's grip on her shoulder tightened, driving her fears for Kit from her head for the moment. He fumbled for the knife at his belt, eyes glowing with drunken bloodlust. She summoned anger as a shield. "Devil take thee, cur! What do you mean by laying your hands on me?" She twisted sharply and jumped back a pace or two, causing her assailant to stumble into the room, releasing her. Her hand was on her own knife but she didn't unsheathe it yet. There might yet be time to end this with words, before her clumsiness with a blade was revealed.

Frizer's unknown companion caught him as he staggered sideways and shoved him toward a table. Poley stepped close to Judith, overwhelming her with the stale scent of his breath. "Begone, little whoreson. Your protector is going to burn and Ingram will sink his knife in your belly if you stay. And that would be a waste of good steel." He tossed her roughly toward the door as Frizer lurched to his feet, bellowing.

Judith fled, raucous laughter pursuing her onto the streets of Deptford. She ran as if pursued by demons, fleet-footed and unassailed for the safety of her room. When she reached it, she slammed the door behind her, her heart racing as she gasped for air and locked the night out. She berated herself for cowardice until she could stay awake no longer. Then she collapsed on the bed, falling eventually into a night of ill dreams, haunted by fearful visions of Kit on the block and her own shamefaced return to her father's home in Stratford or worse.

# Act 3, Scene 1

THE NEXT TWO NIGHTS SHE passed playing a lad on stage in one of the plays that Lord Strange's company was staging. There was still no word from Kit and she began to fear that he was already dead.

On the third day, Will came to see her just before she left for the theater. "I bring you joy of the play, sister. You are as fine a lad as ever tread the boards, myself excepted." He bowed with a flourish and Judith laughed despite her worries.

"Thank you for your kindness, brother. You have been many a fine lad so this is praise indeed. On another point before I must leave, have you had word of Kit?"

Will gave her an impish grin and flourished a grubby bit of paper at her. "Not from Kit but from one close to him."

She took the note, reading and rereading it in increasing bewilderment. "What does this mean?"

Will snorted at her slow wit. "It is an invitation to dine with a powerful man whose patronage can only advance my plays. Surely your foolish jealousy cannot blind you to the advantages of such a relationship?"

"But Will, Tom is Kit's patron and—"

"Perhaps he seeks a better playwright. No, say no more, little sister. I understand that you would stand a friend to Kit but I cannot, nay will not decline such an opportunity."

Judith remembered Tom's cold face when the words "sodomite" and "heretic" were spoken and shivered. He would let Kit go the block or the flames and acquire a new protégé. Still she tried what she could to dissuade Will, but it was no use and she had to leave for the theater. When she returned, she longed for Emilia to come but her beloved remained as absent as Kit. She passed another restless night in frightening dreams, filled with the premonition of ills to come.

The next morning, Judith was awakened by a familiar knock at the door shortly after dawn. Heart pounding, she rose, tugging on a doublet and picking up her knife as she moved to stand by the door. Hand on the heavy oak, she asked, "Kit?"

"Open the door, little one. I'm here alone." Kit's voice, certainly but in a voice that sounded too feeble to be his own.

Judith hesitated a moment, then unbarred the door. Kit stood on the other side, covered in blood, his eyes red and his hands trembling. She recoiled backward, giving him room to enter.

He lurched inside, sinking onto the bed with a quiet groan. Now that he was out of the darkened hall, she could see the marks of torture on him: bruises and cuts too systematic to be the natural result of a fall.

It wrung her heart and she fetched a pitcher of water to wash him clean. He said nothing while she ministered to his wounds, only the hiss of his breath to tell her when something hurt more that it should.

At last, she held a mug of flat beer to his lips and let him lie back on her bed. He closed his eyes and his body went slowly limp as he fell asleep. She looked down at him, frowning for a long moment. But it seemed cruel to wake him merely to satisfy her curiosity; any danger he brought to her door might have found her by other means anyway.

Instead she barred the door again then moved to her chair and table, taking up her quill as she gnawed on a piece of bread. She had been thinking of a play that revolved around twin brothers, not unlike Will and her. The point scratched busily on the page before her as the plot took shape.

# Act 3, Scene 2

She had written a nearly an entire act when Kit finally sat up with a groan and dropped his head into his hands. Judith stood and stretched, her back and hands stiff from her labors, before she spoke. "What happened, Kit? I looked for you everywhere, even in Deptford."

Kit looked up, eyes sharp in his alarmed face. "You went back there looking for me? Did anyone see you?"

Judith shuddered at the memory of Frizer's furious eyes. "That cur who drank with us when we went there, Frizer. And Poley. Frizer tried to draw his blade on me but was too far in his cups. I ran…ran as fast as I could from the place." She hung her head, cheeks burning under her beard. A real man would have stayed to fight. She waited for Marlowe's scorn.

Kit swore, a string of colorful oaths falling from his cut lips. Then he laughed quietly. "They say that he stumbles who runs fastest, yet I'm glad to hear that you eluded the blade so that you might stand friend to me today. As to Frizer, he is a dangerous dog. I advise you to run swiftly away whenever you may see him next." He closed his eyes again.

"Were you in the Tower, Kit? I heard tales of the Privy Council, of charges of heresy." Judith waited but Kit was silent, his face turned toward the floor. When she could stand it no longer, she spoke again. "Will told me yesterday that he intended to steal your patron Walsingham away but since you are here and free, I can see that this is not so." She attempted to laugh lightly but the sound died away when she saw Kit's face. "What is it?"

Kit stood, swaying a little and walked to her table, murmuring softly, "What further mischief is this? What did he say?" He frowned, his face flushing until Judith was well and truly frightened.

"It was an invitation to dine with…Tom Walsingham in Deptford. But the note did not seem as if he had written such a thing. I tried to persuade Will but he would hear nothing of it. Is Will in some danger, Kit?" She caught his sleeve. "Is it the Privy Council or something else?"

Kit's eyes were wild and he pulled a scrap of a note from his doublet. "A note like this one?

Judith stared and nodded. "Whence came this to you, Kit?"

"My jailor gave it to me as he opened the door of my cell. I think we must go and find Will. I do not like this, little Jude; it is not Tom's way to commit more to the page than he must." He paused, seeming to gather his thoughts, "But first, we must disguise me. My looks are not popular on the streets today. Have you still your skirts and maiden's garb?"

# Act 3, Scene 3

It was but the work of a short hour to make Kit into a plain but believable maid. Judith laughed a bit to see him in her old gown and even he began to smile a bit at last. When all was complete, they left to go in search of Will.

But he was not to be found at any of his usual haunts and Judith was struck with a terrible fear. She ached inside, empty of the weight of her brother in her heart for the first time in many years. Kit stumbled at her side, cutting into her thoughts, and she reached out to steady him as if he were a maid in truth. He was exhausted, the dark circles under his eyes making them glitter feverishly in contrast to his white face.

She caught his arm and turned them to walk back to her room just as a coach rattled across the street before them and stopped. Tom Walsingham's sharp-featured face met her gaze impassively from the interior before he swung the door open without a word.

Judith looked to Kit for guidance but found none. He was spent, his complexion grey with pain and effort. She wrapped her arm around his waist and hauled him forward, pulling him into the coach with Tom's help. She followed and Tom signaled to the driver to start up again. He studied Kit in his skirts for a long moment, lips curled in an odd smile. But his expression still held a ghost of tenderness, which helped to reassure her; he might save Kit yet.

Finally he turned to her. "I am astonished to find you here, Master Shakespeare. I had had other news of you that suggested I might not find you in this life again." Judith stiffened but he continued before she could say anything else. "I am glad to see that it is otherwise with you."

"What is it you know, my lord? Do you have some word of my broth…" She caught herself a moment too late.

"A brother? Faith! That would explain it then. I fear I have ill news for you, Master Shakespeare but let us only reach the inn and see what is to be done before we speak more."

Judith stared at him, her mind awhirl with horror and misgiving. Then Kit moaned as the wheels hit a hole and they both turned to him, Tom pulling his cape from his shoulders and tucking it around him. "Poor boy. I would that I could have taken this hurt from you," he murmured. He pulled Kit's head to his shoulder but would say no more until the coach began to lurch its way into Deptford.

The Lincoln Inn looked much the way it had when Judith had fled it last. This time however, Frizer and Poley emerged to meet the coach. Frizer's eyes shifted guiltily under Walsingham's hard stare and he stammered his words a bit. "We thought it a game, my lord. We thought that to teach the young gamecock a lesson while we carried out your other orders…my lord, he drew his blade first. We wrestled for it—" He stopped as Judith threw herself out of the coach, his jaw agape as if he was seeing a ghost.

She shoved her way past him and dashed into the inn. Mrs. Bull caught her eye and pointed silently upstairs. She reached the landing as if she had wings. There she tried each door until she found the one she sought. Tom and Kit followed on her heels until all three stood over a corpse that might have been Judith's own, but for some thickness of the frame, some weight about the jaws.

Judith dropped to her knees, sobbing hysterically and Tom closed the door as she wailed, "It was meant to be me. I insulted them, me, not Will!"

"And I believe that it was meant to be me, was it not, sweet Tom?" Kit's voice was like cold water on her grief and she sat up, tears still pouring down her face. "You feared that I might speak under the Council's caresses and betray you, did you not? Your curs without were to lure me here and slay me alone but they thought to rid themselves of another annoyance as well. Is it not so, sweet Tom?"

Kit and Tom faced each other over Will's bloody body, staring at each other as if there was no corpse between them. Kit's face was nearly as pale as Will's but his eyes were steady. In the end, it was Tom who dropped his gaze first. "I cannot stand against a heresy charge, Marcade. Not that and…the other. I would be sent to the block."

"And if it twere merely my own life?" Kit spoke swiftly, his pain touching each word.

Tom flinched, looking at Judith for the first time since he entered. "Know that I am sorry. He was never meant to die." Judith glared back at him, shaking with fury and reaction. "Still," he continued as if there was nothing more to be said, "this may yet be put to good account."

"I have lost my truest friend!" Judith shouted, lurching to her feet, right hand fumbling for the hilt of her blade. Kit stepped between her and Tom, placing his hands on her shoulders. She struggled with him a moment and he pressed her to him in a tight embrace, holding her until she went limp, body shuddering.

Then Kit turned back to Tom. "You have killed me as well as Will. I cannot stay here with a price on my head. England's theaters may never recover from it. What good account can you make of slaying the future?"

Tom frowned. "Hear my thoughts, gentle sirs. Kit must die, either here or on the block. The Queen's justice demands his blood for his crimes against God and nature. Therefore, Christopher known as Marlowe dies here this day in Deptford." He gestured at Will's body. "The plays may be written in France or Italy as well as here. Will yet stands before us and he has his brother's way with words. He can be your voice in England, Marcade."

Judith slumped against Kit's shoulder, knowing it was the only way to save him. Then it was left only for coin to cross a few palms, enough to say that one Christopher Marlowe, atheist and blaspheming heretic, poet and playwright, had died that day. The witnesses were called, their testimony taken. And by then, Judith and Kit had been dismissed, sent home where her despair would not confuse the telling of the tale.

# ACT 4, SCENE 1

KIT STOOD STARING OUT THE window, a small sack of his goods packed for a journey at his feet. "Well, little Judith, it seems there are just two of us left now to make one good playwright." He said at last. "And I think I must call you Will to grow accustomed to the name in my mouth."

He stared out onto the surrounding roofs for a long moment before he turned back to face her.

She sniffled once or twice more, then rubbed her face with the back of her hand. She found her voice with an effort. "But I have no gift for tragedy."

"Nor I for comedy."

"And the sonnets? What of those?"

Kit reached over and caught up a page from the pile on the table. He studied it a moment and his lips quirked in a wry smile. "I think that together we might manage. The new play?" He reached out a hand to accept the handful of pages she held out.

"But what of your own plays, your own poems, Kit?"

"I am dead, little Will who was Judith. What use have dead men for such things?"

"I can sell them for you. Only give me a letter dated before this week, saying that you left them to me. I will deliver them for you and send you the coin." Judith spoke eagerly. "Think of how they will fight to publish them now that you are…dead." She faltered over the word.

Kit nodded as the idea took root. "And I will send you new tragedies from France, Italy, Spain and whatever other Popish hells I may visit ere I can return to England once more." He looked away from her to the pages in his hands. Like quicksilver, he flipped through them, even laughing aloud once or twice. "Twins, mistaken identities and the lovers reunited at the end of it all. You are in truth the one and only comic Shakespeare." He gave her a deep bow.

Judith shook her head, taking the pages back. "Merely half, Kit. And never quite whole again I think." She wiped her cheek again, picked up her quill and began to write.

# Medium Méchanique

I DID NOT KNOW THE OTHERS seated around the table, their faces dim in the flickering of the gaslight. Since we had not been introduced, it would have been impossible for me, an unchaperoned, but seemingly respectable young lady, to speak to either of the two gentlemen. As for the three other women, respectable or otherwise, none met my eyes and I did not try hard to meet theirs.

So we were resigned to wait for Madame LaFarge in near silence, broken only by the soft whispers of the man and the woman who sat on my right and the occasional popping noise from the lights. These sounds were accompanied by the rustling of silk as the lady in the green dress of that fabric removed her gloves and craned her neck around to look at the room, the ceiling and, unsurprisingly, the door.

Since she was seated across the table from me, I was able to watch her fidgets unobstructed. She was clearly not respectable, or not as was judged so in Her Majesty's England of 1888, where steam-powered carriages filled London's streets, but a certain kind of woman might be killed with impunity in Whitechapel. A bit less silk, a bit less elegance, and she might have joined their numbers.

In another life, I would have wondered why she or, indeed, any of them, were here. Not everyone likes what they hear when they ask to speak with the dead, or so I had been told by those who claimed to know. I suspected that I would not. Yet I stayed. Perhaps Madame would not prove a charlatan like the others I had visited. Maybe Annabel would indeed speak to me through her tonight, saying the things I longed to hear.

I did not care if the others heard those things as well, thereby proving that I, too, was not respectable.

My thoughts turned to the chance acquaintance who had sent me here with tales of a medium who was so close to the spirit world she seemed to dwell there herself. The woman had shuddered when she spoke of Madame and her mechanical eye, until I wondered if she shuddered more at the eye than anything she claimed to have heard.

But I had not credited her talk of unknown terrors and mysterious voices. I cared only that she said that Madame was able to speak with the spirits, unlike the others I had seen. That was enough for me.

My quest had brought me here to these shabby rented rooms near the Thames. I could smell the river from my chair, its scent roaming the city streets as it rode the back of the ever-present fog. They had said that the fog would vanish when all the open fires were replaced with engines and steam, but so far, that had not proved the case. The air remained thick whenever the air was still, though it did not settle for days at a time, as it had when Annabel and I each arrived here by our separate paths. How long ago that seemed!

It must have shown on my face: that terrible longing, the pain that I could barely endure. The lady on my left side reached over to squeeze my hand and broke her silence to murmur something, a phrase that might have been comfort. Or something else entirely. I summoned a tremulous smile of thanks, but gave only a cursory glance at her aging face beneath its black veil. It was not her I had come to see.

That was the moment when Madame LaFarge entered the room, and with her came the chill of purest winter, though the weather outside was autumnal and mild. I felt the cold run so deep run through me that I feared that I might never move again. Not the pure clean cold of a winter's sleigh ride this, but a freeze that made me think of one of Dante's Hells. Or the grave.

The lady on my left withdrew her hand to press it to her mouth, holding back the exclamation that she was too well bred to utter. Madame turned her head, shifting her mechanical eye one way, then the other, as she watched our faces. The maid following at her heels turned up the gas stove in the corner, then turned down the gaslights, casting the room into shadow before she left. All the while, Madame's mechanical eye whirred with a life all its own, glowing pale blue in its Stygian depths.

If I had been able to command my limbs, I might have screamed and fled. I, who had spoken out for women's suffrage before an angry mob, I who was able to face the death of my heart's companion and the ignominy of being cast from my father's house and yet survive, nearly fell captive to my own terrors. But what would Annabel think of me, if indeed she could see me at all?

And Annabel seeing me, to one extent or another, was why I had come. I twisted my hands together until my knuckles ached under the worn kid of my gloves, fighting for control. To distract myself, I thought about the small pistol in my clutch, brought for defense, or for afterward, when this medium failed as the others had before her. I had decided that when that happened, there would be no more need for defense or mediums.

But perhaps she would not fail. I risked another glance at her face.

Madame had a human eye to accompany the other, its muddy brown rendering it nearly invisible when contrasted to the whirring gears and spectral glow of its mate. Yet when it met mine, I found it in me to shudder. This was the eye of a woman who saw beyond the world we dwell in, a woman who knew the spirit world the way an ordinary mortal might know her garden.

In that moment, I wanted to believe most fervently in Madame LaFarge's powers. In that moment, I had no further plans for the pistol except that it would pointed away from me if I needed to fire it. I would give all that I had left to ensure that Madame would not call me from the beyond to a room such as this, to face either eye again.

She released me after a moment, abandoning me to the cold and the terror while she studied each of the others in turn. The woman in green silk gasped at what she saw in that face and pressed her hands to her mouth, eyes wide in shock. Then she rose from her seat, looking away from those terrible eyes. Her complexion was ashen and her hands trembled as if she had an ague. In a moment, her skirts and hat were gathered and she was gone, leaving behind her an empty space that felt even colder than before.

Madame LaFarge sat down and became a small woman in a blue silk turban, her hands large and long-fingered, her face below those eyes slack and dull like a sculptor's putty. Her dress was exotic, composed as it was of a turban, a tunic and a full skirt, with silk scarves fluttering at neck and waist.

"Good evening." The voice that welled out between those thin lips was too large for so small a woman. I wondered if it was her own, imagining for an instant that she was controlled like a ventriloquist's dummy by someone in another room. Or perhaps by whatever lurked in the blue glowing depths of her mechanical eye.

Then she smiled at us and I dropped my gaze to the table, determined to see that face no more for a time. "All of you have come here to speak to spirits who have gone on: fathers, brothers, lovers," I could feel her gaze weigh on my bent head and I bit back a gasp of horror at having my secret revealed. Madame continued speaking but I was lost for an eternity until I could drag myself thought over thought back to the sound of her voice and the darkened room.

"—be quite sure. I am not a charlatan. Are you prepared for what may come when I call? It will not be what you are expecting. Of that you may be sure." She looked at each of us again in turn, this time longest at the man and woman at my side. He stood, though she clutched his arm, and held his hand out to help her rise. His lips were tight with a terrible resolve; I did not think her pleas could move him.

And at last, head bent and shoulders drooping, she did as he wished. He bowed slightly to us, then, taking his wife by the arm, towed her from the room.

And now we were three. Madame smiled to see us still sitting there, waiting on her pleasure. "You are all certain. Good. Please move closer so that you are each seated next to each other."

No power on Earth would persuade me to move closer to her, to cross the abyss of the two empty chairs that shielded me. So I vowed. I prayed fervently to a Heaven I no longer believed in when her mechanical eye focused on me. Its cold blue light called me like a distant star, or the voice of a faraway demon. I rose as if on strings, moved closer to her, and sat as I was bidden.

Madame continued, "Now we will begin. Place your hands upon the table, your fingers touching those of the person next to you." My hands rose to the table of their own accord, fingers outstretched. A part of my mind noticed that I no longer wore my gloves and I wondered when I had taken them off.

The lady on my left trembled out to the length of her fingertips. I could feel her fear when our cold fingers touched. Part of me admired her courage for remaining here in the face of such terror, while another part of me thought her a fool, and myself as well, for failing to follow the example of our fellows and fleeing this dark room full of unseen dead things.

On my right, my fingers touched those of Madame LaFarge, my flesh cringing from the cold dampness of her outlandishly long fingers. They were the hands of a strangler, as Annabel might have said when she was reading one of her penny-dreadfuls aloud to me. I shivered harder at the thought.

Would Annabel come here tonight? And if she did, what might she say to me? Would she know about the pistol, the blackness of my thoughts these last months? Would she wish to haunt my loneliness with more than her memory?

Madame's flesh was gray in the gaslight and looking at it, I thought that perhaps my pistol was a surer route of seeing Annabel again.

There came then a distant sound of rhythmical thumping, as if someone played upon a drum in a nearby room. A sharp, sweet smell filled the air, wafting in from outside. *Incense*, my mind recognized it a moment later. Was Madame then a woman who kept Sabbath and a pew of her own, perhaps in a church nearby? I could not see her as such, not she with that hellish mechanical eye of hers. It would terrify the other devout.

The drumming caught me up as the incense settled like a cloud upon the room. I could no longer smell the Thames, which was a blessing. Instead, I inhaled the sweet scent deeply, letting myself drift upon the heavy air while I waited to see what Madame would do next. With no small part of my mind, I hoped that she might do nothing at all.

But I watched her to find out. Slowly, her mortal eye closed and the light dimmed in her mechanical one, and she tilted her head back. Her profile brought a hawk to mind and I tried without success to stop imagining her swooping down upon her clients and seizing them in her claws. If anything, her fingers against mine grew even icier and the room with them, and her breath the wind that blew ice shards against my cheeks.

There was a quiet hum filling my ears now, louder even than the drums or the small gasps and labored breathing of my companions. The sound overrode even the pounding of my own heart in my ears, and soon I could hear nothing else.

I do not know how long we sat in that sepulchral cold and sound, breathing no air not laden with incense, hearing no sound but the humming and the drum, but it felt as if hours passed before Madame spoke. I was surprised to find my eyes closed, tightly sealed as if I could not bear to see any more of my surroundings. I did not open them at first. Her words ended the humming and the now much fainter sound of the drum. "Hello? Who is there? I can feel you nearby. Do you wish to speak to someone here?"

Hers was the tone of a governess or a nursemaid. I wondered if the dead responded like guilty children caught stealing cookies when Cook's back was turned.

Then I bethought me of Annabel. I remembered her eyes, dark as a moonlit sea, and her skin like damask. But most of all I remembered her laughter: girlish and pealing. I could not hear her laugh without joining in. *Please, love, come to me. Tell me that you still love me.* Even now, in my own thoughts, I could not bring myself to ask what I really wanted to know. What would I do if she said no? I did not wonder what would happen if she said nothing at all.  Instead, I opened my eyes reluctantly to see what the medium might do next.

Madame's thin lips parted in a whisper that turned to a dull growl that resonated through my bones.  I heard the gentleman seated across from me gasp, his eyes gleaming white in the flickering gaslight. His mouth opened and he drank the thick air in gulps like a fish, or one drowning. The growling whisper from Madame's lips was meant for him and him alone, though we heard some words: "Betrayal. Money. Vengeance."

The gentleman stared at Madame until his eyes nearly bulged. I wondered who he had betrayed and why. I wondered what the vengeance would be. But I did not wonder much or strongly as I might have done before I entered Madame's rooms. It was as if I watched from a great distance, somewhere far above the room and its inhabitants. To my relief, I could barely hear her voice from there.

The cold grew worse and something began to form in the smoky air. It was pale and wore no shape that I could recognize. But then, it had not come for me. The gentleman pulled his hands from the table and started to his feet. His gaze was fixed on the shape, whatever it was, and he was pale, paler than Annabel was on her deathbed. His hands trembled as he reached into his pocket.

Madame whispered, "Come!" And the shape drifted forward, not quite so formless now. There was a suggestion of features in it: hands, eyes, a man's arms.

The gentleman stepped back, a flash of something sharp in his hand. "Stay back! Call him off!" This last was said to Madame, who watched him with her mechanical eye. There was a hint of a smile twisting her lips.

My other hand was aching and when I looked down, I realized that the lady next to me was holding onto me, her grip rigid and tight as iron bands. A cry from the man brought my gaze back up and I gasped to see the tableau before us. The gentleman was struggling with something, a formless thing now formed, its fingers locked around his throat.

His hand flashed once, twice. I could see the blade gleam and emerge unblemished, having cut nothing. His arms flailed, dropping the knife and he kicked out once, twice, before he fell to the carpet. I could not bring myself to stand and see how it would end. Instead, I closed my eyes like a coward and waited for his struggles to subside.

There came only silence and a long indrawn breath, one laden with satisfaction. Madame's. I wondered what was next for us and forced my eyes open. The incense was so thick now I could scarce see the room around us and my eyes burned with it. I closed them again and tried to use my other senses. Strain as I might, I could hear no sound until Madame raised her hands and clapped them slowly.

It must have been a signal of some kind because the cloud began to gradually recede, leaving the cold behind like a blanket. I opened my eyes, and across from us, sat the gentleman, seemingly undamaged by his travails. But he had the pallor of the long dead, though I could hear him breathe. He met my eyes for a moment and I shuddered as I turned away, unwilling to think too much on what I saw there.

Had I imagined his fall, spectral fingers at his throat? Why would I have imagined such a thing? The room spun around me for an instant and I could feel myself becoming faint. Madame's grip caught my hand, pulling me back. "Do not leave the circle. The spirits are not done with us yet." Her lips turned up in a smile so dreadful that I feared I might go mad.

And then it all changed. Madame's look became merely sardonic, her mechanical eye examining, then dismissing me. The lady at my side loosened her hold on my aching fingers, and the gentleman, when I looked again, seemed no more than the normal wintery pale of a Londoner kept too long inside.

Was I going mad? I heard Annabel's laughter from far away, but it had a mocking quality that she had never had in life. Was she going to come to us next? I felt ill at the thought. What if what came was no longer Annabel as I had loved her?

The drumming had begun anew, though it might have begun far earlier than that for all I knew, while my thoughts whirled and I was lost in my fears. Now I stared around wildly, determined to miss nothing. I would not lose myself in the incense or the monotonous sounds, not this time! The cold would be my friend and help me stay alert.

Madame's mechanical eye fixed upon the lady at my side this time. I heard a small, animal sound from the lady's throat, but she showed no other sign of distress. I could not read her face behind her veil but she did not seize my hand again and her fingers did not tremble where they lay against mine. I sent a small prayer that whoever she wanted speech with meant her no harm. I did not think I could bear to sit through such an attack again.

If indeed I had sat through it the first time.

I felt ill and faint at the thought. Always, I had prized my reason above all else. If that were gone, what now had I left?

The air had clouded while I was lost in my terror, and despite myself, I let it begin to overwhelm my senses. Madame's head rolled on her shoulders, mortal eye showing white around the edges, and I tried to prepare myself for what might come next.

"Are you there? Who have you come to speak to?" Madame's voice was louder now, as if she had less to fear by speaking in her normal voice. Perhaps she did. The table rocked beneath our hands as if the ocean ran beneath it and I bit back a scream at the unexpected movement. It rose and hovered for a moment and the gentleman gave me a look of pure horror, though he kept his hands on the table. What was she summoning this time?

The table settled gently back upon the carpet and did not move again. Something caressed my cheek, leaving cold and damp behind. My heart pounded loud enough to drown the drumming in my distant ears and I knew that I would never be warm again.

The voice that emerged from Madame's lips was one that I dreamt of each night. "Theresa." My name was so faint that I had to strain to hear it.

I trembled in mixture of terrible hope and mortal fear. She had come for me. Here, we might be together once again. But for how long?

A pale cloud formed before us, driving all thoughts from my mind. "Hello, my love." I knew Annabel's voice as I knew my own and the sound of it, even emerging from Madame's mouth, was enough to make me weep for joy.

"Oh, Theresa, how I have missed you." My heart sang, though my ears could detect nothing of love in the way she said the words. I could feel the lady at my side stiffen, and stare at me, but I could not turn to look. Not when the white cloud before me might shift and turn, revealing her beloved features.

"I have missed you, too," I choked out the words with a sob.

"Tell me you love me, Theresa. Tell me how much you have missed me." There was something in the way she said those words that made me draw back: a pleasure, a hunger that was nothing like the laughing girl I remembered.

The gentleman coughed, as if to remind me of his presence. I had forgotten neither him nor the lady at my side nor Madame with her glowing eye, but what if I said nothing and Annabel left? I had spent all my remaining money securing Madame LaFarge's powers: there would be no second chance.

"I will always love you, Annabel. Just as I promised. You are my soul and my heart."

"Then why haven't you joined me, Theresa?" The question made me start and I could feel my fingers tighten on the table. I flinched at the cruel shift in the voice. Annabel sounded cold and contemptuous as I had never heard her before.

But was she not right to despise me? What was there to stop me from following her? I had nothing left, no one to love me or care what I did next.

With utter certainty, I knew what I should do. I pulled my hand from the table to reach for my clutch.

A hiss from Madame told me that she knew that I had broken the circle, but what was that to me? This life could hold no more dangers. Annabel had come for me and I required nothing more from Madame's powers than that.

Now there was only what I might do for myself. Yet, my certainty faded just enough with the sound that I hesitated, my fingers pausing on the edge of the table. "Theresa," Annabel's voice filled the room, her face forming above the table. "Hurry. I long to embrace you again."

I looked up at her pale, pale face hovering above us, her hair floating in a cloud around it. Her eyes were black holes, not the living blue of memory, and I could see Madame's ceiling beyond her, though misted over as if seen through a veil. But her beloved lips pursed in a little smile and I wanted to kiss them again.

I felt a surge of triumph fill me: Annabel had come for me and me alone. I forgot Madame and the others and saw only Annabel herself, smiling as she had in life. How lucky I was!

Whatever else waited for me I could endure because I would be at her side.

I pulled my pistol free from my clutch and the lady seized my wrist in an iron grip. I tried to shake loose as an oath from the gentleman startled us both. He was staring at Madame, his features twisted in anger and terror. I risked a quick glance away from Annabel toward Madame to see what he saw.

Madame's features were slack and expressionless, with the exception of her mechanical eye. That glowed feverishly and far brighter than it had when she entered and we saw it first. It was too bright to gaze at for long, but in the instant that I met it, I saw such things as I hope to never see again, living or dead. Horrors unspeakable and alien glowed in the depths of that eye as if a demon looked upon us from a shell of human flesh.

My companions each responded in their own ways, the gentleman swearing and jumping to his feet, the lady cringing away and covering her face with her hands. Though my flesh crawled, I looked up at Annabel instead, finding my resolve once again. The circle was broken and my hand had been released. I began to raise my pistol to my head.

"Yesss," a voice that was not quite Annabel's emanated from the spirit, crooning in my ears. The hunger in that voice startled me and I looked away from my beloved, meeting Madame's mechanical eye once again. Annabel looked back at me from the gleaming blue light, her hands held out in a supplicating gesture. It seemed to me that I could see chains on her wrists.

Then I knew the truth: Madame was holding her spirit captive. My sweet, loving Annabel was a prisoner in the demon depths of Madame's mechanical eye. And only I could save her.

My heart racing in my chest, I stood and summoned my resolve. The room spun slowly around me and I heard the gentleman give a distant shout.

A cold cloud enveloped me, wafting in from beyond this room where our fates were to be decided. "Quick, my love," Annabel's sweet voice murmured in my ear, sounding like her own dear self. "Set me free. Then we can be together again." I could deny her nothing and I acted as my heart told me she wanted me to act.

There was an explosion. Then I must have fainted from the noise, like some missish, green girl, because my senses knew no more for a time.

When I revived, I was alone in the room. My beloved's face no longer floated above me and my heart ached in mortal terror and pain. Had I lost her? Was I wrong about what she wanted me to do?

An acrid smell filled the air, quite unlike the incense or the stench of the river that had filled the room earlier. I sat up, coughing and the room twisted in a blur of carpet and gaslight and table.

I blinked and the world steadied itself, and wondered where the gentleman and the lady had gone. Had I merely imagined them? The thought was too dreadful to dwell upon.

Madame still sat in her chair, but she said nothing. I stood, using the table to pull myself to my feet. Then I could see why Madame was silent: her human eye was a smoking ruin.

I flinched away in horror. Who could have done such a thing?

I looked down at my hand and my pistol held tightly in it. I recoiled, as if that hand did not belong to me. I must be truly mad, then. And I had lost everything that I held dear. What was I to do now?

Some force compelled me to meet Madame's mechanical eye and my Annabel looked back at me. Her hands were no longer supplicating, but her eyes were full of longing. She beckoned me closer to her.

And I dropped the pistol, and ran to Madame's side. I touched the edges of the mechanical eye, trying to imagine that I held my beautiful girl close and could comfort her. Madame's damp, gray flesh caught at my fingers, dragging them away from the eye. From Annabel. I could not bear to see this: I must set her free from this as well.

I looked around, frantic to find the means. There was a knife on a nearby side table and I seized it in my trembling hand. Annabel smiled at me, and that was enough to inspire me.

When Madame's eye was finally my own, I held it in my hand and stroked it gently. "We can be together once again," Annabel's voice crooned. The blue light glowed around her, gentle and welcoming now. I wanted to enter it, to speak with the voices that called me from its depths. "Make it yours, my love. Command the spirits and you may command mine as well."

The notion filled me with a fierce, wild joy: this would replace all that I had lost and we would be together forever. The blue light glowed, and a dozen voices spoke to me at once from its depths. They told me what I must do next.

It was but a matter of resolve, and with that, I have always been blessed with an abundance.

When I was done and able to walk once more, I rolled Madame to the door. I removed her turban and her scarves before I summoned the maid. The glow in my mechanical eye compelled her obedience, and together we took Madame to the Thames and left her in its bosom.

Then we returned to the parlor and I commanded the maid to light the fire. "Call me 'Madame Lafarge' now. You may prepare dinner. I am too weary to see any clients tonight, but we will begin again tomorrow." The woman left, trembling.

I placed the turban on my own head and wrapped the scarves around my neck and wrist. Then I spread my hands on the table and listened to the voices of those who had gone before, each one asking me to help them rejoin the land of the living, even if only for a few moments. There would be no trouble commanding them to appear for my clients.

And my love and I would be together always.

From close by, I heard Annabel's laughter, true and joyous as a bell.

# THE EGYPTIAN CAT

ERICA TURNED OVER THE LAST page of the manuscript with a sigh. Somehow, a collection like *Hairballs Over Innsmouth* should have been more fun to edit. She wondered why writers were having such a hard time writing humorous cat-related horror stories that included an homage to H. P. Lovecraft. It should have been a snap. But perhaps the rewrites would look much better.

The thought cheered her enough to go and get the mail, even though it might contain yet more manuscripts. And it did. But along with the envelopes with addresses written in crayon and the one that seemed to contain nothing but melted chocolate, there was a box. She looked at it carefully, noting that although her name and address were printed on a mailing label, the return address was completely illegible.

She wondered if she should contact the bomb squad or something before she opened it. You couldn't be too careful these days. Some of the writers who she'd turned down for her last anthology, *Catnip and Hashish*, had been pretty irate.

Finally, she decided she was overreacting. Her writers were cat people, after all; their limited attention span would have moved on to some new source of fascination or irritation by now. She swept up all the mail and dumped it on the dining room table.

She opened the bills first, of course, then the manuscripts, but her gaze was drawn repeatedly back to the mysterious box. Something about it spoke of unfathomable mysteries beyond human ken.

So, after she had opened everything else, separated the mail into piles and fed the cats when their cries became too inconvenient to ignore, she reached for it. First she held it up to her ear to listen for telltale ticking sounds. The brown paper crackled reassuringly but apart from that, the package made no other sound. She cut open a flap in the paper on one side. Nothing leaped out or blew up.

She slowly removed the paper to reveal a completely nondescript cardboard box. Maybe it was shoes. Would a fan have sent her something as useful as a new pair of shoes? She doubted it. One of the cats uttered a piercing whine and she jumped. The cat, a large tabby named Sarnath, rubbed himself ingratiatingly against her leg while she pondered the box. *Open it*, the cat seemed to be saying. *It might be treats.*

"It might be a bad thing too, Sarny. You just never know." She reflected that living alone had left her with the unfortunate habit of talking to her cats. And listening to them. Sarnath's inscrutable slitted gaze met hers and she reached for the box as if under a spell. She opened it, though not without a remaining qualm or two.

But if she had hoped to see its contents immediately, she was doomed to disappointment. Whatever it was, it was buried under styrofoam peanuts that crinkled and rolled beneath her questing fingers.

But at last they encountered something hard. She shivered, then forced herself to grasp whatever it was and pull it from its nest. For a brief instant, she looked away only to find herself looking deep into Sarnath's eyes. The cat had begun to purr, a deep, rumbling noise that should have been reassuring but somehow only served to fill her with a vague apprehension.

With an effort, she turned her head to look at the contents of the package, now cradled gingerly in her right hand. Slitted emerald eyes stared back at her and she very nearly dropped whatever it was. Regaining control, she found her jaw falling open in astonishment. Her unknown admirer had sent her a statue of a cat. And what a statue it was!

Clearly of Egyptian origin, it was made of some sort of black stone and covered with carvings that appeared to be hieroglyphs. A single gold earring hung from one ear and the eyes were greenest glass. Or were they tiny emeralds? She couldn't be sure. She set it down so that it met her gaze with an impassive expression, filling her with both a nameless dread and an unexpected excitement, as if her life could be completely transformed at any moment.

It was at that same moment the doorbell rang, causing Erica to start from her reverie. Surely it couldn't be Mr. McGillicuddy from next door again. He'd already dropped by three times this week and one could only borrow so many cups of sugar. Perhaps Phyllis and Felicia from her bridge club were right and he was interested in more than the contents of her kitchen. She groaned. If only…but there was no point in dwelling on what might have been.

The doorbell rang again, impatience clear in the length of the chime that echoed through the hall. Erica resigned herself to answering it. "Coming! Give me a minute." She remembered to look through the gauzy curtain that hung over the door before she opened it. Even in Foggy Harbor, Massachusetts, there were criminals inclined to prey on a woman living alone.

But all she could see was that the person on her doorstep was broad of shoulder and wearing an elegant suit and a hat that covered her/his hair. He or she also had their back to the door and was looking out over the garden. She did catch a glimpse of dark golden brown skin as the person, whoever they were, raised one hand to brush away some speck on the beautiful dark gray suit. Erica's pulse raced and she tried in vain to catch her breath. *It couldn't be…*

She admonished herself to stop acting like a schoolgirl. Rashida Simmons was gone for good, along with any hopes she'd had in that quarter. Still she trembled as she reached for the knob and opened the door.

Her visitor turned, almost reluctantly, as if they too feared what they might see. An involuntary cry escaped Erica's lips. The woman on her doorstep pulled off her hat and ran her fingers through her short curls. She didn't look up from the threshold as she spoke, "Hello, Erica. I'm sorry for dropping by like this. I'd have called if…I had the number."

At that moment, Erica forgot the ten years that stretched between them, forgot the professional editor that she'd become and spoke her mind without hesitation or forethought. "Rashida Simmons, you get your ass in here right now! You've got some explaining to do!" She reached out with the strength born of desperation and yanked the other woman's arm, pulling her inside. With shaking hands she locked the door behind her, sealing off any chance of easy escape.

Only then did she turn, chest heaving with pent-up indignation. Her quarry met her eyes this time as she took a deep breath and murmured, "It wasn't like that, Erica. I had to leave Foggy Harbor. Let me try and explain but before I go any further, I have to ask: did you receive a package in the mail today?"

"You just drop by after no word for ten years to inquire about the local postal service? Things a little slow wherever you've been keeping yourself?" Erica shook in every limb, part of her longing to hurl herself into Rashida's arms, part of her wanting to throw her out, never to be seen again.

Rashida winced but persisted. "Did it?"

"Yes. Why? Was it from you? Not that a token of affection wouldn't have been too much to ask." Erica uttered a most unladylike snort.

"Where is it?" Rashida ignored the snort, spinning around on her heels as if the statue would be lying around the foyer. She strode around purposefully, looking into each room as if she were welcome to do so. Erica sputtered indignantly after her as she discovered the study. "At last!" she cried out as she dropped into the chair in front of the statue.

The words were a spear through Erica's heart. She forced that organ to harden around a rapidly widening hole. "Well, now that you've found what you came for, I suggest you take it and get out."

Rashida studied her with large golden eyes, almost glowing amber in the afternoon light. Erica strangled stillborn the memory of what they looked like at dawn when her former lover first awakened. She tapped her foot impatiently, waiting for Rashida to take her statue and go.

Instead, the other woman leaned her arms on the table and gave her a serious look. "I know you better than that, Erica. You could never have changed this much. Besides, you're editing cat horror anthologies. You have to know why I'm here; you'll never be able to sleep until you find out." So Rashida had been following her career? The idea was somehow soothing, warming the coldness of the hard-edged hole in the center of Erica's being. Perhaps…but no. She forced the hope away. Still, it would be nice to know what all this was about. Rashida was right about that much.

She propelled her response out between frozen lips: "Oh, very well. But you'll leave after you're done explaining. I suppose you want tea?" Not gracious certainly, but far more than she intended. She cursed the good manners she'd been brought up with.

"Tea would be wonderful. Thank you." Rashida smiled, and it was like watching dawn over the harbor. Erica very nearly melted, only just forcing herself to flee the room in search of cups and hot water. Rashida trailed after her into the kitchen, giving her no time to recover.

"You've done a lot with the place since your aunt died. I like it." She held the words out like a peace offering and Erica grimaced, knowing that the ceiling was covered with cracked and peeling paint and the random stains of old leaks. Her small inheritance and the income from her books were scarcely enough to pay the property taxes and her own needs, certainly not enough for upkeep in a place this big.

A quiet rage filled her. "I'm engaged. To be married. To Mr. McGillicuddy next door." She blurted the words out, unable to stop herself.

Rashida's dark face paled and she looked away, as if from something she could not bear to see. At last, she murmured, "Congratulations," so softly that Erica barely caught the word.

She cursed the impulse that made her invent such a patent falsehood and longed to throw herself at Rashida's feet to beg for forgiveness. But pride held her upright, made her pour the tea and seal her lips.

Rashida rose, pacing, as she blew on her tea to cool it, her agitation clear. "I had hoped…well, never mind about that now. Can we go back to the other room? I hate to let the statue out of my sight for long." She walked out the door and down the hall without a backward glance or even the saucer that Erica held out to her.

Erica followed her down the hallway, already making up her mind to admit that she'd told a little fib about Mr. McGillicuddy. But when she got to the study, Rashida was sitting at the table, eyes fixed on the cat, and she found she couldn't say it. Instead, she picked up Rashida's cup and smacked it onto the saucer with unnecessary force. "All right, so it's clear that you didn't come back to see me. What's the story about the statue?"

Rashida brought both hands up to her face and rubbed her cheeks as if suddenly exhausted. "All right. You remember when my mother disappeared?"

As if Erica could forget the most traumatic moment of their high school years. Mrs. Simmons had vanished into the night, leaving only the briefest of notes for her husband and teenage daughter. She had assured them that she'd be back and told them not to worry. They never heard from her again.

Erica had spent months consoling Rashida; it had been what had drawn them together. How ironic that Mrs. Simmons' disappearance was somehow instrumental in today's events, too. "Of course I remember. The FBI never found a thing. Your father became a private detective but he never found any trace of her. Why? Have you heard something?"

Rashida reached into the front pocket of her immaculately tailored suit and pulled out a crumpled envelope. Wordlessly, she handed it to Erica. For an instant, Erica contemplated refusing to read whatever it was. After all, what did it matter now?  But her curiosity was aroused. She took it, opening the envelope slowly and carefully as if something inside might bite her. A distant part of her brain noted the two-year-old postmark.

The letter inside was typed on an actual typewriter; there were even smudges where the correction tape failed.

*My dearest daughter,*

*I hope you can forgive me. There's no time to try to explain it all now – it wouldn't be good enough for what you've lost anyway. Just know I always meant to come back and that I love you and your father very much. If I hadn't left, I'd have lost both of you.*

*Now I have to ask you to do something for me. My family, generation upon generation back to our ancestors' time in Nubia of old, were appointed as the guardians of a sacred relic. It is an object of great power and it must be protected from those who would misuse it. The time has come when I must pass it onto you, my child. I know you have started your training and are almost ready to take on this great burden. I will come to you soon to tell you more.*

*If you do not hear from me again, know that I am prevented from coming by forces beyond my control. I will send the object into safekeeping with friends who will guard it until you are ready. Return to the beginning to seek what you need.*

*Your loving mother,*

*Keira*

"I never heard from her again. I believe that she may have run afoul of forces trying to find the statue. I think my aunt and uncle knew what befell her, but feared to tell me in case her fate frightened me from performing my duties," Rashida offered up in spectral tones.

"Not to be overly skeptical, Rashida, but are you sure that your mother was quite…right when she wrote this? Or that this letter is even from her? What 'training'? What sacred relic?" Erica's questions all rushed together until they emerged almost as a single sentence. She bit back a few others. *Nubia? The Simmons family has been here in Foggy Harbor for generations.*

"Still the same old cautious Erica." Rashida smiled wistfully as she took the letter from Erica's hand and carefully folded it before putting it in the envelope and tucking it back in her suit. "My aunt and uncle came to visit about a week before I left Foggy Harbor. They told me some of this back then but I didn't believe it either. Not at first. But then they showed me some things and I…had to leave home with them. It was my duty. Can I trust you with one of my family's greatest secrets, Erica?" Her face was grave and her eyes didn't waver from her former lover's.

Erica bit back a few more responses and thought about it through the numb cloud currently filling her mind. Even if she suspected Rashida was now as crazy as the letter writer, who would she tell? Her bridge club? Her publisher? Not likely. Besides, how different could this story be from anything she'd read recently? There was even a cat in it. She shrugged and sat down at the table. "Disclose away." She sipped at her tea and waited.

Rashida stood and closed all the blinds and curtains, shrouding the room in twilight gloom. Then she walked over to the table and the cat. She raised her hands to shoulder height and a distant look crossed her features, as if she traveled across time. Her lips parted to emit a chant in a language that Erica did not recognize, one that was at once guttural and musical. The hairs stood up on Erica's nape and she shivered despite herself, filled with a heretofore unknown sense of eldritch dread.

Rashida's eyes were pools of molten gold, her face that of a warrior goddess of old. Erica could not tear her gaze away, though her heart cried out in fear that this new Rashida could never be hers again. The statue's eyes began to glow as the hieroglyphics on its sides were outlined in light. A strange humming sound filled the room, vibrating its way through Erica's china cabinet. The hieroglyphs blazed brilliantly, far too bright to look at, and Erica threw her arm over her face.

The humming lasted a moment more before dying away into silence, and the room went dark once again. "It's safe to look now." Rashida's voice was reassuring but Erica still hesitated a moment before lowering her arm. The cat's inscrutable emerald eyes glowed back at her.

She found her voice with an effort. "So does it do anything besides glow and hum?"

Rashida gave her a look of disbelief. "Of course it does. It's an object of destiny, a source of ancient and terrible power."

"Okay. So what does it actually do?" Erica was beginning to remember one of Rashida's less desirable traits, namely a tendency toward the unnecessarily dramatic.

"It can be used as a weapon of awesome destructive power. And it can bring back what was lost and change destinies, perhaps even raising the dead if the user is powerful enough."

*Or it could just be battery-powered and you might be a few scarabs shy of a full complement.* Erica stopped the words before they escaped her lips, focusing instead on Rashida's first statement. "What do you mean 'it can be used as a weapon'? What kind of weapon? Used by whom?"

"Only the followers of Set himself, clearly nothing you'd be worried about." Rashida glared at her and Erica realized that she had been using the same voice she used on Mrs. Grayson, her neighbor who had early onset Alzheimer's. "Very well," Rashida said finally. "I can see that you don't believe me. I'll take the statue and go. I have one last task to perform in Foggy Harbor, then we need never see each other again."

"No, wait. What are you going to do next? At least let me cook dinner for you before you go. For old time's sake." Perhaps she could find a way to bring Rashida back to a little of her old, saner self, she thought. Or get her to spend the night. She squelched the second thought.

The doorbell rang again and Erica rolled her eyes. "Let me just get rid of whoever it is and we can have a cozy chat. I'd really like to hear about what you've been up to." *At least I hope I'll like it.* She skirted around the statue as she headed for the front door. No point in taking too many chances. At least it wasn't changing fate right now, and Rashida wasn't bolting for the door.

The doorbell rang again and Erica found herself looking into Alex McGillicuddy's faded blue eyes through the glass pane. She could have screamed with frustration. Instead she made herself open the door. "Hello, Mr. McGillicuddy. I'm afraid I can't stop to chat. I have a guest. Did you need something?" *Such as a shove off my porch?* She held the words back. Clearly Rashida's return was doing nothing for her good nature.

"Well, hello there, neighbor. I didn't mean to intrude — I was just hoping to get that recipe from you again, the one for that wonderful chicken dish you dropped off when I moved in. I seem to have misplaced the copy you gave me. But it can wait. I've got a frozen pot pie I can just heat up." Alex gave her a look of pure longing that nearly made Erica roll her eyes before he turned away, shoulders slumped with rejection.

*Damn the man.* "Wait a minute, Alex. We can't have you resorting to the microwave every night. Just follow me back to the kitchen and I'll give you another copy of the recipe." She ushered him, trying not to cringe at his beaming smile.

That was the moment when Rashida emerged from the study. Erica couldn't help the tremor that went through her. After all, Rashida still thought… "Hello. I'm Rashida Simmons," she announced before Erica could say anything. "I understand that congratulations are in order." She gave Alex a stiff, wooden smile and clutched his hand in a death grip, white knuckles clearly visible.

Alex looked surprisingly alert, if a bit baffled. "How do you do? I was just stopping by for a recipe. Congratulations, you say?"

Rashida chose that moment to twist their hands so that Alex's wrist was exposed. Erica caught a brief glimpse of a snakelike tattoo before he yanked his arm away and pulled his sleeve down. Rashida and Alex glared at each other as if they were about to engage in mortal combat.

Desperate to end the standoff, Erica began to babble. "Let's talk about that later, Alex. Rashida and I were just going to sit down to dinner and chat about old times. Why don't we head back to the kitchen so you can get on with your own dinner?" She seized Alex's arm and steered him down the hallway with unnecessary force.

She couldn't help but notice the glance he sent after Rashida as she receded down the hallway in the distance. Had he always possessed that gleam of pure malice in his faded blue eyes? It made her think of ancient temples, their walls oozing with ichor and unspeakable evil. The thought made her scowl fiercely at him. He blinked innocently back, which made her scowl more.

She snatched her recipe box from the stove and yanked the card from the front. "Here you go. Just copy it over and give it back to me when you get around to it. Have a lovely evening!" She flung her back door open and gave him a smile that contained no ambiguities whatsoever.

"Your friend seems very nice and of course I don't mean to intrude, but perhaps we could all dine together. She seems as though she'd be very interesting to talk to." Alex smiled ingratiatingly at her and made no move toward the door.

"Perhaps another time. We have a lot to catch up on. Now, if you'll excuse me…" Erica glanced pointedly from the door to her neighbor.

At a glacial pace, he stepped toward the door, mumbling words like "sorry" and "intrude." Erica smiled and nodded, making it clear that her mind was somewhere else entirely. Finally, after what seemed an eternity, he oozed out of her kitchen. She watched him make his way down the garden path and out the gate with a fierce enthusiasm.

Then she raced back to the study. An empty room met her eyes: both the statue and Rashida were gone. Erica delivered herself of several unladylike comments before she noticed the note at the edge of the desk. As she reached for it, a part of her could not help but notice that the room felt better somehow. There was no sense of dread, eldritch or otherwise, only her familiar comfortable furniture and her sleeping cats. She glanced at them as if hoping for answers, but only got gentle snores in response.

She opened the note, knowing what it would say. Rashida was gone for good, driven away by some nonsensical quest and the stupid lie that Erica had told her. In a moment of stunning clarity, she recognized that perhaps even a somewhat unhinged Rashida was worth having, at least to her, and she knew despair even before she began reading. The actual text only confirmed her fears.

> *Dear Erica,*
>
> *I'm sorry to have intruded on you like this. I had forgotten how people's lives change. Please know that I wish only the best for you in your future life and rest assured that I will not burden you again.*
>
> *Yours,*
>
> *Rashida*

Erica was just slumping into the chair Rashida had recently occupied when she remembered something that the other woman had said. Something about "one last task." Where could the long lost scion of Nubian priests guarding a sacred relic perform a task here in Foggy Harbor? She wouldn't have gone back to the old Simmons place, surely. Mr. Simmons had passed on a few years back and the family who bought the place had done a drastic remodeling job. That left his old office and...Mrs. Simmon's mausoleum! Of course, why hadn't it occurred to her before?

Erica leapt to her feet and threw caution to the winds. She grabbed her purse and her shoes. Following some instinct she hadn't known she possessed, she bolted down the hall to the kitchen and obtained a small flashlight and, after a moment of hesitation, a box of matches, several packages of salt, and a longish kitchen knife.

Had there been anyone to ask her why she chose those items, she would not have been able to answer them. Perhaps it was one of her own ancestors advising her, maybe a long forgotten Goodie Somebody or Other who narrowly avoiding meeting her death in Salem. Or perhaps it just was editing too many cat horror anthologies. But whatever the reason, the knife felt good and comforting in her hand and the rest felt like essential tools.

She seized her coat from the hook and made sure the cats had enough to eat in case she was gone for a while. The bridge club would take them in if need be, she reminded herself sternly. Then she was off like a shot on her bicycle, peddling as if her life depended on it toward the Shady Oaks Resting Place out on the edge of town.  Rashida would be there already, if that's where she was headed. Erica hoped for the best and rode as she had never ridden before.

Fortunately, the cemetery was not far away and traffic was light. Erica skidded to a halt in front of the locked gates moments later and wondered how she was going to get inside. Then she remembered that Rashida had another way in, a gap in the fence some ways down that she used when she wanted to visit the family tomb after hours. She rode her bike on a bit further, then chained it to a post near where she thought the hole was.

With a deep breath, she straightened out her coat and marched up to the fence. Her memory had served her well. An impossibly skinny opening met her searching gaze and she despaired. Then she heard the noise of an engine, one that sounded vaguely threatening, if an engine could be described that way. She shrank into the shadows and glanced around.

Alex was parking his car on the street near the cemetery entrance. And he wasn't alone. There were two men with him, neither of them familiar, but both of an aspect that would have caused a braver heart than Erica's to quail. They got out of the car and made for the locked gates of the cemetery.

For an instant, she thought of going home and calling the police. But what would she tell them? Then she thought of the way Alex had looked at Rashida when they met. There had been something in his expression that filled her with urgency. She found that if she held her breath and twisted just right, she was able to squeeze through the fence to fall, gasping, onto the soft green grass on the other side.

She could hear an ominous clicking noise from the entrance; they must be cutting or picking the lock. Brushing herself off, she rose and sprinted for the deeper shadows under the trees. Then she pulled out her little flashlight, and shielding it as much as she could with her fingers, she dashed forward through the tombstones and trees toward the Simmons mausoleum.

It took longer than she expected and she got lost once, but she finally found it. To the amazement of Foggy Harbor, Rashida's grandfather had built the family tomb as a small stone pyramid in the midst of the more standard marble structures. It was trimmed with black stone and guarded by statues of Anubis and Bastet. There were even hieroglyphs, which everyone else in town thought was an unbearable pretension. Erica had thought so herself upon occasion. Now her nerves were so agitated, it was all she could do to approach the structure.

As she got closer, she noticed that the hieroglyphs were glowing faintly. Could Rashida be inside, unaware of her danger? Still, she mustn't overreact. She couldn't be absolutely sure that Alex presented any kind of threat. Perhaps he just enjoyed late night visits to cemeteries with large male friends. Large terrifying male friends.

Erica squared her shoulders and tried to remember where the catch for the door was hidden. Then she reached into the recess next to the door and opened it. The mechanism still worked flawlessly after all these years. Without stopping to marvel at that minor miracle, she slipped inside and let it click shut behind her.

She had expected to walk into Stygian gloom but to her surprise, the interior was lit with a pale golden glow. It was bright enough to illuminate the names on the memorials, including those of Rashida's parents. Erica wondered who, if anyone, was buried in her mother's tomb before she turned away, shivering a bit.

In the middle of the floor, one of the great marble slabs was pulled aside and a flight of steps led downward. From below, she thought she could hear the sound of muted chanting, and it sent chills up her already frozen spine. She considered demanding that Rashida stop all this nonsense and come upstairs to talk to her, but the words would not cross her immobile lips.

Instead, Erica closed her eyes and remembered Rashida as she had been, back when they were first together at Foggy Harbor State, before that first fateful Egyptology class. She caressed the memory of Rashida's golden eyes in the sunset and the way she felt when—she made herself stop and shuffle toward the steps. There would be time for trips down Memory Lane later, once all this was over. Alex and his thugs could only be minutes behind her.

Even so she crept down the stairs at a snail's pace. The sight that met her eyes when she reached the bottom was not one that even her books could have prepared her for. Rashida stood before an altar presided over by the cat statue. The air was thick with incense and the smoke of many candles. Her former lover was naked to the waist, though she still wore her gray wool pants. Above those, she was clad only in massive gold jewelry: a collar, several arm rings, huge earrings. She raised a blood-covered knife as she chanted. Erica could see shallow gashes in her arms, and the sight made her shudder all over.

Rashida was completely unaware of her, her golden eyes rimmed with kohl and focused on another world. Erica shrank back for a moment, too terrified to approach her friend. She could see that there was a dish of blood in front of the statue and for a ghastly moment, she feared that her friend had come to sacrifice herself to the mysterious statue. That thought was enough to break through her fears. "No!" She cried, her voice cutting through the smoke and the chanting like a blade.

Rashida faltered, and Erica could feel the air of the chamber tense and coil, becoming suddenly dangerous to the point of madness. Something unfathomably evil lurked there, somehow, just outside the realm of human senses. Using all of her strength, Erica leaped forward and pulled Rashida to the floor, knocking the knife from her hands and covering her with her trembling body in a vain effort to protect her.

It was at that moment Alex and his minions burst into the tomb. They thundered downstairs just as Erica thought the air itself was about to strike them all down. Alex laughed, a cold mirthless sound in the murk of the chamber. "It seems you received a package intended for me,

Guardian." He stepped forward, towering over them, his eyes cold and clearer than Erica had ever seen them.

*Well,* she thought, somewhat hysterically, *if it's just a post office mix-up, we can all go home. No harm done.* Her glance fell on one of the men with Alex and she was quiet. Harm would be done tonight and it was only a matter of time before it was clear who would be the recipient of it.

Rashida stirred from underneath her, easing Erica off to one side. "It is not for you, oh Servant of Set! It is my sacred mission to guard it and guard it I shall," Rashida's lips were set, a deep fury burning in her eyes. She had not yet looked at Erica, but the latter was not looking forward to the moment when her attention shifted.

She had to cut the tension somehow. "Really, Alex, if I'd know you had such an interest in antiquities, I'd have gone to the museum with you when you asked. Perhaps we can continue this discussion over dinner?" Erica asked hopefully.

"Let her go, she knows nothing about this." Rashida's eyes never left Alex's.

"On the contrary, she has some suspicions about me. And she is curious enough that it is only a matter of time before she wants to know more. Isn't that right, my dear?" Alex gave Erica a mock flirtatious leer that made her grimace in disgust.

*Alex McGillicuddy is a minion of Set? Hard to believe.* At least at first, but when she thought about it more, it gave her some perspective on the attentions he'd been showing her. Clearly she was better off single. Not that that was her biggest concern at the moment.

Whoever or whatever Alex was, he was annoying her greatly right now. She said the most outrageous thing she could think of. "That's it. The wedding's off." She glared at Alex and scrambled to her feet as Rashida did the same. The air around them seemed to have thinned a bit, as if the chanting had stopped calling whatever it was bringing into this world from one beyond.

Alex looked baffled. "The wedd—oh, never mind." His gaze fell on the statue and his eyes brightened with dark emotions. "Take the cat, boys, and we'll just seal up our little friends in their tomb. I'm sure they can comfort each other for a while, at least until the air runs out."

"Wait," Rashida held up her hand. "This is not your Lord's. Its powers will not obey you." Erica could feel a force coiling around them again, could feel something coming to a summons she could not hear. She reached into her handbag and found the packets of salt. As slowly and carefully as she could, she pulled them out. She glanced sidelong at Rashida and noticed that the latter seemed to be preparing to attack Alex.

The cat glowed even brighter as one of the thugs approached it. Alex hadn't answered Rashida's challenge, which was not surprising, since his attention seemed wholly fixed on the statue. But he had a gun out now and was pointing it at them.

Erica reached into her bag with excruciating slowness and pulled out the knife. She handed it to Rashida who gave her a bemused but still angry glance. "Athame," Erica muttered as softly as she could, using the only word she could remember from *Kitties in the Witch House*, her very nearly best-selling anthology.

Rashida smiled and it was an expression that made her face beautiful and terrible all at once. Following the strange instinct that had driven her since she left the house, Erica tore open the packets of salt and threw their contents out around them in a rough circle. "Hold it!" Alex barked at them just as his minion touched the cat.

The air above the altar grew dark as Rashida began to chant again. It swirled around the man, something glowing in its depths that Erica could not bear to look at. She closed her eyes and ducked as a bullet from Alex's gun whizzed past. The words flowing from Rashida's lips were like the ones she'd been chanting when Erica first entered, but they were different in timbre somehow. She was still terrified but she felt protected, as if whatever powers Rashida was calling were no longer harmful. At least to them.

A high-pitched, piercing cry of utter pain and terror filled the room. Erica covered her ears and flinched away and even Rashida stumbled in her chant. The air thickened and tightened above the altar, reminding Erica of nothing so much as a giant serpent. Or a very sinuous cat. Alex's henchman waved his arms and flailed as if trying to fend off some invisible foe. Then with a scream horrific in its finality, he fell to the floor, motionless.

Alex trained his gun on Rashida. "Call it off, witch. Your creature can't kill me before I fire this again." His eyes were icy in the murk of the chamber, even though his remaining thug shook with fear at his side.

Erica gave Rashida a panicked look. She couldn't lose her now, not like this. Rashida laughed, the rich mellow sound filling the chamber around them. The thing above the altar hovered, its face taking shape and growing pointed ears. The face hovered above the bowl of Rashida's blood, a ghastly phantom tongue lapping at its contents. Rashida glanced at it before meeting Alex's eyes. "Bets?" She inquired in a somewhat bored voice.

Erica's eyes widened in horror as she saw Alex's finger tighten on the trigger, then change his mind and point the gun at her. Rashida whispered something that might have been a prayer or a curse. She brought the kitchen knife down in a slashing moment as Alex pulled the trigger. A white cloud rose from the circle of salt around them and Erica watched as the bullet slowed to a crawl, stopping inches from her shoulder. Rashida reached out and flicked it with her finger, sending it to roll on the floor.

Alex's eyes narrowed and his thin lips parted in a chant of his own. Rashida gestured, and the cloud edged closer to his remaining minion. The man stood his ground a moment, then glanced at his fallen comrade, and fled up the stairs. The cloud appeared to have grown paws now, and it circled Alex, a glow that might have been eyes fixed on his upraised hands.

The sounds that fell from Alex's lips were cold and cruel, an ancient evil walking among them. Erica nearly covered her eyes before deciding that she couldn't bear not to watch. A second shadow arose from the cat statue, this one clearly a serpent with a fiery eyes. The cat shadow turned toward it, its spectral mouth opened in a silent hiss.

Then the two were joined in battle as their acolytes chanted at each other across the tomb. Erica glanced from one to the other, wondering what, if anything, she should do. The circle of salt still glowed faintly around them, which was reassuring. She watched the shadows battle for a moment and considered whether or not to simply sit down and wait it out. But that seemed cowardly somehow.

Rashida's face looked strained when she glanced back, and a new sense of urgency filled Erica at the sight. She wondered if she could learn an ancient chant in the next minute or two and help that way, but languages had never been her forte. Next she speculated that there might be something she could do to help the shadow kitty win its battle, but that too seemed unlikely.

Then she looked up at Alex. He seemed stronger, his face twisted in an expression of pure evil. He was also closer than she'd realized, only a few feet away from the edge of their protective circle. There didn't seem to be much time left. A deus ex machina did not seem forthcoming.

It was then that Erica had an idea. It was a weird sort of idea, but she thought it just might work. She reached into her purse and took out her book of matches. Then she took off her sweater and wrapped it around her fake leather purse. She lit several matches and with only the slightest of qualms, she held the sputtering flame to her favorite sweater. As the wool caught on fire, she studied the distance between them and Alex with narrowed eyes.

When at last she made her throw, she threw it underhand, just 'like a girl' as Rashida would have said in disgust back when they played college softball. She lobbed it with care and skill, though, and no one could argue with the results. The ball of flaming wool and plastic landed at Alex's feet, sparks catching on his pants. He hesitated, his chant faltering for a breath, then two, as he stamped and shook his feet to put out the flames that engulfed his cuffs.

With a hiss that knocked Erica to her knees, the cat shadow found some hidden source of strength. When she looked up, she could see the serpent dangling from its spectral kitty jaws. She looked at Rashida, hoping to see that her friend had found the same strength. But to her horror, Rashida seemed nearly spent.

A loud noise distracted her, and she looked at Alex in time to see him drop his gun. She gathered herself and hopped out of the salt circle.

Immediately, mighty forces assailed her and she walked forward as if in a gale. But walk forward she did until she was able to reach the gun. She managed to pick it up and hold it out in front of her with hands that shook convulsively. "All right," she said in a voice that shook nearly as badly. "Enough of this nonsense."

She pointed the gun in Alex's general direction and pulled the trigger, the recoil knocking her to the floor. Her shot missed, but it was enough to make him flinch. Rashida's words fell like hail, faster and more powerful, than before and Alex dropped to his knees, hands pressed over his ears, silent at last. A great rushing sound tore through the chamber and both cat and serpent vanished. The glow of the hieroglyphs faded until only the candles and the fiery sweater still provided light.

Rashida stepped forward and raised the kitchen knife above Alex, her face transformed into the countenance of a goddess of death. "No!" Erica shouted.

Her friend seemed to shift, as if another person was working their way to the surface. "I know you were engaged to him and all, but really Erica, I'm sure you can see he's not the greatest catch."

Erica's jaw dropped open. "I was never engaged to him! I just said that because I was angry with you. That's no reason to kill him." She staggered to her feet. "You won't call on powerful dark forces from beyond this world again, will you, Mr. McGillicuddy?"

Alex hissed something that might have been agreement. His eyes were dead now, as if the spirit which drove him was gone. Looking into them, Erica had another idea. "Besides, maybe he knows what happened to your mother."

Rashida's face shifted, becoming more Rashida again. "Do you, Set-spawn? Do you know something?" She waved the knife threateningly in front of his dazed looking face.

It seemed to be enough to bring him back to life, and his lips twisted in a snarl. "My Lord consumed her, body and spirit, just as he will consume you!" Then he twisted around and kicked out with desperate strength. Rashida jumped back as he pulled himself to his feet. Then he charged forward, straight at the cat on the altar. Rashida lunged after him, but not quickly enough, as he darted past her and placed his hands on the statue.

For a moment, nothing happened. His face twisted and it seemed to Erica as if he was drawing on some unseen source of power. The statue began to glow a little, then a bit more. A tendril of shadow reached out from it and wrapped itself around his body in a hideously companionable fashion. He threw back his head and laughed, and the shadow slipped into his mouth. His laughter changed to a choking cough and he fell to the floor, his body convulsing, until just as suddenly, he was still.

The statue fell with him, meeting the stone floor with a crash. The head broke loose and shadows poured out. They surged out in a mighty gray wave, then just as quickly dissipated. In their wake, they left two corpses and two exhausted women. "Well, looks like that might be it for your task," Erica said in awed but relieved tones.

Rashida stared at her in disbelief, then picked her way across the floor to the statue. She picked up the head and held it as if seeking answers to questions only she could hear. The green eyes twinkled in the cat's face but volunteered nothing. A single tear worked its way down Rashida's cheek.

Erica ran over to comfort her. She wrapped her arms around her friend and held her tightly, and in that brief instant, both of them touched the cat. The statue quivered and shook, light pouring from it instead of shadows this time. It engulfed them, then swept through the chamber and up the stairs into the mausoleum. Then it too vanished as the shadows had done.

"We've released all that it held," Rashida whispered. "There is nothing more to guard."

Erica kissed her bare shoulder and turned her around so she could kiss the tears from her cheeks. "Where are the rest of your clothes, by the way?"

Rashida pointed up wordlessly. Erica took the pieces of the statue and tucked them into her capacious pockets. Then she took Rashida's hand in hers and towed her along as she walked over to pick her house keys out of the smoldering wreckage of her purse. "Let's go home and eat dinner." She smiled reassuringly at Rashida, but the latter seemed lost in her thoughts.

Erica pulled her up the stairs behind her. There was a faint knocking coming from Keira Simmons' tomb. They looked at each other, and Erica shrugged and nodded, the experiences of the evening having completely exhausted her capacity for terror. Rashida pulled on her shirt and jacket before they approached the tomb. They looked deep into each other's eyes for a long moment, then they pushed the lid away. Keira Simmons sat up, clearly alive, her face that of someone waking from a long sleep.

"Hello Mother," Rashida choked out at last. "I asked Bastet to help me find you, and she has." Rashida burst into tears.

Erica nodded politely to Mrs. Simmons as she and her daughter tearfully embraced. She gave Rashida a wan smile before turning and walking out of the tomb. She had no place in this part of Rashida's story. Still, she ached at the thought that she might never see her beloved again. In an acute state of emotional turmoil, she retrieved her bike, and went home where she tumbled into bed and slept for many hours.

She was sitting at her kitchen table the next morning reading stories with titles like "Kittens in the Walls" when the doorbell rang. Once more she shuffled slowly down the hall but this time she flung the door open without bothering to see who it was first.

Rashida looked back at her, golden eyes calm and peaceful. "I was thinking," she said without preamble, "that I missed you." Then she stepped up and took the astonished Erica in her arms for a long kiss. And Erica kissed her back, right there on the doorstep in front of all of Foggy Harbor. Then she took Rashida's hand and pulled her inside, shutting the door behind her.

# At the Roots of the World Tree

So these three women walk into the bookstore on a Saturday night. I know, it sounds like the beginning of a bad joke, which it wasn't. Well, it might have been if it had been someone else's shift instead of mine. The way Fern's always going on about the time the elves came in, she'd go nuts for the Norns. Like elves asking for books on angels is anything out of the ordinary. Puh-lease.

Still, it figured. Fern gets hot blonde guys with pointy ears and I get the Past, Present, and Future personified. And lucky me, they all lined up at the counter so I couldn't pretend to do something else. The young one was drop dead gorgeous, in a glow-in-dark Valkyrie sort of way. The middle-aged one was round and short and would have looked like someone's mom if you didn't look at her eyes. They had stories buried in them, ones that weren't all warm and fuzzy and Victorianized. The third one made me want to curl up somewhere far away and safe. The bones stood out around her eyes until they almost disappeared in the hollow sockets. All she needed was a scythe to complete the look.

I stared at them, and they stared back, until the youngest one cleared her throat with an ominous growl. I became Super Bookstore Guy in a hurry. "Hello, ladies. Can I interest you in our best sellers? We've got lots of new horror right over here, far, far away from the mythology section." And the counter, but no point in offending anyone. I still had nightmares about what happened to the guy I replaced. But they just stared at me and smiled.

The one who reminded me of Death made a weird noise, like heavy machinery. The maternal one raised an eyebrow. Blondie smiled at me; clearly they wanted something more than best-selling horror. Goody.

That was when the store interrupted. "Ask them if they want the special section in the back, Ash." The voice came out of nowhere and everywhere at once. It had this royal thing going on, just like you would imagine the voice of The Cauldron of Ages: Books and Wisdom to sound. Except to me it always sounded like my ex-boyfriend, Kevin. Lately damn near everything sounded like Kevin. Am I screwed up or what?

I reluctantly took the hint. "Er...perhaps you would like to see the special books in the back?" My voice squeaked up like I was twelve or something. *V. smooth, Ash. No wonder you can't get a date.* Great. I wondered what the Cauldron wanted and glared up at the ceiling, hoping for answers that weren't coming my way.

But sooner or later, I had to look down again. The motherly one's big brown eyes melted into mine. "Why? Is that the adult section?" Her voice slithered over the counter and stroked its way up my thigh. Eeep. And I don't even like girls, at least not that way. I turned what I'm sure was a fetching shade of scarlet.

"No! Well, sometimes. That is, The Cauldron likes to keep the unexpected there. You know, for unusual customers." My words huddled together in front of me like a shield.

The old one made a face that might have been a smile if she had more flesh on her face and kept staring at me. She repeated the one word: "Ssspecial," and made a sort of weird sign with her hands. Now I was worried. This was beginning to look like they had some kind of plan for yours truly, and boy, did they have the wrong guy.

Blondie decided to intervene. "It doesn't seem to be his time, dear, and we have to get back to the Well," she said sweetly. "Show us the back room, will you, Ash?" She gave me an arch glance.

"Quessst," said the old one in an evil old voice.

Blondie brightened perceptibly. "Oooh, we haven't done that for a while." She looked me over. "He's got some potential." She gestured at my "I'd Rather be Reading the Eddas" t-shirt with a smirk that said that she didn't believe it for a moment. I was wishing I'd worn a polo when she pulled something from her pocket and looked at it. When I squinted, it just looked like colored wool. Her eyes glowed like a reactor core when she looked back at me. "Oooh, he wants to be a poet. Yes...that will do nicely." The store cleared its throat, a sound that takes some getting used to.

"We just want to borrow him for a little bit. He might buy us more time. You know the others will just sit around carousing until Ragnorak. We should take some initiative to save ourselves. And think of the poetry he'll have when he comes back." She spoke to the air in a wheedling voice.

The store didn't say anything, but those white teeth flashed like a beacon. "Come show us what's so special about the back room, Ash Thor's son." Oh, good. Puns on my last name. I love those. All eyes turned to me. I grabbed the counter to keep from stepping forward. My feet had grown a mind of their own.

"I'm not sure..." My voice quavered. Which was so not true. I was absolutely positive that I didn't want to go anywhere with them.

She smiled. "Not even for the gift of poetry?"

Ouch! That was hard to turn down. A bard in training I wasn't, and even I couldn't kid myself that my stuff was that good. But I couldn't be bought that easily. "Nope, nope, nope. Sorry, ladies, you have the wrong guy." I bolted for the mystery section and found myself at the door to the back room instead. My stomach hugged my toes.

All around us, the Cauldron laughed, the room shaking with the sound. The two over-muscled hero types browsing in the self-help books didn't even look up, but I shivered all over. That did it. Tomorrow, I was applying at a bookstore in a mall somewhere.

The old Norn made a happy sound suggestive of souls in torment, and I headed into the back room like it was the Coming Out Day relays. Kevin always said I needed to be more adventurous. Right now, I would have traded places with him in a minute.

Once through the door, I got a reality check. The Cauldron's back room wasn't like your average bookstore's back room. No, that would be too easy. Instead of being storage, it changed nearly every time you went through the door. Tonight I stepped into a cold, glowing mist so thick that I couldn't see a path in front of me. Two steps more and I couldn't see the room behind me, either.

Near as I could tell, I was all by my lonesome. Terrific. I waved my hands in front of my face and turned around a couple of times to look for the store. No such luck, if luck it was, but after what seemed like forever, a path opened up to my left. Then another to my right. Uh-oh. I looked behind me at the impenetrable wall of mist and took a step into it. Only to find myself facing the two paths again. Damn the Cauldron for getting me into this. But it was too cold to just sit here and hope the mist would clear, so I made a guess and started off down the left-hand path, trying to ignore my sense of foreboding.

Of course, the fog started to lift after I'd gone a few feet, and I could see what looked like a huge tree towering into the mists. I demonstrated my hero potential by stumbling over one of the roots that seemed to be all over the place. My yelp of pain echoed until I decided that I was going to be very quiet for a while. There could be anything running around out here.

Case in point, Blondie reappeared just then on the path in front of me. Her hair trailed off into the fog, blown by a wind I couldn't feel, and she had something in her hand. I guessed that it wasn't the Sangreal and opened my mouth to ask where the bookstore was, but she raised a hand and cut me off. "What you seek lies ahead."

"Great! Now if only I was looking for something," I responded. "Except the bookstore. I really need to get back to the counter. I get paid by the hour, you know."

She held out her hand like I hadn't said a word. I looked at the birch twig she was holding and groaned. What was I supposed to do with this? I asked the question uppermost on my mind instead: "Why me?"

She went on holding it out until I finally took it from her very white fingers. It wasn't like I didn't get the rules for the whole quest thing, after all: take anything that you're given and be nice to animals and old people. Seemed simple enough unless you were prince one or two. "Umm...thank you. What's it for?" I didn't have much hope that she'd tell me, but it was worth a shot.

"You might need it later, cutie. Maybe you can use it on His Scaliness." The scarlet lips pursed in an air kiss, and she disappeared. I didn't like the sound of the Scaliness part. Whatever it was, it needed to be talked about in capital letters. A dragon? The Cauldron wouldn't keep a dragon in the back room, would it? Just the idea made me one unhappy boy.

My mood didn't improve when I turned around to find my other two other missing customers. I decided to try again. "Did you find what you were looking for? Can we head back up to the register now?" I giggled, the sound high and desperate even to me.

They laughed, and the sound was the Kraken rising out of the fog and ships grounding on icebergs. I covered my ears and shivered. "Well, dear, that remains to be seen," said the maternal one.

"It dependsss on you," said the old one.

Whatever it was, I really didn't want any of it depending on me. "I'm probably just a poser anyway, not a real poet. Lately, I've been thinking of taking up actuarial science," I babbled. I loved the Cauldron, I reminded myself. Good books, interesting company, no overpowering sense of routine. I even had a secret crush on that sexy disembodied voice. Maybe I'd tell it about that when I got back. If I got back.

"You will need this," the old one responded.

"Use it well, and remember that a brave man lives comfortably wherever he is, but a coward is never at rest," said the other. Then they handed me a metal cauldron with runes on the side and faded away into the mist like they were erased.

I yelled after their vanishing bodies, "You're wrong about me. I am a coward! A really restless one!" But they continued to be gone, and I continued to have a big metal pot at my feet. I tried to walk away from it, but my feet wouldn't obey me. This night just kept getting better and better. I tried picking it up and found that I could just about manage it if I didn't mind listening to my arms scream.

Something sloshed inside it. Maybe I could empty it out if I couldn't leave it. I started to tilt it, then thought better of it. What came in cauldrons? Poisons? That seemed unlikely. Potions? Now that made more sense. The question was, what did this one do? I stuck a wary finger inside and pulled it out, covered in greenish goop. Filled with trepidation, I stuck the finger in my mouth and licked the goop off. Then I waited. And waited some more until I realized that I probably had to drink a lot more of it.

I tried reading the runes and stuff on the sides to see if they would give me a clue. But all of a sudden, the only thing in my head was bad limericks. "There once was a…" I managed to stop the words before I got to the end of *that* one. Terrific. The Norns had given me the gift of dirty poetry.

I looked at the cauldron again. Nothing ventured, as they say. So I picked it up and tilted it enough to get a small mouthful of the green stuff. It tasted kind of minty but had a really bitter aftertaste. Everything spun around for a second, and I sat down hard on a root. "Now is the summer…" I bit back the rest of it. Okay, I'll take Shakespeare over limericks any day, but I had been hoping for something a bit more original.

I got back up again and picked up Blondie's birch twig from where I had dropped it. Okay, I reasoned, if this Scaly thing got a drop on me, I'd need something to protect myself. And apparently, my defense consisted of a twig and a pot of green stuff that made me quote things. Swell. I rubbed my arms, trying to get warm again.

I decided to slog ahead, cauldron in hands, stubbing my toes on the roots and cursing softly. From the corner of my eye, I thought I saw something moving, but I couldn't be sure. I was willing to bet that the right hand path had gone back to the store. It just figured. I tried to remember something pleasant. Of course, I picked Kevin, hoping to wrap myself in the memory like a blanket. But with that memory came Steve from the Rowing Team. My replacement. I kicked a root. So much for happy memories.

It felt like I walked on through the mist forever, but that might have been because I was hauling a giant metal pot. The me that I was a couple of years ago would have never done this. No, that me was a sensible mall rat with great style. But before I could get too introspective, I saw something up ahead that looked like one of those cheesy lawn ornament things, the kind that looks like it's supposed to be a wishing well. They had to be kidding.

But sure enough, that's what it was. I couldn't see the water at the bottom of it, but the plastic honeysuckle wrapped around it was a nice touch. I dumped my pot next to it and looked around.

"What would you give for a drink from the Well of Wisdom, O former mall rat?"

I jumped about a foot. The voice came out of nowhere and everywhere all at once. It was just like the Cauldron's if it were talking from, say, the bottom of a well next to a bigass tree in a fog.

"What the hell is going on?"

"Decide." The tone was not one you argued with.

What did I have with me? "You want a stick? Or this nice pot?"

The voice piped up again. "Give me something you value or wander the mists forever. Such is the price of a failure to gain wisdom."

I contemplated walking around here until I became pizza for whatever lived under giant trees in the fog. My already buoyant mood dropped a few notches. There was this ominous pseudo-polite coughing noise, like a guidance counselor, so I stopped to try and make myself think about the question instead.

And of course what I thought about just then was Kevin. I wondered if he'd miss me when I didn't come back. I wondered if he'd even notice. The voice boomed out of the well. "So you would give me your love?"

I stared at the well like I was going nuts. Somehow, I hadn't noticed the bucket with the head in it sitting on the edge before. Part of my brain, the sensible mall rat part, screamed in horror and told me to get out as fast as I could. The other part began running through all the Norse mythology I knew.

This was probably Mimir, which meant this had to be Well of Wisdom. He had been quite the looker before his face got separated from the rest of him. Right now, his big blue eyes were fixed on me and waiting for an answer. Did he mean he wanted me to give up my thing for Kevin? Or was I supposed to seduce a head in a bucket surrounded by fog in order to avoid whatever the Fates had in store for me?

Hard to believe these questions had never risen before in my young life. From the corner of my eye, a really big root moved forward in a leisurely sort of way. I turned to look at it as a gigantic scale-covered head reared up and sank its teeth into the bark of the tree. *His Scaliness, I presume,* my brain babbled. Something dark flowed out of the hole that it left, something that looked suspiciously like blood.

Bleeding trees, cute bodiless guys, semi-vegetarian dragon/snake things. Wait. They had said something about buying them more time. Oh, let me guess. I was supposed to take on the dragon. No. Uh-uh. No way.

I turned around and glared at Mimir. "Just what am I supposed to fight that thing with? My keen fashion sense? This twig and a stupid pot?"

His baby blues wandered up me in a way I would have enjoyed from a guy with a body. He didn't quite meet my eyes. "Well...yes."

I threw my hands up in the air. He had to be bluffing about the wandering forever thing. "You can just send me back to the store now, brother, cause it ain't happening." From the corner of my eye, I could see the dragon chow down on another section of tree. Far above us, I could hear something that sounded like leaves whispering and wailing to themselves.

"Then you'll have to go down the well." He looked like Pride had been canceled and replaced with an infomercial marathon.

I breathed a sigh of relief, then looked down the long dark shaft of the well. I could see what looked like bookshelves on the walls at the bottom, just under the water. "Let me guess. The store is the Well of Knowledge. And you're the Cauldron, AKA Mimir. Whatever. So why a bookstore?"

He would have shrugged if he had shoulders. "What else would be a well of wisdom in these latter days? Besides, I like the company, and I have to do something while I wait for Nidhug to finish gnawing through Yggdrasil."

"Who? Oh, the dragon and the tree. Then what happens?"

"The universe ends." His words just sat hanging in the air while we both thought them over. I watched Nidhug take another bite. All of a sudden, the huge tree trunk didn't look very thick.

Mimir said gloomily. "If you're going to go, you might as well hop down."

I looked at the tree again. *Okay, Ash, you've never wanted to save the world. But if you decided that you did, this is your big chance. I bet Steve from the Rowing Team couldn't do it.* I straightened up and took a deep breath. "Okay, let's just say I give you something in exchange for wisdom, then I might be able to stop that thing?"

"Well, not stop, exactly. Delay for a few millennia, perhaps." He was sounding more cheerful. It wasn't contagious.

"What do I have that you want?" I was dreading the answer. I remembered that he'd gotten someone's eye, Odin's I think, in exchange for a drink once. Ick. I was not giving up one of mine, and that was final.

"Your heart." He said it in a weird way, like I was going to laugh at him or something.

What he got instead was a horrified stare and an emphatic, "No!"

"Not literally, of course. You're no good to me dead. It's just... since that stupid would-be warrior left you for his shield mate, I was hoping....Well, it's lonely down here, waiting for the Gods to pop over the rainbow bridge for the occasional quick visit. And Freya won't share any of her boys."

My brain spun around for a while. An immortal Norse demigod had a crush on me? How lucky could I get? What if we actually did get together? Wow, this could be lots cooler than Kevin. I pictured carrying my new bodiless boyfriend around in a bag. Boy, would we be a hit at the clubs.

This wasn't getting me anywhere, so I thought instead about the Cauldron. I really did like it there. A lot. More than hanging out with Kevin's idiot friends, for sure. And Kevin had Steve, and he was right about me. I always was more of a chess geek than a jock, and I did read too much, and I liked it that way. Then I wondered if Mimir had to stay in this form or if he could do something about the missing body problem.

For a brief instant, I also wondered what I was giving up. Maybe this was the real thing: true love. Maybe I was born to write angst-ridden poems to a bodiless head in a pea soup fog at the foot of Yggdrasil until the universe ended. It sounded pretty Goth when I thought about it that way. Cool.

Enough. I made myself back up and think about the big picture. What it came down to was whether or not I could live with myself if I said no. After all, 'a coward is never at rest' and all that. I considered what I had to lose, and it wasn't all that much. Mom and Dad and my friends would understand if I didn't make it back. They were all very into saving the world. Maybe it was time to do my bit.

"I guess so," I said tentatively. No point in sounding too eager. The honeysuckle came alive instantly, and Mimir smiled.

"Kiss me, poet." His voice made it a command, and I got annoyed. Who did this guy think he was? Where were the flowers, the chocolate, or at least a cup of coffee? I glared at him, and he smiled sweetly back.

Then again, I'm always a sucker for big blue eyes. I leaned down and brushed my lips against his. His eyes took on a pleading expression when I backed away. Guess that wasn't enough. I made myself pick up his head. There wasn't any blood or anything. It was as though he just disappeared below the neck. Eeep. I dragged my courage back from wherever it had been vacationing, and I kissed him for real. Ooh. There were fireworks, and if the earth didn't precisely move, it did go away for a while.

When it finally did stop—or when we stopped, depending on how you wanted to look at it—he whispered, "Drink from the well."

Something felt different. I put his head down very gently on the rim. It crossed my mind that if I wasn't careful, he'd just roll away. The idea made me want to giggle or barf, I wasn't sure which. Instead of doing either, I lowered the bucket.

Mimir watched me until I'd hauled the bucket back up and had a drink from my cupped hands. The water was a golden color and strangely sweet. "Two more," he said. "Just to be sure."  I drank again. And again. I met his eyes and everything melted away. When the world flowed back, a great sadness came with it. "A wise man's heart is seldom glad," my love said.

It was true. I knew that the same way I knew both more and less than I had known before. Nothing was ever going to be quite the same again. I looked away toward Yggdrasil and the dragon Nidhug for a span of breaths, and I longed for what I had been before. But that was gone forever. I squared my shoulders, then pulled the birch twig from my pocket and picked up the cauldron. "Drink from the cauldron and go tell it a story," Mimir suggested.

"Well, that does beat trying to kill it with the twig, I suppose." My voice sounded harsh in my ears, and I smiled a little to let him know I spoke in jest.

"A paltry man and poor of mind is he who mocks all things." He gave me an answering smile so I would know that I was only being scolded gently. "No, don't ask what kind of story. You'll know when you get there. Just believe in yourself."

I took a swig of the green stuff, dipping the twig in it for good measure, then I walked slowly toward the dragon. It ran a lazy golden eye over me when I got closer and took another bite of tree trunk. Above us, Yggdrasil cried out, wailing against its fate. Now I understood its every cry, and my heart demanded that I do something.

The twig grew in my hand until I held a staff. Cool, in a weird sort of way. Maybe it would turn me into Gandalf. Only without the useful powers. I looked up at the huge, thick coils above me and gulped. I closed my eyes, hoping it would help me find my soon-to-be-missing nerve.

All right, here goes nothing. I opened my eyes and tightened my grip on the staff, then waved it around menacingly at the beastie. Bark continued to shower down around my ears. Humph. Well, that wasn't it. I looked down, searching for a clue, then, on a whim, I struck the ground between my feet with the staff. And promptly fell over as a bolt of lightning shot out of it, striking Nidhug's nose.

It stopped chewing and looked down at me. Uh-oh. I scrambled to my feet and put both hands on the staff. I would find what I needed, Mimir said. Well, okay, here goes nothing. I waited for something else to happen, more lightning, the staff to turn into a sword, anything. Instead, I got words, lots of them. I started remembering stories I'd read, poems I'd tried to write, grocery lists, you name it.

I closed my eyes again and said the first thing that came into my head. "Hear me, Dragon. I would tell you of what has been and what might have been. Hear now my tale." Okay, so far so good. So what would a dragon want to hear about? Other dragons seemed like a safe bet. I cleared my throat and told it every single story about dragons I could remember. Good dragons, bad dragons, dragons with great powers, dragons with the fate of the universe between their teeth, of these I spoke and more. And, most importantly, it listened, and it did not eat me.

In fact, when I finally opened my eyes, it was watching me and listening. The shower of bark had slowed to an occasional drizzle. I could see Yggdrasil healing itself behind Nidhug's head, the bark creeping back to fill the huge, jagged holes. I kept talking.

Eventually, I ran out of dragon stories, so I started in on unicorns. When I ran out of those, I was thinking about telling it one or two about talking kitty cats, but I couldn't stand up anymore, even with the help of the staff. "Rest," a voice said out of nowhere, and I did.

When I woke up, I was laying by the Well, and the blond Norn sat looking down at me, Mimir's head in her lap. "Well done, Ash." She smiled at me, and I knew her name now: Skuld, the Norn of the Future. "You have saved us all for a time."

I made myself not look up at the tree, even though I could hear the leaves wailing again above us. Nidhug must be at it again. Instead, I met Mimir's eyes, and I knew that I loved him, that I loved no other, and that nothing was ever going to come of it. The big lump in my throat made it hard to breathe for a moment. "Don't you have a job to do?" he asked in the store's voice. I stood up and the back room reappeared around me.

"I get a raise for this, right?" No answer, but I could see him smile. Clearly we had boundary issues to resolve. Later. I looked around. The shelves had books on them now, and I could read the runes on one of them. They spelled out my name: Ash Thorson. Weird.

Somehow, I knew if I opened it right now, it would be blank. I leaned on the staff and looked at the door to the bookstore. This was it, then, my future, the one that would fill the book. I opened the door. There were a bunch of heroes and Valkyries and whatnot hanging out in the store, and they seemed to be waiting for something. Were we having a sale?

"Tell them a tale, Skald," Mimir's voice boomed out around me. Skald, eh? I liked the sound of that. I looked back. The Norn waved a piece of colored wool at me and grinned. Mimir's eyes were filled with something I couldn't read and wasn't sure I wanted to, not just yet. I dragged myself away and swallowed my desire and my butterflies. Then I walked out into the store, his presence wrapped around me like a cloak as I shut the door and began to speak.

# A Scent of Roses

The night it is gude Halloween,    The faery
folk do ride, And they that wad their true-love
win,    At Miles Cross they maun bide.

*Tam Lin*, TRADITIONAL BALLAD

J ANET STRAIGHTENED HER BACK AGAINST the persistent ache that filled her and wiped the sweat from her brow with a grimy hand. The sun was setting slowly, blinding her until she looked away. Time to leave the field and go back to the cottage. She grimaced at the thought. Tam would no doubt have been at the ale. He'd sit by the fire again tonight, singing that witch's tongue the Good Folk spoke and telling her tales about their country as if she cared to know.

With a groan, she picked up her hoe and her bag and began the weary walk home. Almost she wished that she'd not lain with him in the rose garden of her father's house at Carterhaugh. Almost she wished that her courage had failed at the crossroads marked by Miles Cross and that she had not saved him from the Fair Folk. But wishing would not take her back in time, nor restore their babe, sickened and dead in his cradle a year past. If he had lived, her father might have accepted Tam as his heir. Instead, he exiled her and her faery knight to a distant holding, little more than a cottage and a few rocky fields. She kicked at a rock in her path, wincing when it hurt her toes through her thin shoes.

"No longer so proud as you once were, I see."

The voice was cool and sardonic but it fell on Janet's ears like a burning brand. She spun around to face her tormentor but the words caught in her throat. A lady sat on a great stone by the side of the path and her face Janet could never forget. "You!" She spat. "Have you not had revenge enough but must needs come back to mock me in my fall?"

The other woman tilted her head sideways like a bird, but no bird had eyes so fearsome and strange. Janet could not hold back a shiver and the Queen of the Fair Folk smiled to see it. "You fear me now, mortal? I was not so fearsome when you stole my knight away."

"Would your Majesty care to try and take him back?" Janet's fists clenched and her cheeks flushed red. She dropped her tools at her feet, bracing herself as if to box.

The Queen threw back her head with a merry tinkling laugh. "If I did not kill you then, why would I brawl with you like one of your fish-wives now? You won him fair, Janet, and he is yours to mind and tend."

"Then why are you here?" Janet asked, her voice uncertain. "I've kine to tend and bairns and Tam to feed. You've naught to do with me."

"Do I not?" The Queen stood, her gown of green falling to her feet like a river of grass. She seemed taller than Janet remembered and she flinched away, as afraid now as she had been two years before. "There are no bairns, as you know well. Naught but my former knight waits for you and he sleeps before the fire, an empty cup by his chair."

Janet's blood ran hot again. "'Tis your fault! If you had not taken him, he would be an honored knight at the King's court! We should have had bairns aplenty and lands and . . ." Here her voice broke and she wiped savagely at her eyes.

The Queen reached out her hand, her skin glowing a pale green in the dim light. With one feather light touch, she captured one of Janet's tears and brought it to her lips. She gave Janet a hard stare for a breath or two. Then her face softened in an odd smile, one that made her look a bit like any village girl watching her swain.

In a trice, she was gone, vanished like a dream. Janet stared at the spot where she had stood, one hand clasping the cheek those faery fingers had touched. Her skin burned pleasantly, sending a heat through her that she'd not felt in far too long. She took a deep breath and realized that the air around her was full of the scent of the roses of Carterhaugh.

Torn between anger and something she dared not examine too closely, she picked up her hoe and bag and resumed her walk home. Now it was growing dark and the trees' branches twined an arch across the path above her head. All around her the evening was filled with small sounds: the cry of the hunting owl, the soft crackle of a deer's hooves on fallen leaves, and above it all, the distant silver tinkle of bells like those on a bridle. Would the Queen return for her? The thought made her flee for the safety of the cottage, shivering.

She slammed the door behind her and dropped the bolt in place before she turned to look around her, heart racing. Tam sat just as she knew he would: handsome sleeping face lit by the dying flames and an empty jug beside him. As she watched, he blinked and sat up, blue eyes puzzled as if he had dreamt of other times and places. Perhaps his dreams were full of eyes that had no color Janet could name.

Anger filled her with the thought, driving out the fear that held her silent in the doorway. "You drunken sot! Have you done nothing but lay here all day? Did you even go to the castle to see if Lord Edmond would have you as a guard?" She stalked toward the fire without waiting for an answer, for she knew there would be none that would please her.

"Ah Janet, lass, you know they'll have none of me up at the castle. Better I should come to the fields with you and work the soil at your side." He ran trembling fingers through his brown curls, leaning forward so his elbows rested on his knees.

"You cannot till the soil, and the cattle tremble when they see you. You are good for nothing but the sword and the lute and pleasing the Fair Folk's Queen until she saw fit to tithe you to Hell!" As soon as the words were spoken, Janet wished she could call them back.

Tam Lin gave her a look of pure agony, all cloudiness gone from the blue glory of his eyes for a moment. She felt his pain as if it was her own and she dropped a gentle hand to his shoulder as she went to stoke the fire. It was not all his fault that he was not raised to the farm and that the castle would not have him. Yet if he would try harder and drink less, they might yet make their living from this farm and the herd her father gave them as a parting gift. She sighed, wondering if she must fight the battle anew tonight.

Instead, he stood unsteadily. "I'll fetch the kine."

"No, Tam, they fear you. I'll do it." She turned toward the door with a sigh.

He was there before her, wordlessly unbarring the door and vanishing into the darkness beyond. She started to follow him, then changed her mind and went to put on the remains of the morning's porridge for their dinner. Perhaps the beasts would grow accustomed to him with time. Unthinking, her hand caressed her cheek as if the Queen's fingertips were still there. She watched the fire for a span of breaths, seeing a beautiful face out of dream instead of her humble cauldron.

She was still standing there when Tam came back from stabling the cattle. He barred the door quietly and came up behind her to wrap his arms tight around her waist. She could feel his lips in her hair as he held her, desire stirring sluggishly inside her as if waking from a long sleep. She smiled at him over one shoulder, then swung the pot of porridge away from the fire before turning to kiss him. When they paused for breath, some impulse made her whisper, "Do you still dream about her?"

Tam pulled away from her as if stung. "Why must you ask these questions? You won me, heart and soul. Must you have all my thoughts as well?"

Janet gaped at him and stammered, "I only . . ." She stopped at his upraised palm and the shake of his head. Perhaps there had been too many words already tonight. Silently, she ladled the porridge into the wooden bowls and equally silently, they ate. Little more passed between them until Janet, weary of the silence heavy with unspoken thoughts, went to their bed alone, leaving Tam to brood before the dying fire.

The dreams that came to her that night would have seen her barred from their humble church. The Queen rode through each of them, the bells jingling at her horse's bridle to signal her coming. Each dream began with her touch, sometimes her fingers on Janet's cheek, sometimes her lips. As the night wore on, her fingers and lips tasted Janet's breast and her tongue traced the outline of her belly. Then the curved roundness of her thighs. Janet started awake before that tongue could go elsewhere, sitting up to gasp for air and shudder at the burning in her loins.

Beside her, Tam slept like the dead, hearing and feeling nothing of her distress. She put out a tentative hand and rested it on his bare shoulder, then lay down at his side, pressing close against him. How could she want such things? Surely, this was the Devil's work and she was under a glamour. The Queen had tasted her tears. That must be how she did it. Tomorrow, she must go to the kirk and beg for shriving. Only that could save her soul. She lay awake, listening to Tam's heavy breathing and shivering under the burden of her thoughts until dawn.

"I must go to the priest," she told Tam when the cows were fed and they had eaten their meal. "Will you come with me?"

He shook his head but did not meet her eyes. "The damned fool will scrub all with holy water if he sees me. I cannot bear the stench of fear and hatred that hangs about the old man. Today I will feed the cattle and go to the field." His jaw was set and his face was grim when he described these simple tasks and Janet could not help letting a small sigh escape her lips. A quick and furious glare came hard on its heels to meet her eyes, then Tam caught up the tools and was gone.

She bit back the impulse to tell him not to lose the cows or burn down the cottage. It would do no good and was best left unsaid. At least it was better than that he should spend the day awash in ale. She was off to the kirk then. Still she found that her feet moved but slowly down the path despite her resolution. The old priest was foolish, just as Tam said. Perhaps he did not have the power to stand against a glamour like this. "Do you want him to?" The unspoken question whispered against her ear like a soft breeze carrying the breath of a lover.

Janet trembled against the words, the heat of strange longing filling her until she was near to feeling the Queen's lips against her own. She fought it with a howl more like an animal's than her own voice. "Yes!" When the word passed her lips, she dropped to her knees in the grass and prayed as she had never done before. Desperation lent her thoughts an earnest fervor that cooled her heated limbs and drove all dreams from her until she could stand and resume her walk. It would be enough. The priest would shrive her and there would be no more dreams, no phantom touches to give her unclean thoughts.

But the old priest was nowhere to be found when she reached the church. When she asked in the village, one had him at a deathbed in the Highlands, another at a baptism in a village some hours walk away. Discouraged, she went into the tiny church and knelt in prayer for a time. She could not say how long her head was bowed, how hard it was to send her thoughts toward heaven but when she stood at last, she swayed with hunger and the priest had still not returned.

She made her way out and followed the stream that ran through the churchyard away from the village. She walked until she reached a clearing ringed with berry bushes nearly past their full ripeness. These she added to the hard bread she had brought in her pocket and the water from the stream. Then she sat a time, watching the water flow past.

Her thoughts unbidden turned to Tam's tales of the Faery lands. Wild tales they were, full of a land in eternal spring, ever blooming and flourishing. There were green forests to ride through and clear streams to drink from and marvels to see with each passing day. The Queen's palace was made of silver and gems, flashing in the pale sunlight and all her folk were beautiful to hearts-breaking.

In all, he made it seem a paradise that she had kidnapped him from. Her jaw tightened with the thought. Once and once alone, he spoke of the other things he had seen there: the redcaps, the Jack-in-Irons with his clanking chains and the other nightmare creatures of fang and claw. They, too, dwelt in that fair land and haunted its corners and dark hollows, lying in wait for the unwary.

He spoke then too of the day he heard that the Court paid a tithe to Hell every seven years to keep them safe from the flames of God's wrath. The Fair Folk whispered that it must be he who went in place of them, for he had a soul and they had none. How he shuddered when he spoke of it! Janet herself shivered to remember it now, even in the warmth of the summer sun.

To drive the thought from her mind, she rose and went to the berry bushes. In the thicket was the biggest, juiciest berry she had ever seen and she reached for it, straining until her fingers clasped it. A thorn caught her then and she pulled her hand quickly from the bush as a bright red drop of blood spilled over her skin. She raised it to her lips only to feel the weight of another's gaze hard upon her. Janet whirled, heart racing, to find the Queen watching her from under a great oak tree a few paces away, a white horse at her side.

"Have you no servants, Madam, who can be trusted to spy on me but that you must do it yourself?" Janet asked when she caught her breath.

"Ah, but it pleases me to watch you. I stole Tam because he was brave and beautiful and bright with mortal promise, but you, you are something more." The Queen tilted her head as if considering what that might be.

Janet crossed herself frantically. If only the priest had been there to shrive her! She could not fail to notice that the gesture made the Queen smile and she shuddered, closing her eyes against desire and fear. Something caught her hand and she felt lips as tender as the dawn capture the blood welling from the scratch the thorns had left. All strength left her and she fell to her knees, heart pounding and flesh burning until her hand was released.

Then she forced herself to her feet and dragged her eyelids open. The Queen was far too close and Janet staggered back away from her, welcoming the bracing trunk of a giant oak at her back. The other's face had a glimmer of wonder in it. "You still resist me. Tam was mine for a fall from his horse into a mushroom ring, yet you can stand apart from me, despite what I have taken from you. I have never seen your like before, Janet. Can you still wonder that I come to try you myself instead of sending others?"

Janet shivered against the tree. "What glamour have you thrown on me, fiend?"

"I cast no spell. Come to me of your own free will, Janet, and I will show you all the wonders of Faery. Only come to Miles Cross to ride at my side on Hallows Eve." With one last near wistful smile, the Queen of the Fey vanished into the woods with only the faint jingle of bells and the frantic racing of Janet's heart left to mark her passage.

Janet seized her bag and took to her heels, running toward the village as fast as she could, her long skirt tangling in her legs. Only when she staggered into the churchyard could she bring herself to look at the scratch on her hand. The flesh had begun to heal itself under a gossamer web like a spider's. Staring at it in horror, she fled into the church, the priest's name on her lips. Her words echoed into emptiness and she fell sobbing on her knees before the altar.

It was anger, finally, that drove her to her feet and onto the path that led back to their cottage. It seemed God's reward for saving Tam's soul was to put her own in danger. Bitterly, she cursed the impulse that had led her to Miles Cross and the night that she first spied the Queen of the Fairies in her bold, bright fury. Would that she had left Tam to his fate and born his bastard in the comforting concealment of her father's castle. He would have married her off to one of his knights and she could have continued a life free from want and desire alike.

Frowning, she imagined a life without Tam or the Queen. The thoughts sat heavy on her shoulders until the cottage came into view and she quickened her pace to reach it. Enough of might-have-beens. She made her choices at Miles Cross and Carterhaugh and there was no more to it than that. Now she had the kine to tend and the porridge to make.

Her cousin had even promised her a chicken and a rooster before winter came. They would make their own ease and if she loved Tam a little less for the life they now led, it was not so different from other married folk.

Her back was straight and firm and her jaw set in resolve when she entered the cottage. The fire was cold in the hearth, but at least there was no silent figure in the chair, no empty jug on the floor. Tam must still be abroad in the field. Well and good, she must be about her own chores then. With a will, she set to setting the cottage to rights, starting the fire anew and placing the pot on the flames to boil. The floor was swept and the cobwebs in the corners cleaned away with scarce a shudder when Tam returned from the field.

He looked weary and red with the sun but she could hear the cattle outside. All was well and her lips curved into a welcoming smile as she kissed his cheek. He gave her a startled look and a shy smile in return and so they sat down to their stew at the table. "Did the priest shrive you then?" He asked after a few moments' talk.

Janet jumped in her chair, her hand going to her cheek as if the Queen's fingers still lay there. She made herself shrug as if it was no great thing, as if her fears and wants were like the washing and the mending. "No. He was away in the Highlands. I will go back another day for shriving." Tam nodded and returned to his stew, leaving her lost in her thoughts.

That night, they tried to recover some of what they had lost in the warmth of kisses and hot skin against skin until they fell asleep wrapped in each other's arms. No dreams about the Queen came to trouble Janet that night or the next or the ones that followed.

Instead, she began to see herself as she would be ten, twenty years hence when hard work on the farm had taken its toll. By then, she feared that she and Tam would have no more love for each other but would remain together from long habit and fondness. A great emptiness filled Janet when she woke from these dreams and more and more her fingers stole to her cheek or to her hand. She remembered the wild elation of Miles Cross, the knowledge that she alone had succeeded in defying the

Queen of the Faeries. She remembered feeling alive and the dreams that she had now were repugnant to her.

More than once, she tried to speak to Tam of it but the harder he worked in the fields, the more silent he became. Sometimes she found him polishing his old sword and once she saw him fight an opponent that none could see but him. His dreams at night seemed as troubled as her own but she found no words to ask him what he feared. Nor did she tell him anything of the Queen, though once she tried to get him to tell her about his time at her Court. He gave her a sharp look and asked. "What have you to do with mushroom rings and those that dance within them?"

"Nothing. I but remember the tales you told me before." She stumbled over the lie and she could see that he knew it for what it was. He said nothing more, only reaching over to press her hand, a look of pity in his eyes.

It was two mornings later that a well-dressed man rode up to their gate on a fine horse and spoke long with Tam. She heard none of their words and cared little more, thinking the stranger only a lost traveler. It was only when she came into the barn later to find Tam with his sword in his hands, his feet treading a measure with an imaginary opponent that she thought to ask, "Who was he? What did he say to you?" She sat on a pile of hay, admiring despite herself the sweep of the blade and the rusty grace with which he held it.

He spun, beheading a shadow before he rested the point of the blade on the dirt in front of him. "He came to speak to me of a fool's errand beyond the sea, of fighting and glory and all else that a farmer's life does not offer. He spoke of gold to be won, Janet, and a name to be regained." Tam did not meet her eyes, looking only at the sword in his hands. Even so, she could see that his eyes held a fire to them that she had not seen since Carterhaugh.

He put up the sword then, sliding it into its scabbard with an ease that his hands knew well. But she saw how his hand lingered on the hilt and she knew what his answer must be. She said nothing more, remembering with a start that tonight was Hallows Eve and Miles Cross was not so long a ride from the cottage. Her heart beat madly then for all she went about her work as though it was a day like any other. Tam, too, seemed lighter of heart but still they did not speak of their thoughts to each other.

And such thoughts they were! She shuddered at the tithe, bit back a wail at the thought of the monsters of Faery, of what she would leave behind. Still and all, what would she do with Tam gone, even if he sent back whatever gold he won? There was nothing for her here but to grow old and lonely and bitter until even the Queen of Faeries would have no use for her. But to live at the Queen's side, that would be worth the risks surely. Her thoughts ran round and round until dusk.

Her choice when it came found her running to the stable. She led their old plow horse out of the barn as quietly as she could. She had only just saddled the beast when there came Tam with his kit over one shoulder and his sword buckled at his side. They looked at each other for a long moment in the fading light until he spoke at last. "You go to her at Miles Cross, then?" He frowned, his hand reaching up to caress her cheek.

She held his hand there and kissed his palm. "And you away beyond the sea to fight?" He nodded and she smiled at him in understanding. Together, they released the cattle from the makeshift barn and doused the fire in the hearth. Together, they stood side by side looking at the cottage and the rocky fields around it.

Tam spoke first. "I loved you true, Janet, with no glamour to compel it. I will miss you." He pulled her close and held her tight. "Beware the tithe, love. If I may, I will come to Carterhaugh a year hence. If you need me, leave word for me there."

Janet wiped away a tear and smiled up at him. "Go well, love. May you be safe from all harm and find what you seek." Their lips met briefly in a final kiss. Then she mounted the old horse, glancing back to wave him on his way as they parted. Her heart almost failed her then and the night seemed full of secret sounds and whispers. Her hands trembled on the reins and she watched the shadows on either side. From far away, she heard music and laughter but she forced herself to stay on the path and closed her eyes so that she would not see whoever made the sounds. Still she rode on, turning neither to left nor right until the moon rose and the great stone cross appeared before her.

Then she had naught to do but wait for what seemed an eternity. When she had come to rescue Tam, she had hidden in the bushes, catching the Queen all unawares, but tonight she sat in full moonlight at the crossroads like a knight from a tale. Before she had her love for Tam and their babe inside her to buoy her courage, but tonight she had nothing but her dreams and the very longings that she feared. Almost she turned her horse back, almost she rode for her father's court to ask his forgiveness. Always something held her there, waiting.

It was nearly midnight when she heard the jingle of bells on bridles and saw the glow of riders through the trees. Her heart beat so fast she thought it would jump out of her mouth and the old horse fidgeted beneath her as he caught her mood. The faery knights came closer, the ladies of the Seelie Court on their heels and she could see that their eyes shone with colors that she could not name and that they were beautiful to hearts-breaking. All fell silent to see her there and the faery riders came to a halt at the edge of the clearing. She stared back at them, a wild excitement rising in her.

The Queen came riding through her courtiers and smiled to see her waiting there. Something broke inside Janet, like a river when the thaw comes and she laughed as she had not in years. The Queen rode closer and spoke, a victorious smile tilting her lovely lips, "Come and mount behind me, my Janet. My horse shall bear us both." Janet shook her head mutely and held her horse's reins all the tighter. The Queen looked amused. "Give me a kiss then and ride at my side."

She reached for Janet, who did not pull away. The Queen's lips burned against hers until she broke away laughing, enchanted by a glamour all her own. Then, bright and full of mortal promise, she urged her horse into a gallop and rode with into Faery with the Queen at her side.

# At Mother Laurie's House of Bliss

Ren Harath, trusted right hand of the Sunlord himself, was in a playful mood. There was a twinkle in his dark eyes that stood out despite the mask he wore to disguise his face each time he came to me. It amused him to think that he might hide behind it, as if Mother Laurie herself had not told me who he was when he first began to come to the House of Bliss.

I helped him slide off his heavy cloak, rich with the fur of some animal I'd never seen before. Then I knelt at his feet for a moment, reaching for his boots as much as to appear appropriately humble as to undress him but he gestured me up on to the bed instead. This was new. I wondered, with a mild mixture of boredom and apprehension, what he wanted from me tonight.

But I let none of that show on my face. Instead, I lay down and summoned my most welcoming boyish grin. Mother Laurie didn't like it if we didn't at least pretend to look enthusiastic and her displeasure was not something I wanted to risk. Of course, privately I wondered how enthusiastic she'd looked, back when she was in my place. Back before one of her lovers, some wealthy Sunborn or other, gave her enough to set up her own house and give up lovers like Ren.

But this wasn't the time to wonder about that too hard. Instead, I thought hopeful thoughts about how some of the other boys in the house had told me that nobles like Ren sometimes left a jewel or two behind when they left. Perhaps even enough to put aside for a House of my own someday, once I'd bought my freedom.

Thus far, he'd left me three gold pieces and some handfuls of silver, but nothing more valuable than that. Still, he kept coming back and it was something to be able to say that one of the King's most trusted advisers was one of my lovers. Or at least it would have been if I were allowed to talk about it. As it was, Mother Laurie had told me that only she and I knew the identity of my mysterious lover.

I tilted my head back to show off the taut muscles in my neck and chest and thought about the virtue of discretion. It was at once the most valued and least appreciated of my skills. Ren gave an appreciative grumble from the foot of the bed. I worked on looking overcome with desire.

In response, he tossed his sword and scabbard aside and smiled. "Arin, you have served me well, perhaps even begun to earn my love. Since you have moved me, tonight I shall favor you as I have favored no other. I shall read the poems that I have composed under the spell of your inspiration." He yanked a piece of parchment from the saddlebag that hung over the chair. Then he seized his gold-plated cup and downed the wine I had poured into it with what seemed like a single gulp.

My seductive smile locked into place. Ren's poetry was not like the kind made by two men together, joined by love and lust. Or not like any such poetry anyone was willing to pay me for. He also seemed to have forgotten that I'd been present at Lady Iridice's birthday celebration last month and well remembered his impulse to declaim there. The sidelong glances and smothered titters at his skills were startling in their openness, given his rank.

Now I wished that I'd had the wit to pour myself a cup of the wine as well. Ren began to read from the parchment while I stilled my face to vapid admiration. His words were as foolish as I remembered them and I wondered how long he planned to go on. I practiced drawing in my breath slowly and letting my body ease seductively back into the silken coverlets as Mother Laurie herself had taught me when I first came to her.

Then Ren's voice faltered. He choked on his words and coughed, his shoulders shaking with the effort. I sat up; surely this was more than bad verse. I watched in horror as his face paled beneath its normal dusky hue and he gasped. His legs began to buckle and he staggered.

I uncoiled from the silken covers as fast as I could and rushed to his side, catching him as he collapsed. I lowered him slowly to the expensive carpet as he stared up at me, eyes rolling, a white foam pouring from his lips. "Ser! Ser! What is it? Mirana!" I howled for our witch. She would know what to do, if she was in earshot.

But no one came. His body convulsed and then Ser Ren Harath, adviser to the King, noblest of the Sunborn, went still in my arms. I placed him gently on the floor and ran, naked as I was to the chamber door. I flung it wide. "Mirana! Mirana! Come at once!"

Mother Laurie appeared in the doorway as if by magic and I fell backward at her frown. I wondered if she'd been waiting outside. "What are you doing, fool? All that screaming will frighten off business." She stepped in as I retreated, stopping only when she could see Ren's body on the carpet. Then she pushed me aside, closed the door and knelt next to him.

Her hands were at his face, then his neck. I could see her broad features change as she realized what I feared. "Put some clothes on, boy. Then fetch Mirana." She seemed to think of something else. "And don't imagine that you can run from this house. I still hold your bond." An unpleasant glint shone in her blue eyes for a moment and I shivered, my hand going to the nearly invisible silver collar around my neck. If she willed it, it would tighten like the grip of the King's executioner until I joined Ren Harath in the Lady's dark caves.

I scrambled into my tunic and leggings and went down the stairs like I had wings, dodging the inquisitive hands of several older gentlemen and at least one lady in my passage. Mirana was in the kitchen, as usual this time of night. She looked up from a smoking cup of something that the cook had just handed her and I shivered despite myself. Looking into her cold dark eyes, it was almost as if she knew what I would say before I said it. "It's Ser Harath! You've got to come! Mother Laurie's with him." I gasped.

She gave me an odd look before she rose and caught up her stick in one hand, my arm in the other. "Come then." Her voice rumbled up from some place deep below our feet.

My legs began to shake as I looked at the cup the witch had just put down. Now I remembered who had poured Ren's wine. If he had been poisoned, I was doomed. I went limp in the witch's grasp. She yanked hard, pulling me back into reality. "Smile at the clients, Arin. I don't know what's happened but you're not in the King's dungeons yet." I stared at her and she bared sharp blackened teeth back at me. It brought no comfort.

We were back in my room almost as fast as I had left it. Mother Laurie was sitting on a chair and studying Ren Harath's body on the floor before her, a thoughtful look on her face. "Mirana, do what you can, please." She and the witch exchanged odd, cool glances and I shut the door, sealing us all in.

I tried not to look down at Ren and found myself looking instead at the parchment that he never finished reading. Unthinking, I reached toward it only to have my hand knocked aside by the witch's staff. "Don't touch anything until I'm done!" Mirana barked.

Nursing my knuckles, I watched her circle the body, leaning on her stick as if she was pulling the boat of her body forward with it like a steersman's oar. The moon of her form eclipsed Mother Laurie's each time she moved and I wondered if it was a portent of things to come.

At least Mother Laurie was familiar. A witch exiled from the Lady's Temple in Idrenpur, on the other hand, was a stranger everywhere she went. Given the manner of sinister arts they taught there, I could not imagine what would be evil enough to result in being cast out. A cold shiver crept over my flesh.

Mother Laurie beckoned me over, making a circular gesture with one thick hand to indicate that I should not get too close to the witch and Ren's body as I crossed the room. As if I needed encouragement. I nearly pressed myself through the walls and beyond as I circled around the macabre scene in the center of the room.

As I went, I tried to read Mother Laurie's expressionless face; would she throw me to the Guards unheard? Was there a chance of proclaiming my innocence? I knelt at her feet when I reached her side and stared down at the thick carpet below my knee.

Then I noticed that Ren's purse had fallen from the saddlebag and was now spilling its contents on the floor under the chair. He must have grabbed it when he fell. I wondered if I could reach it before the two women noticed, seize it and run for the street, bond or no bond.

"You are a foolish young man, Arin," Mother Laurie rumbled over my bent head. "The question is: how foolish?"

I jerked back and stared at her. Always, I could read the men who came to me, very nearly knowing their thoughts, but this woman was a stone wall. What did she mean?

She sighed, the movement shaking her big frame. "Did you know the Ser's wine was tainted?" She scowled down at me as if reconsidering the phrasing of the question. "Did an enemy of the King persuade you to kill his minister?"

My head shook like a marketplace puppet's. "No!" I stared up at her in horror, all the while thinking of reasons to want the man dead. Not my reasons, but reasons nonetheless. He had been rich and powerful, his heirs contending for his favor. The King's other favorites were replaced when he arrived at court. It was even said that he had been the King's lover as well as that of other powerful Sunborn. Harath had been ruthless, sometimes cruel, and a dreadful poet. Any of these things, or perhaps all of them, might have been inspiration enough to kill him.

Mirana cleared her throat. Harath's body, the parchment and the goblet all glowed for a moment. She murmured some words I didn't catch, then made a sweeping gesture with her hands. The glow gradually dimmed until all looked as it had before. The witch glanced at Mother Laurie. "Poison, as you guessed. Dragonsbreath from the western mountains, I believe."

I froze, my breath trapped behind my lips. I knew Dragonsbreath, as did every child in my village. The old women warned us away from its red flowers and deceptively sweet smell from the moment we could walk. I wrapped my arms around my legs and lowered my head, a moan I could not halt leaping from my lips. There were no other whores from my valley at Mother Laurie's House of Bliss, nor even elsewhere in the whole city of Hidrath that I knew of. And Dragonsbreath grew nowhere else in the Sunlord's lands.

My reaction had not gone unnoticed. "Mirana, see if he speaks the truth about the Ser. Use your powers." Mother Laurie's voice was implacable, cold as the northern snows. I flinched away and she grabbed me by the shoulders, holding me still.

Mirana held up her hands, rings flashing on her fingers, and whispered a phrase. I could see a dark pattern on her skin now and the lines of it moved like snakes. My bond circlet burned around my neck and I screamed, the sound cut off by Mother Laurie's hand over my mouth. "Silence, boy! It is this or the Sunlord's torturers and I want answers before I give you to them. Let Mirana do her work."

The witch reached for me, the patterns writhing on her skin from her fingers down her arms. Her eyes were all black now, the magic of Idrenpur and something more besides filling her like a vessel. I knew that whatever it was, she would pour it into me and it would force me to tell her anything she wanted. It was familiar and yet it should not be. Had this been done to me before? When?

I shoved back hard against Mother Laurie, my panic overriding my fear of death as I tried to yank myself free. But I was too slow. The witch's hand closed over my head, holding me in place. The pattern fell from the flesh of her hand, dropping over my face like a black net and I screamed as I had not since I was sold into bondage. I had sworn that no one would make me scream like again, yet here I broke that oath without a second thought.

The net tightened, its touch making my flesh flinch away from its tendrils, its knots. They quested out across my face until they covered it. I could feel my body bucking away from their unclean touch as they sank into my skin.

Then, my mind was no longer my own.

From as far away as if she was still at the cook's table in the kitchen, I heard Mirana's voice. "You will speak the truth, Arin. Anything less will mean your death." I tried to look at her from behind the veil that covered my face, but I could not move. I heard the truth in her words though, fearing only my own answers.

"Did you desire Harath's death?"

I heard my lips form a whispered, "No," and I went limp with relief. That much at least was true. What whore desires their best client dead, if he has not been cruel?

"Do you remember anyone speaking to you of his death?"

My lips formed another, "No." And yet, someone had done this to me before, perhaps even given me orders. Who knew what they had spoken of? My "No" was a greater effort this time.

There was a stillness in the room. There was a rushing in my ears as though I swam in a river, with only the net holding me in place. Then Mirana spoke again, "Did you put poison in the goblet?"

My "No" froze on my lips this time. Instead, to my utter and complete horror, I heard myself say, "Yes." A tear, then another rolled down my cheek under the webs that covered it. How could I have done such a thing and not remembered it? Again, there was silence in the room and neither Mother Laurie nor Mirana spoke for a moment.

"It is settled then. We give him to the Guards with a confession." That was Mother Laurie's voice, implacable and cold. I wondered if she was disappointed in me, her finest pupil. I wondered if I was disappointed in myself.

Mirana's voice came again and it echoed with the Lady's power. "Wait. There is more he has not said. I can feel it."

Mother Laurie snorted. "I doubt it. Remember that your powers are not what they might have been if you had stayed at Idrenpur. I pay you for hedge witcheries, to keep the whores free of disease and babies, but to divine the whole truth is work for a fully trained witch."

The webs retreated a little, not enough to free me, but enough for me to see their faces clearly again. Mother Laurie looked contemptuous and Mirana looked as if the fires of the Lady's caves were burning in her eyes. When the witch spoke again, her tone was full of winter's frost, "But of course, Mistress. And the Guards will not think it at all amiss that a bondwhore, held by *your* hand, was able to act on his own to murder Ser Ren Harath. Of course, no one will suspect you of any involvement."

The breath hissed between Mother Laurie's lips and I could feel her hands tighten on my head and shoulder. She had held me thus when my collar was fastened, just before my training began. My flesh remembered that day as if it had been only moments ago, rather than six long years. Some part of me fought free and I mouthed, "I'm innocent. Innocent," into the room though I knew no one would hear me.

Finally Mother Laurie spoke again, "Then you must prove me free of this crime as well. Otherwise, everyone in this house is likely to die along with me. You are right in thinking they will not believe he acted alone."

Mirana gave her an odd smile, black teeth hidden this time. She reached toward me once more and the webs pulled away from my face, leaving me gasping for breath. Neither one paid me any heed as the witch turned back toward the body. This time, she placed her staff in the bowl of the goblet. Nothing happened for so long that I thought she was asleep. Finally, she growled, "There is magic here, but it is from long ago."

"How long ago, witch? Is every goblet in the house corrupted? Shall I have them all brought?" Mother Laurie's voice was tense but she released my head, shifting her grip to my other shoulder.

Mirana leaned down and held her hand just above the goblet's bowl, being careful not to touch it. "Perhaps three moons, maybe more. Whatever the spell was, it seems simple. So simple it should have dissipated by now." She was frowning.

I found myself wondering why a spell would simply vanish. Weren't they supposed to last? Then I wondered what else a witch might learn at Idrenpur once she or he completed their studies.

It mattered little to me now, of course; Mirana was only trying to prove herself and Mother Laurie clean of my crime. I was doomed no matter what. Despite my terrors, I curled my toes around a gold piece and began to slide it slowly sideways under one of the chairs. Perhaps a chance for escape would present itself.

Mirana turned again to Harath's body and I could feel Laurie stir restlessly behind me. Soon I knew that the Ser's servants would begin to look for him. He would never stay the night here. If they could not see him when they came here, they would call the Guards. "Maybe," I ventured cautiously, "the goblet was poisoned in the kitchen."

They both stared at me as if I should have been unable to speak. Mirana nodded slowly. "It's possible. Do you remember fetching it?"

I frowned and tried to weed through my thoughts. Where had the goblet come from? I looked at it hard as if hoping it would answer my questions. "I remember...one of the kitchen boys bringing the wine in before Ser Harath came up." I couldn't remember which boy it had been, though I tried until my head ached.

Mirana looked at me and I could tell that her magic still held me. "He speaks the truth on this."

I went limp with relief. Perhaps I hadn't poisoned Harath, at least not intentionally. Not that the Sunlord's executioner would care. If I was to free myself, I had to find another to take my place. I dragged my memory back to before Harath had walked through the door. The boy—was he black-haired or was it more silver, like the Eastern nomads? My life might hang on the answer. I remembered that he seemed familiar and I recalled all of the boys I knew by name, matching a face to each.

None of them was the right one. "Is there anyone new in the kitchens?" I could hear the despair in my voice.

Mother Laurie's lip curled. "No." She glanced back at Mirana. "Perhaps we can blame one of the clients, say that they put a spell on him?"

"Who would you like to have die for this?" Mirana's face was without obvious expression, but for the first time, I thought I could read it. She bore no love for Mother Laurie; something boiled beneath the surface between those two and I was desperate to find out what it was. And if it would be of use to me.

"Use your magic to find the most likely candidate. Surely you learned that much at Idrenpur," Mother Laurie stood, looming above the two of us.

Mirana's eyes narrowed and I shifted sideways, moving myself from between them as much as I could. The witch said nothing for a moment, then glanced down at me. She made a gesture and spoke a single word and the webs shot over my face again faster than I could scream. The world went dark.

I do not know how long it was that I sat there or what I might have told them but when Mirana's magic released me, the witch was pulling her hand away from my face. I made myself another promise: that no one would ever use me this way again.

Mother Laurie gave me a contemptuous look and turned away. I turned to stone. Part of me had hoped that I still might be too valuable to sacrifice, but now I knew that I was doomed. I must be guilty. I could feel the wetness of tears on my cheek and I dashed them away. Instead I made myself look at Ren's body and I wondered why I killed him. I truly did not know.

"I didn't ask you that," Mirana's voice was cool, indifferent. I flinched, thinking her still in my mind, but then I realized I had spoken the words out loud.

That was too much and I broke down and wept. The women said nothing at first, at least not to me. Mother Laurie hissed something at the witch after a time but I could not hear it above my own misery.

But Mirana's next words were a dash of icy water on my pain. "I am not the only student of Idrenpur here in the city. They say in the alleys and kitchens that others, even others in this very house, studied there. Perhaps one of them might unravel this mystery."

Mother Laurie spat her words, "Lies! I do not pay you to gossip, hedge witch."

The witch took in a sudden breath and hissed something back at her. Then there was a sharp snap and a bright flash of light. Mirana screamed and dropped to her knees. Her hands went to her throat and for the first time, I could see the silver of a bond circlet, mate to the one I wore. It smoked under her hands, glowed, then turned black and split open.

She dropped forward onto the carpet while Mother Laurie snarled a curse. Her hands moved in an arcane gesture, like to the witch's movements. I could feel my jaw fall open. Was Mother Laurie also a student of Idrenpur?

The witch looked up and gave her a terrifying smile. "I'll be taking back my bond today. You will agree to it if you want my help this time."

I looked from one to the other of them. What was this? Laurie had bought me from the village elders after my parents died of summer fever when I was thirteen winters old. It had been six long winters at the House of Bliss, six winters where I had been trained, beaten when I failed and praised when I did not. I could not say that all of that was sufficient for me to know her.

But Mirana clearly did. I could see the fear on Mother Laurie's face now, her skin pale as I had never seen it before. Her hands moved again, this time as if she did not know what she did. Mirana laughed and they went still. Finally, Mother Laurie walked to the door and flung it open. She bellowed for one of the kitchen lads, and when he came, she stepped forward to block his view of the body.

I heard the word "Guards" and I dried my tears. They would not help me here. At least I could go to my death bravely. I stood up slowly and waited for my fate.

Mother Laurie did not look at me or Mirana. Instead, she looked down at Ren Harath's body for a moment. Then she smiled. It was a triumphant smile, etched in with a bit of pure loathing. I wondered what she had to smile about.

And then I knew who had poisoned Ren. I met Mother Laurie's eyes as I heard the Guards enter below. My circlet tightened, closing off my power to speak. I grabbed for it, trying to voice my suspicions. Instead I felt hard hands on my shoulders and was shoved toward the door. I would die in the Sunlord's dungeons and no one would hear my screams.

"Wait." The command behind the voice was enough to stop the Guards for a moment.

Mirana stepped forward. "Take her instead. Hers was the hand that felled the Sunborn." Her hands moved and for a moment, I saw the webs between them.

Mother Laurie screamed and leaped for her throat but two of the Guards held her back. The Guard Captain looked puzzled, even angry. "How do you know this?"

Mirana's hands moved toward me, then pulled and it was my turn to scream. A second self appeared beside me, this time myself as the boy I had been six years ago. I looked at the younger me and wondered if I could warn him about what was to come, urge him to run up into the mountains to escape his fate. He looked baffled and docile and fixed his eyes on the witch like a puppy.

Webs grew over his face a moment later and I cringed away. "Did you put something in the Ser's goblet besides wine?" Mirana asked.

"Yes," he spoke, as if in a dream, and I choked. He was my memory, my former self. If they executed him, what would become of me?

"Who ordered it? And who called you forth?" He pointed at Mother Laurie.

The Guard Captain stared from one to another of us, his face displaying his astonishment. Mirana looked at the boy again. "Who are you?" He pointed this time at me.

The witch's eyes pierced me through. "Now. Did you kill Ren Harath?"

I looked down at the body then back at the boy. I was innocent of the crime but my own innocence now stood before me. There was a hollow place inside me where he had been and I would be the lesser for it. But I would be alive, if I told the truth, and that might be enough.

Now…what was the truth?

"No." I said the word tentatively, as if I was not sure how it would sound in my mouth. Then my mind cleared like it had when Mirana's spell was removed. I gestured at the boy, "And I don't think he killed him either. You said the spell had worn off the goblet, that what remained was old magic?"

Mirana nodded. She reached into her clothes and removed an insignia that she showed to the Guard's Captain. I was startled to see the Lady's sign, such as only the priests and priestesses wear; perhaps she had not been driven from Idrenpur after all. He gave her a shallow bow and stepped back. "The goblet contains an old spell, too weak now to kill the Ser."

I looked at the boy who had been me. "Did you poison the goblet?" He looked puzzled. I looked at Mirana, "Could that old magic have been reactivated by something else?" She nodded. "So perhaps the poison wasn't what killed him." I shot a glance at Mother Laurie. "I left you here with him when I went to fetch Mirana. You might have…"

My bond circlet locked tight again and I gasped for air. A moment later there was a flash and Mirana's hands yanked it free from my neck.

She turned back to Mother Laurie. "Now," her voice purred, "Let me show you what I did learn at Idrenpur." The web that came from her hands this time had a foul glint to it, as if it had come from the Lady's caves directly. Mother Laurie screamed when it touched her and I turned away, unable to watch.

It was over moments later. Mirana forced a confession from Mother Laurie that Ren Harath would have recovered from the small dose of poison in the goblet, but not from the spell that she used to activate the older magic.

The Captain picked up the goblet and stared at it warily until Mirana made him put it in a silk bag that she stuffed away in her garments. As to the whys of what Mother Laurie had done, there followed a tale of intrigue and politics of which I understood not one word in ten. I had been merely convenient and close to the Ser.

There was more, but I ceased to listen. Instead I studied the boy who I had been and wondered what I might do to become him again. He seemed so happy, free of murder accusations, a life of bondage and bad poetry alike. At last Mother Laurie was done and the Guards took her to the door. Mirana followed close behind and I knew that soon the Ser's servants would come to retrieve his corpse. But what was I supposed to do now? "Mirana…" I could not find the words to ask.

She turned and gave me another black-toothed smile. Her hand moved once more and I nearly fell to my knees as the boy merged back into me. I was whole and, I remembered as I touched my neck, free. The thought left me stunned and silent as the witch, the Guards and my former mistress vanished down the stairs.

I wondered what the boy I had been would have done. I thought of the Western mountains, of Dragonsbreath and happier times. Then I gathered some coins from the Ser's purse. Not all. I was no thief so I took only what I needed to go home. Then I stood, stretching out as I felt the years and the weight of bondage drop away. After that, I left The House of Bliss to seek myself.

# Spell, Book and Candle

M OM ALWAYS TOLD ME TO stay away from the love spells. She would know; she and Dad tried them all, back in their "Let's stay together for the children" phase. And we had the therapy bills to prove it. I resolved early on to learn from their mistakes and get my dates the traditional way.

Most of the time.

That didn't apply to selling the tools to others, however. Love and lust are big sellers here at Lovejoy's Magical Books and Mystical Goods Emporium. You name the spell workings and we sell it. Still, I usually just sent the fairly benign stuff out the door with the herbs, the candles and the little books in the customers' shopping bags. It wasn't like they could do much harm with them. Or at least that was store policy until Mona Santiago stopped by.

Mona and I had history, provided 'history' refers to major dyke drama. I dumped her in college for some sweet young thing who seemed like less work. After that, Mona made it her mission to break up every college relationship I had. It got to be a game. I'd pick up girls just to see how long it would take her to seduce them or drive them away.

We feuded right up until graduation, then went our separate ways, her to the big city life of corporate magic she'd always dreamed of, me to run the family business in the burbs. We hadn't done more than exchange the occasional email in six or seven years. Except, of course, for those dreams I had about her from time to time. Okay, almost nightly. So sue me.

Even so, I'd forgotten just how…compelling she was in person. Especially when she was standing in front of me in my own little shop. That gorgeous face with those huge dark eyes, the most kissable lips I'd ever seen, that spectacular body with those luscious curves. I made myself stop inventorying and plastered on a nonchalant welcoming smile that fooled no one.

"Selena, honey! It's been ages!" Mona lunged around the counter and clutched me to those  curves in a way that made me feel more than friendly. She followed it up with a kiss on the lips, which was good, except it was the kind you give your ex: no tongue and less passion.

Not the kind of reunion I'd hoped for, alas. I bit back a sigh. I hadn't dated in months and Mona was looking better than good. But then, she always did. I made my lips form words. "What brings you out to the burbs? Need some candles for that thriving corporate Santeria practice of yours?"

"Sweetie, that's old school." Mona gave me a blinding smile. "I use circuits and wires for the work stuff now, not candles. But you do have some things I need." She looked around and wrinkled her nose at the stuff piled on the shelves. And hanging off the shelves. And sitting on the floor. Hey, at least I knew where everything was.

This visit was beginning to depress me so I switched modes, "Then what can I help the corporate director with today?" With any luck, she'd buy enough of the special books in the back to pay my property taxes this year. After all, hot is hot but business is business.

"Still your repressed New England shop keeper self, I see." Mona wrinkled the perfect cocoa butter skin on her almost equally perfect nose. Someone had clearly had some work done since college.

I couldn't help but notice her lack of shared enthusiasm about my current look. Maybe it was time to be less repressed. "Not all of us can handle those cool corporate jobs. But since you're out here in the sticks anyway, how about I show you the books in the back and maybe take you to dinner for old time's sake?" I leered hopefully and managed, just barely, not to bat my eyelashes.

For an instant, it looked like she was reminiscing about the good old days. Then, as if oblivious to smacking down one of my favorite fantasies, she shook her head, spilling glorious jet-black locks over her shoulders with abandon. "I'm sorry, Selena. Sometime soon, I promise. I have to get back tonight for work. And I still need this stuff." She pulled a list out of her bag and dropped it on the counter.

I looked down as I picked it up so that she wouldn't see how much I wanted to plead with her about going out with me tonight. At that moment that I realized how bad I still had it. I wondered if she felt even a ghost of all that college passion. Some crazy part of me parted my lips to ask.

"You can see what I want it for. I mean it seems nuts, right, me trying to use a love spell to get someone infatuated with me? But it's only a little one, just enough to give her a crush on me. I can do the rest but I need a way in." Mona leaned against the counter and stared dreamily past me like I was part of the wall.

I cringed inside and made myself read the list. Red candles, the ultimate lovespell cliché. The usual herbs: jasmine oil, lavender, laurel and some other miscellaneous greens with a kick. Then, the title of the first book caught my eye: *Making Them Your Own* by Owen Lovejoy. Dear old Dad's first book, the one where he explored using love spells for manipulation and control. I shuddered. Maybe she didn't know what she was asking for. "You sure you want this book? I've got a lot better titles."

She had the good sense to look very contrite; it suited her. "Oh hon, I'm sorry! I know how you feel about your dad and all that mess between him and your mom when you were growing up. I didn't mean to be so thoughtless. I can get it somewhere else if you'd rather; I just figured you'd have it. And could use the business." This time she frowned at my poor shelves and they sank under her stare.

"Hey! Stop torturing my furniture!" I was frowning now too and Mona had the good grace to switch from contrite to guilty. "At least tell me why you're doing this. You, of all people, should have women eating out of your hand without using magic."

"I'm in love and she likes me, I know she does. But I can't tell how she likes me. My regular magic doesn't seem to work on her. I'm starting to worry that she might be…straight." Mona blushed scarlet and stared down at the carpet, then looked up defiantly. "But she'll be hot for me within in the week once I work this spell."

I was horrified; this kind of stuff always ended badly for everyone involved. It was at that moment that my duty became clear. I had to save Mona from herself and I had to do it soon. Plans galloped into and out of my brain. I dismissed several at lightning speed until I got to the last one. I could do what I'd wanted to do since college and make Mona fall in love with me again, just for a little while until this infatuation wore off. Once that notion took root, I was like a missile pointed at a target.

I walked out from behind the counter over to the shelves without meeting Mona's eyes. She had a gift for seeing the truth and I was guessing that my expression wouldn't look very honest. "Just hang out for a minute. I know where everything is – I'll bring it all out," I called over one shoulder.

Then I made a mad dash for the shelves in the back. I kept the serious stuff there and given Mona's powers, I was going to need everything I could find. I got the stuff from her list as I went, leaving the herbs and the books I needed until last. My Book of Shadows came easily from its hiding place and I greeted it like an old friend. It had been far too long since I'd done any real magic.

I found Dad's book where I'd hidden it, on the darkest bookcase on the bottom shelf. This was where I kept that stuff that actually worked, even for novices, mostly because it had unintended consequences. The tourists never made it back here; a simple 'Don't Notice Me' kept them out of trouble. But then, trouble was my business, more or less. And I was about to have plenty of it.

I headed back out to the counter. "I've got everything. Had to grab a few more things for a mail order while I was at it." I gave Mona my cheeriest smile.

She frowned suspiciously. "Aren't you going to say anything more about what I said?"

"Like what? Chasing het girls is a bad idea? You know that. Using love spells on the wrong person isn't that great of an idea either? Think you've got that one down too. What more can I add?" I bared my teeth in something like a smile.

"I dunno. Maybe 'Why is this one so special, Mona'?"

Great. She wanted to talk and I just wanted to bewitch her back to our red-hot salad days. I found myself momentarily distracted by a vision of what she looked like when she was wearing a lot less than she had on now. She must have read my mind since she scowled at me long enough to bring on wrinkles. "I guess I don't want to know right now." I mumbled.

She looked apologetic, then shrugged. A few moments later, money had changed hands and I was watching her perfect butt swing its way out the door. If I were a TV witch, this would be the point where my chatty familiar would give me sound advice, which I would then ignore. But then, if I were a TV witch, I wouldn't be a dyke with the hots for her old college sweetie. Not to mention the fact that my familiar, Pyewacket, never said much except 'Meow.'

I pulled my Book of Shadows from my back pocket and flipped through its stained and dog-eared pages to some notes that I remembered making a few years back. Ah, there it was: Rekindling Lost Loves. There was the light and fluffy version, all scents and candles and romantic dinners. Then there was the one I adapted from Dad's original, with a few extras from other sources. I'd never had the nerve to try it before but this situation called for something special.

Whatever rational parts of my brain that I had left were making unhappy whimpering sounds right about then. I overruled them. I had enough control now that I could make this work without permanent damage or side effects. I was sure of that. I hoped. In any case, I could always call it back and what I was doing was no worse than what Mona was planning. At least I was doing it to someone who I knew for sure liked girls.

I concentrated on that thought while I read my notes, dismissing the last of my guilt pangs. The spell wasn't as complete as I remembered it being and my notes pointed me to another book. I found myself staring at the cover of *Spells and Enchantments* by Lady Isabelle Hubert as it sat there in all of its crumbling leather splendor. I couldn't shake the sense that the tome was looking back at me.

I made myself touch the cover. For a book with such an innocuous title, it had the worst magical feel of any book I kept in the store. Lady Isabelle was an ancestor of mine and family history claimed that she had narrowly avoided the stake, back in the seventeenth century. The witch finders had lost much of their clout by then anyway, but the fact of the matter was that Isabelle had a way of seeming to be someone else whenever there was a problem. She lived to a ripe old age, using her powers to get whatever she wanted well past her hundredth birthday.

One thing that Isabelle liked was reliable companionship. She was a woman ahead of her time so gender was less important than susceptibility to her magic. There were one or two grim little stories about her taking over her lovers' bodies, but I wasn't after those spells. No, what Isabelle had to offer was love spells possessed of great speed and effectiveness. Anything else I had would take months to reel in my prey but one of hers would take no more than a few hours, even on the most magically astute subject.

I flipped her book open and paged through until I found the spell I wanted written in Lady Isabelle's flowing script: *Finding and Holding Love*. She wasn't big on titles. I looked over the wording: calling on Hecate and Aphrodite, calling on various powers, blah, blah, herbs, something of the beloved's, something of yours. Mostly the usual stuff, with a few exceptions. One was the added line: "Let the one who belonged to me once be mine forevermore until death or I release them." The other was a few lines in some language I'd never learned; I decided they must be footnotes since they didn't seem to be part of the ritual itself.

In a more lucid frame of mind, the whole "until Death do us part or else" thing always gave me the shivers. Anything could happen with that in a casting. Sometimes the person you used it on decided to take death as an out the minute your control slipped. Sometimes the witch got too power hungry and did things to the object of the enchantment just because she or he could get away with them.

Then there was my own internal moral compass. Despite Mom and Dad's general instability as a couple, they always brought me up to be responsible for the outcome of my spells, good and bad. Sure, I wanted her now but did I want Mona to be mine forever? It wasn't a question I could answer for certain. I wondered if I could edit the spell a bit when I read it.

I checked the calendar to see which moon phase we were in. Not perfect, but it would do. The sun had set so I went and locked the door and pulled down the shades, officially closing shop a bit early. I looked at the phone and thought about calling my parents or someone from my coven for advice. Then I looked at Mona's receipt on the counter and thought about her.

After that, I called the local Chinese place for delivery instead.

An hour or two later, I gathered up the various things I needed and headed out to the little private patio in back of the store. I drew up my pentagram in chalk and sprinkled the salt around it in a circle. Then I lit the candles at the appropriate points and did some of the other odds and ends that I usually did before I began a ritual. I made a mental checklist and looked around, feeling vaguely uneasy.

But I decided I was imagining it. Pyewacket wandered out and stretched herself over a lawn chair to watch me. I scritched her behind the ears, then I went to work on my notes and Isabelle's spell.

First of all I decided to make the language of her spell less dire. I took out the call to Hecate and opted for a lesser power than the one she used for the original. I tweaked one or two other things and decided I was as ready as I was going to get. Then I recited the spell aloud, Mona's face hovering before me as I changed the last line to "Let the one who once belonged to me renounce the one she now desires and turn to me instead for the next three months or until I release her."

There. It was official. I was now the wimpiest practitioner of the dark arts in the entire metro area, but at least the spell wasn't quite as awful as the original. Even so, there was a cold wave of power that washed its way through me when I was done, followed by a flash of heat that made me sweat. It surged over me, then out into the world toward its intended target. The sensation of raw power was disconcertingly wonderful. I closed my eyes for a minute to savor it, which lasted until Pyewacket started howling.

I looked at my normally imperturbable black cat as she shook her head and raced around the patio. Her ears were flat and her fur was standing on end from one end of her plump body to the other. I lowered my hands and blessed the circle to end the ritual. Then I tried to call her to me but she went to ground in the farthest, darkest corner of the yard.

Her eyes had an odd blue gleam in them when I followed her over. Her expression was starting to freak me out so I left her alone to go back into the store and turn the patio lights on. At least I'd be able to see what was wrong with her. The phone rang just as I hit the switch and I reached over and picked it up automatically.

Mona's voice hit my ear like a gentle sigh. "Oh good, you're still there! Listen, I've been thinking. I need to stop by and talk to you about that spell again."

I smiled at the empty shop. Nothing like that old black magic, courtesy of Lady Isabelle. "Of course, hon. Come on over." The phone clicked off like Mona couldn't wait to be at my side and I hung up the receiver with a huge grin. This time, I wouldn't give her up for some twit. No, I was all grown up now and I knew what I wanted. She was the one and we would grow old together, scaring the neighborhood kids from the porch of our rambling Victorian.

I heard a growl from the patio and remembered Pye with a guilty start. I dashed outside to see what was still bugging her. Now, instead of hiding out in the corner, she was up on the table, staring down at Lady Isabelle's book for all the world like she was reading it. She was even wearing what looked like a little kitty frown of concentration and she was warbling some little cat song at it. I laughed as I shut the book and tucked it away in the store, along with the rest of my paraphernalia. Mona didn't need to know what I'd been up to.

Then I came back out to give Pye an ear scratch and her eyes slitted in pleasure. Her fur settled down and she started to look normal again. Judging from the way she was purring, whatever had scared her was getting erased from her little brain. Nothing a few treats wouldn't completely wipe out. I walked back inside and opened up a can of Pye's favorite food.

She sauntered, rather than ran in when I called, much like a queen accepting her due. The regal air lasted until she got a whiff of what was in the bowl in front of her. She unleashed an unearthly howl of pure indignation and hissed at the food.

I gaped. "Pye, what's the matter? You love this stuff!"

There was a sharp rap on the door behind me and I jumped about a foot. Mona's face stared back at me through the glass when I looked around the shade, then unlocked the door. My heart was racing as she charged inside, almost knocking me down. She stared around, her eyes wild, her face haggard as she demanded, "Where is she? Where is my precious darling?"

I said the first intelligent thing that popped into my head. "I'm right here, love. Who else are you looking for?"

That question got answered the split second Mona and Pye spotted each other. Next thing I knew, my once and future girlfriend and my cat were wrapped in each other's arms, figuratively speaking. Mona murmured, "Is that bad witch trying to feed you icky canned cat food? You just come right home with me, snookums and I'll cook you up something delicious." She mumbled some endearments and Pye purred back at her like she was the coolest thing ever. She turned and headed for the door with my cat in her arms.

"Snookums?" Mona could barely tolerate cats; she was more of a purse dog kind of gal. Something was clearly very wrong. I stepped in front of them. "What the hell do you think you're doing? You are not walking out of here with my cat. Besides it's me you're supposed to want."

Pye turned her face so her ears framed Mona's eyes and her head blocked out the rest, just like Kim Novak's cat in that witchy film of hers that was great up until the end. Kind of like now. Mona's expression was completely blissed out but Pye gave me a look of purely malevolent intelligence. For an instant, her eyes were blue, not green. I stumbled backward in shock, catching myself on the doorframe as Mona and the cat swept out of my shop and into the night.

My heart was still racing and my legs shook as I watched them climb into Mona's sporty little car and drive off. I had to do something and fast. What had I called up that had taken over my cat? And what did it intend to do with Mona? I forced myself into action as the taillights disappeared and pulled out the books that I had hidden away behind the counter and spread them out in front of me: Book of Shadows, Isabelle's book and Dad's book: the answer was in here somewhere.

I flipped Isabelle's book open and almost screamed when it opened to the print of her face, just after the title. There was something so fierce in that face, something distinctly…feline that I couldn't help but recognize it. A ghastly realization shook me. I'd brought Isabelle back somehow, and stuck her inside Pyewacket. How the hell had I done that?

I paged quickly through to the spell and read it again. Nothing registered the first time. But the second time through I looked at the line I didn't understand. This time I recited a charm to translate it. The words flowed across the page: "Let the recitation of this spell by one of power call me back from wherever I am that I may resume my mortal span of years as I have enjoyed them ere now." Okay, I got the calling back part down but how was she planning on resuming much of anything? It wasn't too clear until I remembered the other story. Lady Izzy was some sort of body snatcher. And I had just put my cat and my ex-girlfriend in her clutches.

I needed help and I needed it right away. Dad's book practically wiggled for my attention until I gritted my teeth and opened it up at what I thought was random. The chapter title made me cringe: *Consequences and Quandaries—The Aftermath of Love Spells.* "All right, Dad. You've made your point," I growled down at the page. I nearly tossed it onto the nearest shelf but somehow, my hand wasn't cooperating. Instead, I started reading.

By dawn, I had read my way through Dad's words of wisdom and everything I could find on our family history. I drank my fourth copy of coffee and packed the things I was going to need. This time I went for the charm bags, the oils and one or two other things. For one thing, Lady Izzy needed a new shell and I wasn't volunteering so that meant bringing along the best spirit holding receptacle I could find.

Then I went out, got into my battered little Corolla and headed for Mona's condo. At least, I hoped she still lived there; it was where I sent holiday cards. This time, I knew what I was getting myself into. She'd probably never talk to me again once she figured all of this out, but at least she'd be okay. The thought gave me a sharp pang in the vicinity of my heart but it was too late to worry about that now. I'd put things right, then worry about the rest later. Maybe there was a 'Making friends with your ex after you screwed up colossally ' spell floating around somewhere.

The drive was much shorter than I remembered it being, probably because hardly anyone was out and about yet. I buzzed downstairs and didn't get an answer so I spoke a minor cantrip into the security lock and walked in. The elevator was mysteriously out of order so I hiked up to the fifth floor, swearing quietly under my breath. Someone knew I was coming and it wasn't Mona.

When I got to the right floor, I was struck with the realization of how silly this all was. Clearly, I hadn't been successful in casting a spell on Mona since she wasn't in love with me so why was I here? I could just go grab breakfast at my favorite diner and open the store up early, maybe get all those mail orders done.

Uh huh. "I know what you're doing," I said to the empty air of the hallway as I waved my hands in a gesture of dismissal. For added emphasis, I whispered a spell that caused misused magic to return to its source. Something thought dark thoughts back at me, but the feeling that this was all wasted effort went away.

I walked down the no longer apparently endless hallway to Mona's door and pulled one of the charms from my bag. I fastened it to the doorknob, then used the same spell I'd used to get into the building. It didn't work this time so I broke out the angelica and the vervain, sprinkling it over the hall side of the threshold to drive back evil. Then I tried the knob again.

Mona's apartment was dark. I stumbled over and opened one of the blinds so I could see my way around, stumbled being the operative word. I wasn't sure my toes would ever recover. Once I got some light on the living room, I could see why. Mona's apartment was filled with all kinds of ottomans and cushy chairs, most of them fairly low to the floor. An elaborate scratching post tree filled one corner. It couldn't be like this all the time. This had to be Lady Izzy feeling her catnip. I wondered what else she could control Mona to do and shivered.

My quarry was nowhere to be seen so I started for one of the doors that I thought would lead to the bedroom. I uncorked a bottle of Ava Rosa for binding evil and let its scent cloud around me as I walked. Something wasn't happy but I made it across the room unscathed.

The first door turned out to be a closet so I went for the next one. Bingo. Mona was sprawled on the bed, mouth open in a gentle snore. I gave her a regretful glance before I focused on the being I had come to see.

Lady Isabelle Hubert stared back at me from Pyewacket's now completely blue eyes. She growled and hissed as she tried unsuccessfully to form words with her kitty vocal cords. I had the feeling that intent was more important than execution so whatever I was going to do, I needed to do fast. There would be no time for the candles that I usually used or any of my usual ritual.

Instead, I reached into my bag and pulled out the object that I'd brought with me from the shop. Holding Dad's book at arm's length, I started the chant, my eyes holding Isabelle's the whole time.

She shivered, then wailed in Pye's voice, a tiny cry of pain that made me falter for just an instant. Mona sat up, eyes blazing. I had always thought that was just an expression, but apparently it wasn't. I was nearly singed. She spoke, her voice a snarl of fury, "What the hell are you doing to my cat?"

For an answer, I opened Dad's book and shouted the last few words of the entrapment spell. It was like being hit with a tornado. A sharp force slapped me against the far wall, knocking all the air out of me. I wrestled with it, trying to ignore the hideous feeling that it was working its way inside *me*. It was like struggling with an anaconda.

After the longest minutes of my life, it started to feel like something was pulling at it, drawing it away. Then the force shot past me and into the book with a hideous wail. I dropped to my knees and slammed the book shut. I shoved it into my bag. Just not before Mona was released from Lady Isabelle's hold in time to see me doing it.

She recovered fast. "What the hell did you just do? And why are you and your cat in my bedroom at the crack of dawn?" She and Pye shared a baffled stare before turning back to me.

I held out my carryall. "C'mon Pye. Let's go home." Pye jumped in without a struggle, which was an indication of how shook up she was.

"If you think you're walking out of here without an explanation, you've got…" Mona's eyes narrowed. "You did a love spell on me, didn't you? Did you make me do all that obsessive crap in college too? I've suspected it for years now." Her jaw was tightening and her beautiful kissable lips were getting thin. Her hands were beginning to make gestures that I knew would probably lead to me spending the next year as furniture if I didn't get out.

"No! Not after the first month or so! At least, I think it expired!" I was babbling when I should be fleeing. I was also starting to reassess my college memories and this wasn't the time for that. Pye chose that moment to whimper quietly and I snapped out of it and bolted for the front door, running as fast as I could.

I slammed it behind me as something hard smashed into the area my head had just occupied. Then I hauled my butt down the stairs like I had wings. Hell hath no fury like the ex you emotionally jerked around because you hoped for a different outcome. I drove away, swearing off love spells for the rest of my magical existence, sure that I'd learned my lesson.

Dad's book slid a little ways out of my bag and I thought about Lady Isabelle. There had been something in the way she handled herself that I liked, now that I was almost over being terrified. I thought about her portrait and how long it had been since I'd had a girlfriend who really understood me over the screams of my common sense. Maybe one more spell, if I did it really carefully…

# Beauty

I F I SAID I MET my vampire prince at a ball at the King's palace, would you believe me? Of course, it is easier by far to believe it now. But then it seemed an impossibility. The King was my father and the Queen, my mother, or so I thought. I was merely the fourth son and sixth child of the King and Queen's eight children, with no hope of the throne. When have you heard a story about the fourth Prince before? I flatter myself that this maybe the first.

But at least my status meant that the courtiers and servants did not trouble themselves to hide their thoughts from me. I learned much of what happened in my father's kingdom from them, most importantly that none of my father's subjects had any reason to love him. I also heard the whispers before Prince Raven arrived. "Did you hear? One of Princess Aruna's suitors, he's a real vampire! From beyond the mountains of the Western Wall, I heard." And so it went until I might have pitied the fellow were I not so intent on pitying myself.

Still, something about him intrigued me and I imagined what he might be like before he arrived. I wondered, along with the servants and no few of the courtiers, why one of the vampire princes would aim so low as one of my sisters. Not merely because I loathed each and every one of them, mind, but because the vampire kingdom beyond the mountains was rumored to be full of beautiful beings.

It was also said that the vampires were rich beyond the dreams of mortal men and deathless in the bargain. They seldom intruded on the lands of men since their infatuated victims often gave themselves up by choice. Why bother with a human bride, especially one like Aruna who was neither beautiful nor kind? True, there were other tales that said that the vampires' powers were fading and that they could no longer hold their lands as they once had. But I had no way to judge the truth of any of these rumors and thus gave them small consideration.

On the night that the vampire prince arrived, I sat sulking in my usual corner of my father's banquet hall with Kriun the jester. Kriun, like me, was short and blonde, slender and elfin in the court of dark-haired giants that ruled over the peasants who looked like us. That was one reason I liked him better than my kin, the other being that as the butt of all the jokes that weren't directed at me, he was my companion in suffering.

Not that he saw it as such. "Fine fish, tonight, lad. Eat up! We may not eat so well again tomorrow." He belched contentedly as the last of the fish he had purloined from the waiter's trays vanished into his gullet, then scowled at the door. The scowl made the scar on his cheek twist into something fierce and harsh for a moment before his face lapsed into his usual foolish smile.

I turned to see what he was looking at and saw that the vampires had arrived. The word does no justice to the way they appeared, their eyes old and full of secrets, their faces perfect in their weird splendor. They came in, silent as cats but for the clink of their armor, trailing in the wake of their prince.

To see a score of them in company, shining in my father's court like small suns, was a magnificent sight. And yet there was something about them that sent shivers down my spine, as if they might turn and begin to hunt amongst us without warning. There was a bit of the monster about them still, despite their wisdom and beauty.

Then it was that I caught my first glimpse of my sister's suitor. He was tall and slim like the others but somehow gave the impression of a speed and strength that would be hard to match in battle. His face was pale, white and beautiful, and his hair flowed long and black in a queue down his back. But it was his eyes that made me believe that he was the creature of the rumors. Their silver-grey gaze swept the court with a cold, hungry look like a hawk newly unhooded.

He caught my own stare in their grasp from across the room and I gasped, struggling like a fish on a line. There was something in his gaze that felt as though a single black-gloved hand held my soul and saw all that I thought and felt. I blushed and tried to look away, afraid of having been caught gawking. The strange prince smiled a thin smile with no hint of fang and slowly, oh so slowly released me from his eyes.

When I was able to breathe again, Kriun was giving me a strange look. "Don't look at him directly again, lad. He can command your soul if he's all they say he is. The King would kill you with his own sword if he saw even a hint of that come about. Let Aruna lie down with the living corpse and have whatever good there is of it."

He spoke true. The King, my father, had wished me left to the mercy of the wolves when I was a child a thousand times. I could not have said why he hated me so, other than I was the only one of his children to resemble my slim, golden, and long dead, mother. Perhaps it was more than he could bear to see her in my face. Whatever the cause, any infraction, real or imagined, could spark his rage and give him the reason he craved to be free of his least-loved offspring.

I glanced at the scar on Kriun's face, a relic of a time when he stepped between the King and the object of his wrath, my ten-year-old self. It took no effort to nod my agreement. What was he to me, this vampire prince from beyond the Western Wall who desired the hand of my most hated sister? I turned away.

Once the pleasantries were complete and the prince had been presented to Aruna and the important folk of the court, the evening began in truth. My father had not stinted the flood of gold necessary to bring about the most magnificent feast I had ever seen or heard of. If all manner of delicacies and gallons of sheep's blood alone were enough to sway the heart of the prince, then Aruna was as good as wed.

Idly, I wondered if the blood had truly come from sheep or if my father was bleeding the unfortunates in the dungeons. I spared a small thought for their agonies, poor souls. The cold distance of my father's face as he sat on his throne brought me no more comfort than usual. In fact, the vampires looked almost kindly in comparison. I shuddered and turned to the small plate of food that Kriun had seized from the main table.

The banquet went on around us, turning from food to entertainment and from thence to dancing. I would have sat on in my corner at peace were it not for my sister Eria. When the dancing began, nothing would please her than that her ugly brother would stand up to dance with her, painting her as a beauty in comparison.

Eria simpered and pretended to smile down at me, her eyes cold as the prince's, withholding all her usual taunts behind closed lips. Yet her face spoke volumes and it was as if she spoke aloud so her silence was no boon. By the time we finally danced in a pairing with Aruna and her prince, I would have given anything to be forgotten.

He glanced at me again, eyes burning through me with a mocking stare. Aruna whispered something to him and he looked deliberately away, contempt written all over his features. At that moment, I hated him more than my entire family, were such a thing possible. Had I any skill with a sword, I might have challenged him at once but since I had none, I finished the dance with what dignity I could muster. Then I turned on my heel without a word to Eria and left the hall to begin the long weary climb to my half-ruined tower room. I was done with feasting.

I seized a flagon of my father's finest wine as I left and I gulped it as I walked, remembering the prince's eyes. He had looked at me as though I was nothing, as though I could never be worthy of his notice. The realization made my flesh start and burn as though I had been struck and my heart raced with anger. I stormed along the passage, paying little attention to my surroundings.

That was why I didn't see Aruna's vampire when he appeared in the corridor before me so suddenly that we collided and I dropped the flagon. He looked down his nose at me. "Are you always so rude, dwarf prince of the Northern Kingdom? You leave your sister unpartnered and unescorted, you smash your unwanted self into your father's guests—these things do not bode well if we are to be one clan."

He towered above me, as did all at the Court except Kriun, and blocked my passage so that I could not ignore him. "Move aside, sir. My sister may barter her body and soul to you but you will never be a brother to me as long as I draw breath." I was shaking with fury now, glaring at him as if I could force my way past.

With a speed that made me gasp, he spun me back against the stone wall and braced his hands against the rock at either of my shoulders so I could not flee. His face was inches from mine as he hissed, "You are quick to assume that your sister is good enough for one whose lineage stretches back to the Elder Kings, foolish brat. I see that the blood of your kingdom's Old Ones runs true in your veins, yet even they are children compared to the years of my people."

What was he talking about? Who were the Old Ones? I had heard the tales of the people who lived here before my great-grandfather conquered the kingdom but all of those folk had been destroyed or enslaved in the distant mines. There was nothing left of them but some tiny, blonde peasants and they had naught to do with me. I nearly shrugged as I dismissed my thoughts. Who knew how the vampires entertained themselves? Perhaps he simply lied.

His eyes burned into me as if he read my doubts. I was wrenched back from my thoughts to find myself still held captive by a being I despised. I found the words to say as much. "What do you want with her then? Our lineage is as good as yours, creature of the night. My sister can marry any one of a dozen lords."

"You were simple-minded farmers when my people took the Western lands. Your sister is worth nothing more or less than the alliance she brings and the lands that will be linked to mine. As her husband, I will occupy the throne of this sty and this kingdom will be mine or have you forgotten that?"

The blood burned in my veins. "Sty? I wonder that you bother to soil your hands with us then, great Prince! Or are the tales true? Do your powers fade with time and your lands slip from your fingers?" I did not expect an answer and he did not grant me one.

"As for you…" he bared his teeth as he hissed, "Do you think I could not command you to love me if I wanted to? You would beg for the honor of my notice then."

I could see his fangs when he spoke and I knew that some of what I heard was true. He might control me or even kill me in an instant and I was powerless before him. I looked deep into his eyes, forgetting Kriun's warning and took a long breath. He smelled of wild magic and other things that I could not name.

I found my anger again. "Oh all-powerful Prince! Now I see the error of my ways and prepare myself to adore you in any way you see fit! How weak do you think I am, monster? Save your powers to bend men to your will for my father and my sister and let me pass."

His eyes darkened at my sarcasm and for a moment my knees trembled. I could feel the cordlike strength of the muscles in his arms on either side of mine and I knew I could not defeat him in battle. So we remained for an eternity until he dropped his arm and turned from me with a curl of his lip. He stalked away before I could demand to know what he was doing in that corridor so far from the guest quarters.

I opened my mouth to call after him, to demand an accounting of his actions but no words came. Instead I, too, turned and continued toward my tower, trying to ignore the shaking of my hands and knees. I reached my room without further incident and bolted the door behind me before I collapsed on my hard bed. There I lay, wrapped in my thread-bare blankets and tried to forget what I had seen.

But even after I fell into an uneasy sleep, his face haunted my dreams and nightmares. When at last I fell from the bed to land on the cobbled floor, it was because in the final dream, he ripped my tunic from me to sink his sharp fangs into my neck. His flesh was cold as ice against mine and my body craved his, even as he stole my life away. It was my struggle to deny him that landed me on the stone floor, forcing me awake to the dawn outside.

I groaned and passed my fingers through my hair with a shudder. What had that creature done to me? Even now, my flesh was still hard from my dream and it made me sick to see it. Was I so reduced that I wanted a monster to take me and consume me like a pheasant at my father's banquet? And the monster was not even one of the beautiful vampire women from the tales. I retched and dove for the icy harshness of the washbasin, determined to wash all such thoughts from my head.

When I went to the kitchens to break my fast, I avoided the corridors near the guest quarters. Perhaps the legends that said that the prince and his people must spend the daylight hours asleep were not true. I wanted to see no more of my monstrous brother to be than I was forced to.

But despite my precautions, it was clear when I reached my destination that I could do nothing to avoid hearing about him. All the talk was of the prince and his retinue, his wealth, his thirst for blood. True, he had drunk sheep's blood last night and seemed pleased enough with it then but what would happen once the lovely Princess was in his bed? And on it went until I fled to avoid hearing more.

I chose the library as my hiding place for the day, knowing that I would not be discovered there. I curled up in one of the decaying chairs with a dusty leather book that none of my brothers or sisters would dream of reading. But eventually, the dry history was too much even for me and I fell asleep.

I do not know how long it was that I drifted in slumber but there was a fire on the hearth when I awoke. I smiled to see it, warm for the first time all day. Then I stretched my stiffened limbs, swearing softly at the small pains. It was then that I realized that there was a cloak spread over me and that I was no longer alone in the library.

The prince sat watching me, an unread book open in his own lap. I started and the book I held fell unheeded to the floor with a loud thump. "What are you doing here? You startled me." My words sounded unnecessary, hovering in the air amid the cloud of dust from the books.

"Afraid to wake and find the monster feeding from your open veins, princeling? I'll trouble you for my cloak if you're done with it."

I scrambled to my feet, holding the cloak out to him as if its touch stung me. He took it with a wry and twisted smile that did not reach his eyes. Somehow it gave me my courage back. "You visit a room you'll never see Aruna in when she comes to your castle." I smirked in the knowledge of my own superiority.

The prince rose so fast I leapt backward only to be stopped by his hand under my chin. He tilted my face upward so I had to meet his eyes and they swallowed me. Almost it felt as if his lips brushed mine but I knew that could not be. Instead I heard the sting of his words. "You bore me with your assumptions, princeling. Mayhap I come here only to feed my people and not to wed at all. Do your nightmares not tell you as much?"

I found my voice with an effort. "It's a long way from the Western Wall to my father's court. Were there no peasants or barbarian ladies you might have tasted along the way with greater ease? Or is the throne of this 'sty' temptation enough?" I hated him more in that moment than I had ever hated anyone before and my hands trembled with the strength of my anger.

"Perhaps it might be. If I wed Aruna," his lips twisted, "I shall live here in this delightful castle with her equally delightful family. I might even come to their chambers on moonlit nights to sample all they had to give me. What do you say to that?"

"Let me go. They say you do not take unwilling victims. My sister is willing to give herself to you. She should be enough." My anger cooled just enough for me to feel afraid and I hated myself for it.

"What do you know about it, Princeling Beast?" I flinched. How kind of Aruna to share the family's nickname for me with this *thing*. He ran his thumb over my lower lip, tugging it downward and leaned in close to whisper in my ear. "I think I will always call you that. It suits you."

"Am I to call you 'Beauty' then?" I snorted as I jerked away. "Begone, monster!" I fumbled at my neck for the old silver cross that my grandmother had given me and yanked it free of my clothes. The vampire prince looked at me and laughed. It was a hearty laugh, one that showed his fangs and made me shudder. Then he turned and left the library, still laughing.

I shivered and shuddered at the heat coursing through my veins and the anger that filled me from head to toe. And yet...I could feel such sensations within me that I could scarcely bear to contemplate. My lip burned where his finger had touched it and my ear echoed with the sound of his whisper. Some part of me longed to encounter him again. My senses reeled with confusion.

Clearly he was a monster and nothing more, and yet he laid his cloak on me while I slept. He had a servant start a fire or had started it himself so that I would be warm. In a life unaccustomed to kindness, he had shown me a little and it was more than I could bear. I flung myself into the chair by the fire and gave vent to my helpless anger in silent weeping until my hunger sent me to the banquet hall for dinner.

There I sat in my distant corner and ate my usual fare of the King's leavings. I watched the prince and tried to hate him more than my father who sat at his side. But I could not find it in me since I had hated my father far longer. A voice pulled me from my thoughts. "The Prince sends this with his warmest regards." Cheeks flaming, I glanced up at one of the prince's servitors. He set the tray he carried down on the bench next to me and vanished as silently as he appeared.

For a moment, I thought about throwing it to the dogs. But there was Kriun watching me askance and a plate of food finer than I had ever eaten set before me. I ate, sharing it with my father's jester, fearing that my father or Aruna had noticed this strange act of kindness and would make me pay for it later. Or that the prince himself sought only to fatten me up for his own future meal. Still I ate, savoring the sweetness of the roast bird and tried to ignore all that it might mean.

My father called Kriun to entertain his guests but I could not bear to stay and watch my friend play the fool. Too often I had helped to ease his bruises when the King or one of the courtiers did not find him amusing enough. My intervention would only mean more punishment later for both of us so instead I slipped quietly from the hall.

This time, it was Aruna and not her prince, who found me in the corridors. She slipped up behind me, wrapping a meaty arm around my throat and squeezing until I flailed the air with my arms, trying to get free. "I've seen the way he looks at you, Beast and I won't stand for it. He's mine and I won't have any of his misplaced sympathy for our mother's mistake interfering. You are to stay away from him or I will have you brought to the dungeons and tormented until you beg for death."

"Father would never permit it," I gasped, barely able to get the words out.

Aruna laughed, a harsh cruel sound that echoed off the stone walls. "Father would help heat the irons. You're none of his get, fool. Surely you've realized that by now. You live only because our mother protected you. Now that she's gone, it's just a matter of time."

I flailed harder, breaking her hold as the sound of approaching servants came up the corridor behind us. She watched me scamper away, her look burning its way through the back of my tunic. So the King thought he was not truly my father? This was almost too much to hope for, despite my terror. I ran up the stairs to my tower, barring the door and barricading it with the old bureau. My sister was quite capable of carrying out her threats, as I knew of old.

I spent a sleepless night turning what she said over in my mind. True, she might have lied but her words had the ring of truth. When the sun rose the next day, I had decided on a plan. It would take me several days to steal all that I needed but once I succeeded in that, I would leave my father's castle and go out into the world. It could be no harsher than my family and there would be no monsters to haunt my sleep or baffle me with periodic kindnesses and harsh words.

The decision brought me some peace as the day passed in a blur. I darted from hiding place to hiding place, taking an apple here, a pack or a waterskin there. Since I was able to walk I had explored every hidden cubby, every secret passage in the castle until I could vanish for hours, completely undiscovered. It was in one of these that I hid what I found, confident that no one would find it there. When I thought I had purloined all that would not be missed in a single day, I went openly to the kitchen and begged some bread and cheese. This I took once more to the library, though trepidation filled me at what I might find there.

I would say that I didn't think of the beautiful, monstrous prince during the long hours of hiding and stealing but there would be no truth in it. I imagined his thumb on my lip, his teeth in my neck, until it seemed as if he might emerge from any one of a thousand hidden corners. I berated myself soundly for this sickness of mind that seemed to hold me whenever I thought of him but to no avail.

Still I was relieved not to find him in the library. True that meant no fire and no warm cloak but the cold was a small price to pay to be at peace for a time. To my surprise, there was enough wood in the hearth to make a fire myself so I indulged myself in this small luxury and sat watching the flames and warming my half-frozen feet. Idly, I found that the flames reminded me of his eyes and I wrinkled my nose in disgust at the quality of my own dreams.

At the time, I thought that this was how he was able to appear so noiselessly at my side but then I was not so used to his powers. "Little Beast. We meet again." His voice was dry, richly amused and I started a little from my chair, heart pounding.

"My sister has threatened my life if I speak to you again, my lord." I was afraid of Aruna but I said it mainly to ruin her chances. I would be gone long before their betrothal was announced, surely. And he should know that he had found his match for brutality. I looked up at him, noticing the open neck of his shirt and the lean muscles it exposed, and I tried to look away.

He knelt before me with a soft crackling of wool and leather and black silk so his eyes were level with mine. They went on forever and I was not surprised to feel his gloved hand on my chin. "Are you afraid of your sister, beautiful little Beast?" I nodded, unable to take refuge in a brave lie. Part of me wondered about his new name for me; no one had ever thought me 'beautiful' before. I wondered then if he spoke to all his meals this way and I shuddered.

"Then I'll speak and do you keep silent," he murmured. I tried to tug free of his hand, his eyes, but found myself immobile, frozen. He fastened his mouth on mine, leaving me to howl my protests into the muffling softness of his tongue.

I flailed, trying to free myself from the awful pressure of his mouth but he held me in a grip like iron, pulling me close to his cold flesh. I made the futile gesture of shoving at his breast, gasping for air as his mouth relentlessly claimed mine. I could feel the edge of his fangs against my tongue and wailed in pure terror. He broke off his terrible kiss then and reaching his hand up into my hair, bent my face backward so that my neck was exposed.

"Let me go, monster!" I found my voice in a single burst of sound.

"I could take you now and make you one of us. I can tell that you are not unwilling." He murmured the words against the skin of my neck, sending shivers all over my flesh. I could feel his fangs rest against me like a dagger's edge and I writhed to get away but he held me fast. He opened the neck of my tunic to bare more of my shoulder and he showered me with burning kisses, agonizingly slow.

Then his hand found its way down between my legs, cupping what it found there. To my shame, I hardened even more at his touch and he laughed at my flesh's betrayal of my spirit. He lowered his face, still holding me in place and kissed his way down to where it strained at my leggings. He kissed me through my clothes and I moaned, a small tortured sound. I burned with sickened desire, feeling it engulf me like a wave even as I fought it with all my strength. He murmured, "Such a beautiful boy should be immortal. Don't you agree?"

Sheer terror took me then and I kicked at him in a fury. He laughed and raised his face to my neck. His fingers continued to stroke me, cupping and caressing until it was almost more than I could bear. "Stop it! I'll kill you if you make me one of you! I swear I will!" I screamed the words as he bit me gently at the base of my neck. My body was betraying me to his touch but I would not let my weakness deny me vengeance. This I swore to myself.

"You seem to be enjoying my touch." His fingers lingered until my breath quickened in pace with my heart.

"No! Let me go!" I wailed even though my body begged for things I could not bear to imagine.

"So fierce a princeling should be taken willingly and in the full knowledge of what he does." He smiled down at me, fangs barely visible at the corners of his lips and gave me a final kiss, more gentle than the first. He released my face and removed his hand from between my legs, leaving me to spit and swear at him from the safety of the chair. "But I am accustomed to getting what I desire, little Beast. I do not think that you will be an exception. Remember that."

"My name is Allain, not 'Beast,' you foul creature. I'm not a boy, either! I came of age this year." I spat the words as I managed to fling myself from the chair and leap behind it, giving myself the illusion of security.

"In that case, you may call me Raven, little Beast. And I will call you whatever I please."

The arrogance of this...*thing* left me as breathless as his ruthless kiss had earlier. I stared after him as he left the room in a swirl of black cloak, fuming but unable to find the suitable words to hurl at his departing back. I made due by wiping my mouth furiously as though that would clear his kiss from my lips. How dare he make me feel this way? My entire body still shivered and shuddered at the memory of his touch.

Finally I could bear it no longer and doused the fire. I was ravenous and I needed to eat more than bread and cheese or I might faint the next time I had to elude my sister or her suitor. I would also require all my strength to flee before the next banquet three nights hence. That was when the prince would make his official proposal to her and I could not bear to sit and watch that particular farce.

That determination filled me as I darted into the kitchen and tried to beg some tidbits from the cook. There it was that Kriun found me. From the dark frown creasing his normally cheerful face, I knew something was amiss and my heart sank even before he spoke. "Hello, lad. It seems that your sister's suitor has a desire to see her entire family at dinner. The King bids me make sure that you're ready and present." He looked as though the words burned his lips in passing.

I met his eyes and knew that he would pay the price if I failed to appear as ordered so I gave him a cheerful smile. "Well then, let's make me look like as much of a prince as we can before the ordeal begins." He smiled back at me, gratitude and some other fleeting emotion crossing his face in rapid succession.

We climbed up to my tower in silence, holding back all questions until we were far from prying ears. But a startling sight met my eyes when I flung open the door. Stretched across my pallet was a tunic and cloak made, seemingly, of silver and moonlight, with leggings and boots to match. I reached out cautiously to touch the fine silk and embroidery, almost as if I was afraid that it would vanish once caressed. This must be Raven's doing, since I could imagine it coming from no other. I would be fortunate if my sister did not poison me at dinner.

"That prince of Aruna's takes too great an interest in you, boy. Nothing good can come of this," Kriun grumbled.

"That's why I've decided to leave, old friend. I need only to steal some coin and warm clothes to sustain me until I can get further south.

I've already got food and waterskins and the other supplies that I need hidden away." I yanked off my threadbare tunic and stripped out of the rest of my old and nearly outgrown garments. Kriun looked away, as if he could not bear to watch.

I felt a moment of shame that I had not thought of the effect of my news on my only friend. But the words could not be unsaid so I went to the washbasin and cleaned my face and what I could of the rest of me. When I was done, Kriun was staring out the window at the mountains outside. "There's something I must tell you, Your Highness." He paused and I froze at his tone. He gestured and I sat, sinking slowly down onto my bedding. He never used my title unless he was very serious. Hoping he would not attempt to dissuade me, I waited for him to continue.

"You know that I served your mother; the past is common knowledge in the kitchens and servant's halls." I nodded. There were even whispers that he had been her lover but I had never given them any weight. Now I wondered. He continued, his eyes still fixed on the mountains outside, an audible knife-edge of hatred in his voice now. "She was the last of her line, the last of the rulers of the Old Blood who were not wiped out by the present King's ancestors. I remained at her side as her counselor as long as she sat as Queen."

"So the King is not my father? Aruna said as much." I trailed off at the look in his eyes.

"That monster! The creature who sits on the throne of this land is as much a thing of evil as the one who seeks Aruna's hand. He stole the throne from you and rules your people with the sword. Remember that, my Prince. Your mother had a lover of the Old Blood, one of the last surviving scions of the merchant houses who stayed faithful. He was your father. This is why the King hates you so. He cannot kill you openly because he acknowledged you as his to stop tongues from wagging."

"Where is my real father?" I felt the relief of placing down a great burden. I could not keep a smile from my lips.

"He's long dead by your father's hand, lad. And now you have come of age and have no protection. We must flee to the wild lands of the border. There we might be able to raise an army of your people and retake your throne." He held up his hand to stop my questions. "I must go with you. I swore to your mother that I would always protect you."

I watched his face for a span of breaths, imagining a life far from the castle that was all I knew. My mother died when I was but nine winters old and my memories of her were fading, despite my best efforts. She had been kind and beautiful, teaching me to read in the old library and training me in the ways of the land. Now Kriun and the blood in my veins were all I had to remember her by. I went to embrace him, wrapping my arms tight around his shoulders. "Thank you, Kriun."

When he turned, there were tears in his eyes but all he said was, "Come lad, let us get you ready for tonight. Do not trouble yourself to steal since I have enough coin put aside for us both. I also have some of your brothers' clothes that should fit. We can leave tomorrow night." I grinned my agreement at him as he helped me put on the magnificent clothes.

Once he was done and I was dressed, I caught a glimpse of myself in the bit of broken mirror that served me for a glass and paused in shock. I knew myself to be plain and drab. I had been told as much since I was a child. Now I barely recognized the figure I saw. A prince in truth rather than name alone stared back at me and the sight filled me with foreboding. Aruna would recognize the source of the change and either she or my father would make me pay dearly for it.

But, alas, we would be missed if we did not come to the banquet tonight so I could not flee yet. I squared my shoulders and slipped my eating knife into the sheath that hung from the magnificent silver-embroidered belt. Perhaps the Prince would pay no attention to me and all would be well. My heart ached a bit at the thought and I swore silently at myself for my strange weakness. But Kriun had begun the long climb down the tower stairs so I forced myself to follow at his heels.

We arrived in the hall just as the King and my half-brothers and sisters entered. I was able to sit several seats down the table from Aruna and the empty chair next to her, something that I hoped would keep me from notice. The others favored me with nods and predatory glares, but nothing more. But that changed subtly when the Prince arrived with his retinue.

Raven's gaze took in my family with a lazy contempt that sent a thrill through me. In it was all the loathing I feared ever to let them see and I very nearly liked him for it. But I remembered the library and thought instead of throwing my eating knife at him. They made me feel ugly and unlovable. He had made feel unclean and ashamed. I could not be away from them all soon enough and it was all I could to remain at the table.

At that instant he caught my eyes in his own and his thin lips curled in a smile both wanton and cruel. I gasped for breath, my heart racing and cheeks flaming as he tilted his goblet toward me before he turned to Aruna and the King. Now my half-sisters and brothers watched me sidelong and a frown darkened the King's brow until I trembled in my chair. I forced myself to eat and drink as though nothing was amiss but it seemed an eternity before it was done and the servants began to clear the table.

All rose and I was able to slip from the hall unnoticed in the confusion, or so I thought. Kriun was nowhere to be seen so I followed the corridor that led to his room in hopes of finding him. Aruna's retainers must have followed me from the hall because it was there they found me and seized my arms, stopping my mouth with a gag so I could not cry out. A sharp blow to the head ended my attempts to break free and I sank into a cold darkness.

When I woke, I was chained facing a dank stone wall, my arms and legs outstretched and fastened so I could not move them. From the corner of my eye, I could turn enough to see that I was in one of the lower dungeons and that all the men present were my sister's creatures. I knew then that I would be shown no mercy and I gave myself up for lost.

That feeling only worsened when Aruna herself entered carrying a long carter's whip in her hands. She would think nothing of beating me to death or nearly so. I tugged frantically at the chains when I realized what was about to happened but could not free myself. She laughed to see it and I ceased rather than give her amusement. "I told you what I would do to you, Beast. And I am a woman who keeps her word." She snapped the whip through the air and I bit my lips to hold back a whimper.

The first blow stung a little but since they had not removed my tunic, I was able to bear it. I found my thoughts turning to Raven and marveled that I should be punished for attracting the attentions of a prince whom I hated. Still, a part of me rejoiced that I had taken something from Aruna, even if she killed me for it.

The fourth blow made me moan and the eighth to shriek as my sister's whip began to cut through the fine cloth to my skin. Now I stopped thinking, stopped imagining the vampire's face as I had seen him in the library when he caressed my flesh. Once my tunic hung in shreds and each blow landed on my bare flesh, I ceased to count or to attempt to hold back my cries. Thus it was that I failed to hear the door creak open.

"My, what an interesting entertainment. I had no idea that you enjoyed the sight of blood so much, my dear." Raven's voice was bored, slightly cruel with twisted amusement. Over the sound of my labored breathing, I could hear the hiss of my sister's displeasure. He continued, "Perhaps we can add to your enjoyment once my hand is joined to yours. For the moment, however, your brother amuses me and I intend to take him with me. I assume you're done?"

Something dark and menacing crept beneath his tone, like a snake coiling and the retainer who had brought me the food now appeared at my side with a key. In moments, I was released from my bonds, crumpling to the floor as my legs failed to support me. The vampires carried me from the dungeon and their prince followed behind them still chatting with my sister as if naught was amiss. I hung half-swooning from their arms and wondered a little at what my fate was to be. I saw him kiss her hand as the darkness took me and I surrendered to the pain.

When I awoke, I found myself in the Prince's chambers. I was lying naked and face down on a huge soft bed. My wounds had been treated and they pained me far less than they had earlier. For that I was grateful.

But then Raven chose to lie down at my side and drowned that feeling in a flood of pure terror. He had removed his cloak and tunic and the white flesh of his breast gleamed in the firelight. I forced myself to turn and sit up despite the agony of the motion. A tear I could not hold back leaked from my eye.

He reached out his hand and ran a white finger down my cheek following its track. "It seems that I am to blame at least in part for your punishment, princeling. Your sister is quite vicious in her defense of what she feels to be her own." He was much closer now, leaning so close that I could feel the coldness of his bare flesh. Somehow, I could not move away, despite my terror.

He stroked my shoulder, caressing me lightly. "Let me atone for my sins, little Beast, little Allain. I can make you forget the agonies of the whip if you let me.

I shuddered and thought about turning away but he held my face and kissed me, a long deep kiss that left me breathless. I tried to summon the strength to defy him but somehow it had all fled under the whip's caress. I wondered if his desire was heightened by the sight of blood pouring from my back as my clothes were flogged from me. I tried to ask him as much, though I had no longing to hear the answer.

Somehow he understood what I was trying to say, despite my inability to form the words. "Your blood was every bit as sweet as I imagined. I took only what you had already lost, princeling. It is my nature to drink even if I do not often kill to take it." He pressed himself against me, stirring my reluctant desires until I reached out my hand and touched his face.

Then he pulled me up against the pillows with a care and tenderness that brought fresh tears to my eyes and I wept as he kissed me again and again. His lips and hands were everywhere on my naked flesh and I hardened, longing filling me until I could remember nothing for a time, except wanting him.

When we were done, my mind whirled. What had I done? What could I do now? This bout of madness would cost me dear. Aruna would kill us both.

Kriun. I had to find Kriun. We had to leave tonight before all of this got worse.

I twisted out from under Raven and gathered all my remaining strength to roll from the bed with a painful wrench of my flayed skin. I found the rags that my silver clothes had become and pulled them on as if they would still cover me. The prince watched me from the bed, his lips twisted in a wry smile. "You know, I like them better that way." I looked down. My tunic and leggings hung in rags from me, exposing more of my flesh than they covered and I blushed despite myself. "There's a small cloak in the wardrobe if you insist on leaving."

He got up, body gleaming white and beautiful in the firelight. I watched him approach as the mouse watches the snake, knowing it is doomed yet unable to flee. "I never thought to find so beautiful a boy in one of the barbarian mortal lands. Come with me to my kingdom, Princeling Beast. Leave this clan that is no clan and join me." He circled me, running caressing fingers over my bare skin then pulling me close so he could kiss my neck and bare shoulder.

I pulled away, determined not to succumb to him again. He would kill me eventually; this I knew in the depths of my very heart. He would make me a vampire catamite, forever young and forever enslaved. And Aruna would hunt me down and stake my sleeping body during the day. I knew what she was capable of.

I exerted all my powers of resistance and to my surprise, I was able to limp to the door. I flung it open to flee into the darkened corridor beyond. Once there, the madness of the night overtook me and I loped until I went to ground like a hare in one of the secret corridors. Both sister and prince knew where I slept so there was nothing to keep either or both from my tower room. I was safer in hiding for the moment. Despite the coldness of the stone around me, I fell into an uneasy sleep filled with unclean dreams.

Perhaps it was one of them that awoke me some time later. I could hear noises in the main corridor beyond the wall, the swishing drag of something being hauled across the stone floor. I wondered what it was that would be dragged instead of carried. Surely, I thought drowsily, moving whatever it was that way would simply rub holes in it and let the contents drain out.

Then I heard Aruna's voice and tried to curl even deeper into the darkness of my hiding place. At first I could not make out the words but then she drew closer to the wall and I heard her say, "This will bring the creature out of hiding. Then he is mine." And she laughed coldly, sending echoes through the hollow stone that made me cover my ears.

Did she mean Raven? Why would he be hiding? And what could they be doing that would bring him into my half-sister's unkind hands? Of course, it was no concern of mine if she sought to harm her own suitor. So I told myself and so I tried to believe. But as hard as I tried to tell myself that his fate was nothing to me, I could not drive his face from my mind.

Finally I could stand it no more and I rose to follow the passage I occupied as far as I could before it ended in an exit in a hidden alcove. I slid out as soundlessly as a mouse, my skills honed by years of practice, and found myself in the corridor behind my sister's men. An ancient stone statue hid me for the moment but I was very cautious as I peered around it to see what they were doing.

I could see little at first but as they passed under one of the few torches well down the corridor from my hiding place, I could see that they dragged a limp body behind them. I wondered who the unfortunate was, since all who went to the dungeons in my father's house were unfortunate or soon would be. I could not see his face but a strange and morbid curiosity took hold of me. I needed to know who this was. I crept along the wall behind them, avoiding the circles of torchlight as much as possible. Then they paused beneath a torch well ahead of me and tossed the limp body onto the shoulder of the biggest guard. Its hood fell off and I saw the flash of golden hair. *Kriun.*

I managed to strangle the cry that leapt to my lips. My heart raced and it was only with difficulty that I imposed order on my thoughts. If they saw me, I would join him and they would simply kill us both. I had to see where they were taking him first. Then I could devise a plan to rescue him. My heart was in my throat as I trailed after my sister and her men, hoping they would do no more than chain him up in the dungeons.

Yet something in my sister's voice made me fear that was a vain hope. Trembling with fear for my only friend and myself, I followed them down and down into the depths of the castle, into the darkest levels of the dungeons. Eventually they stopped and I managed to hide myself in a recess as they carried Kriun inside. I slunk closer, my back always to the wall, my feet sliding over the stone as if I walked on air. As if our very lives depended on it.

Finally I got as close as I dared to the open door, just near enough to make out some of what they were saying. I heard Aruna laugh before she spoke and the sound sent chills down my spine, "Your life will be short but less merry than you might have dreamed, fool. You should have left the kingdom after the Queen died instead of troubling yourself about the boy. What does it matter to you who sits on the throne?"

Kriun's voice was faint but stern. "The Prince is of the Old Blood. He bears the right to rule the kingdom, not your family of usurpers." I pressed myself against the wall, imagining myself as King, the dungeons emptied and the peasants free, those demons I thought my family in exile. The vision filled me with indescribable joy. Not that it mattered since I had no army to take back what was mine. Better to flee, perhaps to build an army in hiding, perhaps only to live in a less hostile world.

But not without Kriun. His words were followed by the sound of a ringing blow, of flesh meeting flesh. How long they beat him I could not say because I fled. Not from fear, you understand, but because I realized that I could not aid him by myself. There were too many of them and they might kill him while I lingered, trying to find a way to trick them away from his side. That realization lent wings to my feet and I scrambled up the stairs toward the upper levels with every bit of speed I could find in my trembling limbs.

When I reached the corridor with the guest quarters, I slowed, appalled by the only option before me. I had no other friends in the castle. The King and his children would turn their hands against me and though some of the servants were kind, I could not trust them to aid me in this. There was only one who had the might to help me rescue Kriun. But the price would be all I had.

I froze before the door to Raven's chamber, trying to find my courage. I remembered how Kriun had stood between myself and the enraged King. I remembered how he had soothed my back after beatings, had listened to the futile wailing of my young heart at the cruelty of my family. How he had stolen food and clothes for me and done all that my true father could have done. Then I knocked on the wooden door, praying that it was still dark outside and that the vampires were yet awake.

At first, I heard no sound within and I rested my head against the wooden planks of the door and knew despair. Then at last I heard the bolts being pulled with a great shrieking of iron on wood. The door was opened by the same servant who had brought me food from the King's table. He raised an astonished eyebrow to find me there but stood aside to let me enter the same chamber I had fled hours before.

Raven was buckling on his sword when I entered and several of his people appeared to be donning armor. All paused to stare at me in what seemed to be astonishment. "Ah. It appears that our rescue efforts were a bit premature." Raven smiled at me and I made myself smile back. He tossed me a piece of parchment with a scrawled message on it. *Prince Allain is in the Princess' hands. Please, please as you have been kind to him, come and save him now.* It was signed with Kriun's name.

I flung it to the floor in disgust. "It's a trap! Kriun never wrote this! She must have thought you would come to rescue me. It's Kriun who she's imprisoned. I fear that she may kill him." The words came out in a rush while the vampires looked on impassively. "Please, Your Highness, I beg your aid as one Prince to another. Help me rescue my liege man."

No one even blinked. Finally, Raven broke the silence. "Who is this Kriun to you?"

"He was my mother's counselor. You have seen him at the banquet—" I stopped, aware for the first time that I was begging a group of vampire knights to save the King's jester. I hunted for the words to persuade them.

"The jester with the scar? The one who bears the look of the Old Blood of this misbegotten land?" Raven sat on the edge of the bed, one eyebrow raised in cynical astonishment.

"He is my friend, my liege man. The only one who called me 'Prince'." I thought of mentioning love but such an emotion would be too alien to these creatures. Loyalty, I thought they might comprehend. "I am prepared to…" I stumbled over the words until I could force them out, "to give you whatever you desire in return for your assistance." I drew in a deep breath, preparing myself for the sacrifice that I intended to make.

Raven frowned, then waved his hand at his people. "Wait for me in Lord Nekaron's room until I call. Prepare the others." His people filed out, taking the servant with them and leaving us alone. I closed my eyes and waited. "Now, Prince, perhaps you might tell me what it is that you think I want."

I moved as close to him as I could bear, close enough to reach out and touch his face. Then I leaned in and kissed him, my lips tentative and nervous against his cold ones. I pressed my body against his but still he did not reach for me. For a long moment I thought I would fall weeping to the floor at his feet. Then I realized what I must do.

I pulled his dagger from his belt and stepped back. With an effort that made me tremble, I rolled my sleeve up to expose my arm. Then I ran the knife's edge in a line from my hand to my elbow so that the red blood gushed to the surface. The pain was intense but I made myself remember Kriun and I did not faint. "Take me. I am yours." It was the only command I had ever issued and it rolled from my lips with an assurance that I did not feel.

Raven watched the blood run down my arm and I could see the monster rise in his eyes. He was fighting it, looking away. I brought the dagger up to cut off the rags of my tunic, exposing my flesh.  I cut off the remains of my leggings too and stood before him naked. His nostrils flared, breathing in the scent of my blood, but he still resisted it for what seemed an eternity.

Then he met my eyes, his face going cold and fierce like a wolf's. My heart raced as I saw him become the thing I feared. I was shivering so much I thought I would swoon but I forced myself to hold the dagger up before me like a shield. "Will you honor our bargain, Prince? My blood, my body, for Kriun's life?"

He tilted his head sidelong to study me from those cold eyes and for an instant, he was the Raven from the library. He nodded and I knew that this was the only reassurance I would receive. I could only hope that I would be alive to see Kriun safe. It was my last thought before he moved, his hands a blur as he seized my arm and brought it to his lips. This time he sank his teeth into me without hesitation and drank, pulling me closer as I swayed on my feet. I watched him draw the life from my veins for what felt like hours before I fainted.

When I awoke moments later, I could feel his lips trail icy kisses up my bare arm. I wondered that one so close a kin to the wolf could be so brutal, yet so tender. The thought was too complex for me in my present state and I soon abandoned it in favor of contemplating Kriun's fate. I have never known such an effort to form words before. "Please. I will give you all you want. Kriun. You must help." I collapsed into the pillow, unable to summon my legs beneath me to rise from the bed.

"You did indeed, little Beast. Where is the jester being held?" I remembered the corridor that I had followed and murmured some incoherent instructions. He held my eyes with his own, seeming to read my thoughts. Then he nodded and rose from the bed. A single clap of his hands and his servant appeared, silent as a cat.

Raven's servant applied a healing ointment to my back and arms before flinging a soft blanket over me. By the time he finished, Raven was appareled for battle, long sword at his side. His knights emerged to join him and the sight was as the coming of a terrible dawn. For the first time, I wondered what I had done, calling such beings as these to slake their thirst on my fellow humans. But it was the only way. My head dropped to the pillow and I surrendered to oblivion before they left the chamber.

It was some time later when I awoke with the hand of the Prince's servant on my shoulder. We were no longer in the prince's chamber. Instead, I recognized one of the disused passages where I was accustomed to travel, far from the watchful eyes of the court. I wondered that Raven's servants would know of such a place but spoke another thought first. "Kriun?"

The servant pressed a finger to his lips and gestured at the other servants around us. Only Raven and his knights were missing and we were in hiding. The descent of despair was so sudden and so black it took my breath away. Raven had failed. His life, Kriun's life, all of our lives were forfeit. I blinked tears away, trying to prepare to hear the worst. "Is he dead?" I whispered the words, realizing that I could be speaking either of my friend or Raven, unsure which loss would bring me greater pain.

"We don't know, Highness. Our prince bid us hide here in case he failed, but it is daylight outside now and he is not returned. We fear that he is dead or captive." The servant met my eyes in the flickering light of the torch and I read a despair nearly as great as my own. In that moment, I realized that he was a mortal like myself. I marveled that he would choose to serve the vampire lords, at least until I remembered the cold perfection of Raven's flesh against my own. Then I knew how close I was to the Western Wall and what lay beyond.

I looked up along the stone walls, noting that the pale light of dawn was trickling through the arrow slits on the wall behind me. I closed my eyes to shut out my fears, to shut out the doom that might have befallen my one true friend. One thing I knew beyond all doubt: if I lay here doing nothing, then all hope was lost. I did not know what I could do to save them, if indeed they could be saved, but a way must be found. Else I was unworthy of Kriun's love and unworthy of the throne of my fathers.

I forced myself to my knees, relieved to see that I was clothed once more. I rolled up the overlong sleeves of the tunic and winced at the sight of my arm, ravaged by Raven's teeth. I forced my trembling knees to hold me as I stood and the Prince's man rose with me to hold me steady. We stood swaying together a moment as I thought of what to do next. I knew well the secret passages of the Castle. Perhaps there might be more beyond the ones that I knew. Perhaps even some that entered the deepest of the dungeons.

The determination to begin, to know the fate of my friend and the prince, propelled me forward as I muttered my thoughts in a rambling surge of words to the servant. Then I realized that I had not even asked his name, he who had saved my life by hiding me. "What is your name?"

"Raoul, Your Highness."

"You will accompany me, yes? Good man. Are there any others here who might be of assistance?" I gestured at the other servants and Raoul beckoned to two of them. No plan came from my fevered brain at first so I simply began to walk. My strange escort moved behind me as I walked, held upright by Raoul's strong arm.

Soon, I knew where we were and I began to lead us down broken stairs and through deserted corridors. Betimes, we stepped warily across the open corridors to reach more of the secret ways. And all the while my blood beat with the rhythm of fear warring with hope.

I would say that I thought of Kriun and I did, hoping and praying that he was yet alive and unharmed. But it was the vampire prince's face that rose before me and lent wings to my feet, despite all I could do to banish it. I hoped that my fears would lend me strength to do whatever I must at our journey's end.

Lower and lower we descended through stone-lined passages dank with cold. Now I had to stop more frequently to find holes to look out of, doorways into the known passages to see where we were. Once we hid when some of the King's troops walked past, one of them wiping blood from his hands. I shuddered, praying that it did not belong to ones I loved. It seemed an eternity before we found our way down to the level where I thought Kriun was held.

I opened the door from the hidden corridor cautiously, unsure of what I would find on the other side. My heart raced to see nothing but an empty corridor before me, lit only by the sputtering of a single torch. I stepped into it, staggering a little as I was still faint. Raoul steadied me. "From here, I am lost," I whispered to my companions. "We need to find out where your master is being held captive." I gestured in either direction.

One of the servants shrugged and slipped down the corridor to see what he could see. After a moment, the other went the opposite direction while Raoul leaned my swaying form against a wall. An eternity passed before the man who had taken the right-hand path appeared and waved from the far end of the corridor. I walked toward him, my hand against the rough stone for support while Raoul went to fetch the other servant.

For some reason, the fellow seemed further and further away with each step of the winding corridor, almost as if he moved away from me deliberately. I followed him around several turns and past some other passages, still vainly trying to catch up with him. Finally I opened my mouth to call to him to wait only to find that there was no need as I turned the corner.

He lay on the stone of the corridor at my sister's feet. The King stood at her side, wiping his dripping sword on the body's clothes. Behind them stood ten men at arms. Aruna gave me a smile that might have been birthed from deepest winter. "Hello, 'brother.'" She reached out, catching my arm in an iron grip and rolling up the tunic's sleeve. "You see the wounds, Father? He has given himself to the vampires. No doubt the fool told him that he was the rightful ruler of the land or some such other nonsense before he died. The Beast thought to make an alliance with my prince, using his grotesque little body and his tainted blood. How pathetic."

News of Kriun's death shot through me like an arrow and I bit my lip hard to hold back a sob. The King glowered down at me from under fearsome black brows. "I have spared you until now, traitor's get, for your mother's sake. Now it seems my mercy was misguided. Your father, my idiot jester, is dead at my hand." Here he seemed to spit the words, his cold eyes alight with hatred. I gaped at him in astonishment. Kriun, my true father? Why had he not told me this?

The King smiled grimly at my surprise. "He did not tell you then. He did not speak of the Old Blood or that you might rule in my place, were I as weak as he? How droll. As if a race of weaklings like you could drive us from this land." Aruna laughed but he waved her to silence. "I give you to the Princess, who you have wronged. She shall determine your punishment." He turned away with a look of contempt.

I was in truth doomed; I could see it Aruna's eyes. Still I found the strength to be defiant. "At least my body was sufficient to gain an alliance, my 'sister.' Can you say the same?" I growled the words, somehow twisting free of her grip. For an instant I thought to run but the armsmen circled around behind me and I knew that I could not succeed.

Aruna's slap knocked me to the ground a moment later and left my head ringing too much to think further on the subject. Then I was seized by the arms and dragged down the corridor. I cursed the King and his daughter with every drop of the Old Blood in me, hoping it was strong enough to do them some harm.

The King growled an order at the guards and Aruna laughed, the sound trailing fingers of ice down my spine. I had failed and now she would succeed in killing all of us. And she would  marry Raven if he still lived. The realization that this was a cut near as unbearable as all the rest made me groan, made the hot helpless tears threaten to spill down my cheeks. I could not bear to see her win, could not bear to see him kiss her. I would die before I would see that happen.

Soon it became clear that my wish would be granted. The guards dragged me into a cold stone chamber and chained me to the wall by my neck. A second set of manacles were fastened on my wrists and I was left alone for a few moments to mourn the loss of the only being who had loved me since my mother's death. It seemed only moments but my eyes were raw with weeping when Aruna entered, five of the guards at her heels.

I backed away from them as far as the chains would permit, my eyes anxiously searching the gloom for the whip she had used on me before. "No whip this time, Allain. Now I'll make the punishment fit the crime and there will be no rescue. Your monstrous lover sleeps until sunset and by then you will be dead. But not before you know what it means to try to take what is rightfully mine." Her eyes were feral in the dim light now and I shuddered, making the chains rattle with it.

She stepped away and waved her men forward and I knew fear greater than any I had known before. They encircled me, each one bigger and uglier than the last. One of them grasped the flesh between his legs and said something in a lower-class accent that I did not understand, though it made the others laugh. But the gesture, that I understood and I bit back a wail of pure terror before it could escape my lips.

Then two of them reached down with knives in their hands while the others seized my arms and legs. I struggled and flailed but to no avail and the shining blades descended to cut the clothing from my trembling limbs. Once I was naked, they held me up suspended before the largest guard. Lenash, Aruna's lieutenant. I remembered his tortures of old and I very nearly begged for mercy. He smiled and one of his huge hands went to untie his trousers, exposing a fleshly spear of such a length and breadth as could split me in two.

I stared at Aruna in horror. "Your body will not seem so desirable to my prince when they are done, Beast. And I shall enjoy your screams as they all take their turns with you. Now beg for mercy until Lenash plugs your mouth for you." She leaned against the wall, anticipation lighting her features.

I was forced to kneel before him. The others had unfastened their own trousers and watched me from eyes turned savage with lust and rage. I drew a breath and closed my eyes, but I would not beg. I was a prince of the Old Blood and my enemies might break me but they would not humble me. So I promised myself. Lenash's huge fingers closed on my nose, trying to force my mouth open. I fought as best as I could, determined to suffocate before I drew breath.

The room had begun to whirl around me when a mighty slap jarred the side of my head. My gasp of pain was enough and he crammed his filthy length inside my mouth. His pawlike hands held the back of my head while I choked and gagged, trying to push him away. He thrust his way inside me, nearly breaking my jaw and forced my mouth wider. His movement jerked him against my teeth and tongue while I tried to bite him. The effort only amused him and earned me another cuff on the head.

Then all at once, the torture of my mouth was over and he withdrew to run his fingers down his spear. "Nice and wet now for what comes next." He grinned at his companions and I was seized and bent at the waist. My arms were held and they kicked my legs apart. I braced myself, dreading what was to come. Lenash stood behind me, pressing himself against me, pawing at me in his efforts to force his way inside.

I tried to pull away, tried to think of Raven and pretend that it was him instead but it was no use. Another guard seized my head and shoved himself inside my mouth as Lenash pushed up against me, beginning to wrench me open, to pierce me through until it killed me as I knew it would.

The sound of voices from corridor could be nothing, must mean nothing. There was none to save me or even to avenge my death. Raven would marry Aruna and forget me, once he awoke. The vision pierced me with a pain of the heart, greater still than that of my body. I screamed as well as I could with the guard's spear in my mouth. He yanked my head forward so that his length choked me and I could scream no more, could make no other sounds than the low animal-like grunts that fell from my lips that I could not suppress.

Only Aruna's scream was louder. Lenash released me with a bellow and the other guard pulled himself from my battered mouth. I fell to the cobbles, too weak for a moment to lift my head and see what had forced them to stop. All around me the guards grabbed for their swords and I was kicked once or twice in the melee. I curled up in a ball as swords clashed over my head. Lenash's head dropped to the floor nearby and I smiled to see it, no matter who wielded the other sword.

Suddenly, Raoul was by my side and I was pulled away from the fight to the safety of the opposite wall. Raven and several of the vampire knights still faced the last two guards but the latter were no match for them. My vampire prince turned as they fell, fangs bared and face awesome and fearsomely white with rage. I quailed and rejoiced at once but realized that his eyes were not fixed on me.

It was then that I saw Aruna being held near the door by one of his knights. Her face was nearly as white as the prince's, even down to her lips. She struggled against her captor's grip, but it was to no avail. For a moment, her gaze fell on me and I thought that she might beg me for mercy. But she read the answer on my face though I could not speak and looked away. Instead, she threw herself on her knees before Raven as best she could. "Mercy, my lord! All I did, I did for love of you!"

Raven stood before her, his blade dripping with the blood of the fallen guards and said nothing for a moment that seemed an eternity. Raoul dropped a cloak over me then and I wrapped it around me and sat up slowly to see what the prince would do. Aruna tried to bare her throat but the knight would not release her arms. Across the room, Raven's knights fed on the fallen; the sight seemed to stir her greatly. She cried out, "Take me, highness! Make me one of you and I will serve you for the rest of my unending days."

I saw Raven's face change, become wolflike as he sniffed the air, laden now with the scent of blood. He looked first at me and I huddled deeper in the cloak, as if it was enough to conceal me. Then he turned back to Aruna. Time seemed to stand still and I wondered if he fought the monster he held within. If so, it was not for long.  I watched as he pounced on her like a cat with a mouse and sank his teeth into her throat with a growl. Aruna gave one short scream and her back arched. She pushed against him with hands growing weaker as he drained her.

When she stopped moving, Raven looked up and met my eyes. I shuddered and looked away; there was no prince there now, only a monster. The blood of one who I had thought my kin ran down the alabaster flesh of his chin, red as rubies. His fangs dripped with it and I found I could not bear to look at him again. In that moment, he was more like the King and his children than like the prince I had known. True, I had hated Aruna but her fate was more than recompense for all she had done to me.

Then Raoul lifted me, carrying me from the chamber of the horrors I had witnessed. I was weak, far too weak to walk unassisted and soon I found that my eyes closed on their own and I rested my head on his breast. Darkness took me soon thereafter and I knew no more for a time.

When I awoke next, I was dressed and we were in the palace stables. Raven's horse was saddled and his people already mounted. Raoul picked me up and handed me to the prince as if I was a feather to be passed among them. The memory of his fangs carmine with blood came back to me at a moment and I flinched away with a cry. His cold arms wrapped themselves tight around me and he tilted my face up so he could see my eyes. "Are you so afraid of me now, little Beast?" His cold fingers stroked my cheek and he searched my eyes for an answer.

Was I too afraid to go with him? True, my fear wailed within me that he would feed on me as he had with Aruna. That my broken corpse would be flung from his bed to be taken away by the servants. But if I stayed, the King would kill me. It was then that I remembered Kriun and what he had told me. "I must stay in my lands if I am to become the King. Yes, I am afraid of you but I am more afraid of what will become of my people if I abandon them." As I spoke the words, I knew them to be true. A weak king I might be but better by far than one who ruled awash in blood.

Raven spoke at last, interrupting my thoughts. "We must go into hiding then, at least for a time." With that, he set spurs to his horse and we loped swiftly from the stables, vampire knights and servants at our heels.

For the first time, I realized what he had sacrificed to save me. Both knights and servants were fewer in number and they crept away at his heels, who had ridden into the court in triumph. They were fugitives for my sake unless they returned to their own land. What right had I to ask this? I resolved to send Raven away when next we stopped. For now, there could be nothing but flight and pursuit, for I knew the King would seek to avenge his favorite daughter.

Night had fallen and the moon shone brightly down on us, lighting the stone road before us. I saw the guards at the gate felled before they could raise the alarm, saw the torches and beacons lit on the walls behind us. For the first time, I cursed myself for not knowing the lands outside the castle. I could not guide us to sanctuary. Instead I clung to the monster who had saved me while the motion of his horse's galloping hooves jarred me until I was sore. Exhaustion forced me to ignore the questions that boiled in my brain, begging to be asked.

So passed much of the first night. We stopped to walk and rest the horses once we were in the mountains and away from the road. I saw then that we were bound for the mountains of the Western Wall and I thought for a moment that I might flee, hide myself away before we journeyed to the land I feared above my own.

The moon came out from behind the clouds then and a single beam lit Raven's face. It was pale and wise and beautiful as he spoke to his knights and they decided on the route. My heart twisted inside me as I watched him, sending a pain so sharp through me that I gasped for breath.

Then behind him, I saw distant torches on the trail. "They have found us," I whispered, pointing. Raven snarled, a trapped animal staring from his eyes and I flinched away in horror. He leapt up into his saddle, catching me by the arm as he rode past. His arms were iron bands holding me prisoner as he guided horses and men higher and higher into the mountain passes. I knew I could do nothing to save myself then. In my secret heart, I wondered if I wanted to.

Our flight went on forever or so it seemed. We hid in caves by day and I watched Raven sleep when I could not. He lay so still that it wrung my heart to see him, fearing him dead each day until he rose at dusk.

Once Raoul managed to steal fresh horses. Once the King's soldiers were so close that I could hear them breathe but they so outnumbered the knights that we hid, flattening ourselves against the rocks and behind bushes. Raven told me nothing until the third evening after we left the castle though I knew he could see the questions in my face.

Finally, I could bear it no longer. "Where are you taking me? And how were you able to save me? All the stories say that you cannot walk when the sun is in the sky." I did not ask why he had saved me; I was not sure that I could bear to hear the answer.

"Don't believe everything you hear from the bards, little Beast." He smiled at me to take the sting from his tone and I almost forgot what I knew of him. Almost. "I have trained myself and my men to walk before sunset if there is need enough. There is a price to be paid for it so soon we must eat and feed." His gaze lingered on me like an icy caress and I felt the hot blood rise to my cheeks.

"And where are we going? I have never been so far from the castle before." I detested the whine in my voice. I sounded not like a future king, but rather like a child and a foolish one at that. I spared a thought for Kriun, my father and resolved to act more as I had seen him behave when not obliged to clown for the court.

"Do you grieve for him, little one? I am sorry that I failed you. He was dead when we reached his cell." Raven's face showed nothing but the disappointment of a noble lord who had failed in his purpose but there was pain in his voice. I wondered how I could ever begin to understand this creature, this strange mix of kind and cruel.

"He was my true father, my mother's secret lover from one of the families of the Old Blood. I did not know this until it was too late."

"Ah. Then my grief on his behalf is the greater." Raven turned away, jaw working a little and my heart burned inside me.

Despite my terrors, despite anything proper that I should have felt, I reached out to him, turning his cheek so he faced me. Then I pressed my lips to his, slowly and cautiously. He tasted like metal, like the tang of blood. He pulled me to him, half-straddling his legs as his tongue sought mine. For the moment, I forgot the rest of our company, I forgot the danger of pursuit all to lie safe in his arms for a moment.

Then I remembered my shame and the face of the one who I thought my sister. I remembered the eyes of the wolf watching me from Raven's face and I pulled away, trembling in every limb. His grip on me only tightened and he pulled me closer, his lips caressing my neck until I was torn between desire and revulsion.

It was the sentry giving warning who saved me from going any further. Raven put me aside and went to him, leaving me gasping for air and my flesh burning wherever he had touched me. I could not look at any of the others. Raven vanished for a time, followed by some of his knights and there followed the screaming whinnies of terrified horses, then silence. A thin trickle of blood ran down his chin when next they stepped back into the firelight and my flesh turned cold.

Then we fled again, riding all night toward the Western Wall. Always, I rode before Raven on his saddle, and felt sometimes his lips at my ear or caressing my hair. I wondered if my blood called out to him the way my flesh did. Part of me wondered what it would be like to be immortal. I rejected it firmly yet it appeared again and again. To be beautiful and wise, for somehow I believed that his deadly kiss would remake me, and to be at his side forever. A vision came to me of what it would be like to be in his bed forever as well, sending a rush of heat and horror through me. These were my dreams despite all I could do to think purer thoughts.

So we rode, each wrapped in our own thoughts and fears until the mountains of the Western Wall loomed above us. Once on the other side, we would leave my lands behind and, I feared, all chance of reclaiming them. Never had I desired the throne so much as when I knew that it was mine yet I could not attain it. My head spun with plans, each stranger and more complicated than the last, each discarded as impractical in turn.

I nearly missed it when Raven turned from the road we followed and sent his horse in a weary gallop up to a tower, overgrown with vines. Looking about showed me the remains of an old castle, with enough of the wall still standing to make it defensible. "Here we shall find sanctuary until you gain your throne," Raven whispered in my ear, sending chills through me.

I looked around at my new domain and knew not whether to laugh or cry. Still, I must begin somewhere. With that thought, I dropped from the saddle to the ground. I helped the servants and the knights as best I could to clear the tower's floor and stairs and to build a fire. Raven hunted, bringing several hares for us to cook and eat once he and his people had drained their blood. We covered the windows and the door and prepared for the coming of day and sleep. Thus we ended our first night in our new home.

But I am forgetting to speak of what passed when Raven laid out his bedroll for us to share. I will not say that I approached it with the same terror that I had before. The press of his body against mine as we rode had accustomed me to the cold feel of his flesh. But this was not the same as being naked before him once more. Almost I found it in myself to flee rather than let him remove my clothes.

"Allain." His voice was tender and he said nothing more than my name, yet he had not spoken it before now. I came to him then, no more master of my feet than I was of my kingdom. He undressed me with gentle cold hands, his lips finding the scars from the bites he had inflicted as well as the marks of beatings both fresh and old on my body. Each of these he kissed slowly and carefully until I buried my fingers in his hair and pressed myself close against him.

This time when his hands slid between my legs to caress me into hardness, I did not stop him or cry out in protest. My memory of the wolf inside him had faded a bit but not so much that I did not realize that the prince I longed for and the demon were one and the same.

Still, I did not offer him my life's blood this time, only my body. That he took gently, pulling more pleasure from my weak form than I thought any mortal could withstand. When we finished, my legs could no longer hold me and we fell to the ground in a tangle of limbs. I twined my arms around his neck, all power of speech lost as we kissed once more, our bodies hot and cold flowing together until we were as nearly one as was possible between mortal and immortal. He held me close and buried his face in my neck, making me flinch away.

He stroked my cheek in the darkness. "Little Beast, I will not take your blood unless you give it to me."

But Aruna's dead face hung before my closed lids and I could not stop shivering. The birds outside began to twitter and it was time for him to enter his deathlike sleep. I sat with him as he lay down and covered his face before I found my scattered clothing. I was too tired to sleep so instead I began climbing the tower stairs in hopes of seeing where we were.

The steps were rotting but I was able to traverse them by the early light, following their spiral curve upward to the top. They emptied finally into a room whose windows looked out on the mountains of the Western Wall and my vampire prince's lands on the one side and my own on the other. I went first to look at the mountains and tried to imagine life there. I realized then that Raven had never told me why he left, only mocked me when I thought he was my enemy.

With that thought, I turned to look out on my own land and wished with all my heart that Kriun was by my side to see it in all its beauty. I could see a tiny village some distance north and figures in the fields. I looked back toward the castle, the only home I had ever known but it was too far away to still be visible. I thought about the Old Blood in my veins and the bloodstained swords of my family's conquest. I wondered what I could do to undo the wrongs that had been done until I fell asleep facing the windows.

Raoul woke me when the day's shadows had grown long and I knew that Raven would be awake soon. The thought filled me with longing, desire, terror all somehow mixed in a way I had never imagined. I followed Raoul down the stairs and shared the servant's meal of stewed rabbit. We heard the sentry cry out and Raoul and one of the other servants slipped out to see what it was. Curiosity overcame me and I followed them, staying well back in case of danger.

But it was not so far back that the old peasant woman on the path did not see me. She gaped and pointed at me before sinking to her knees. Raoul, who had moved to intercept her if she had any evil intent, spoke in wondering tones, "She recognizes your golden hair and bows to you, thinking you her prince."

I went to her side and raised her then, realizing that her hair had once been as yellow as mine and that she was bit shorter than me: one of my people then, the people of the Old Blood. Inspired, I remembered my true father's words then and gave the second command that I had ever issued. "Tell your neighbors that the true King is returned and that those who would serve him should gather here by sunset three days hence." She kissed my hand, a wondering look in her faded blue eyes, then vanished into the brush.

"Was that wise, Highness? Your father will be able to find you too." Raoul frowned at me in the fading light.

"My army must come from somewhere, Raoul. Do not fear for your prince. I will send him back before I will let further harm come to him." I rested my hand on his shoulder for a moment and watched the reluctant dawn of trust in his eyes.

"Send me back where exactly, Princeling? I'm the third heir to our throne, sent forth to marry and build alliances, perhaps to make more like myself. Do you think my Queen wants me to return?" Night had fallen and Raven stood behind us, listening to all I said.

Raoul vanished silently and I trembled a little to see him go. If I provoked my prince into a rage, would he serve me as he had my sister? For I still could not think of her otherwise, having thought of her that way for so long. He continued, his voice a low, steady growl. "And since when do you have the skills to command an army, even one composed of untrained peasants?"

"I meant no insult. Only that I could not bear—"

"To perish, as you surely would without your consort's aid? I thought as much." His lips curled in a mocking smile and something else, an expression that went through me like an arrow and deprived me of speech. "Or did Kriun not mention that particular tradition among the ancient rulers of your land? Several centuries past I believe one of my ancestors sat on the throne next to one of your own. We'd have to find you a noble lady to bear your heirs, of course. "

Now I knew he mocked me and I grimaced back at him. Surely I could not mean so much to him. He could not want to be a mere consort when he might rule as King himself merely for the price of marrying a mortal princess. I concealed my hurt as best I could. "Teach me to use a sword, demon prince. There is much I need to learn."

He smiled then bowed slightly. Moments later, I stood before him holding the lightest sword any of the company possessed. Some hours of practice passed, first through a series of movements like a dance, then in combat with a figure of bundled wood.

It lasted until I could stand no more and wove in my stride as if overcome with drink. "Enough, little Beast. Rest now and we will do more again tomorrow." Raven swept me up into his arms and took me into the tower.

He laid me carefully on the bedroll and removed my clothes but tonight he did no more than kiss me before he vanished. I wondered where he went but was too tired to think about it for long. I slept until the sun was high in the sky. This time, there were several baskets of food by the path and a trio of peasant lads standing before the tower when I emerged. I broke my fast with them awhile before the others woke. Thus I learned some of how the peasants lived under the blades of my family's conquerors.

More joined us that night, including one of the border lords with his small retinue. He had been driven into exile by the King and sought to take back his lands and his standing. His sword was mine if I would return what had been his. He watched critically as Raven took me through the exercises and arms training, shouting the occasional suggestion as I learned to swing the sword. When I could do no more, he produced two staffs tipped in metal from the pack on his horse and tossed one to Raven.

Wordlessly, they faced each other as all of us gathered to watch. Raven dropped into a fighting stance and the lord made the first attack. A moment later the staffs whirled, their metal tips gleaming in the firelight as they clashed, then fell away from each other. The border lord was gasping moments later but my prince showed no sign of weariness.

It could not last and finally Raven felled him with one deft swing. The lord bowed his head unsmiling but took his hand to be helped up. He gave Raven a nod of approval then he sent one of his men away and sat down to break bread with us.

More farmers trickled in as the night wore on, no few with mighty spears and bows. The borderlands were perilous ones. At dawn the lord's man returned, bringing word of more of the border rulers coming down from their mountain castles. For once, I might be grateful for the wages of cruelty. My army grew apace until by the third night, it numbered near a hundred men and boys.

"Now what?" Raven asked me as we looked down from the tower. "It is not enough to fight the King's armies yet, even if all the rest of the land rose up to join us."

"Ah, but that would be enough. Only a few men are needed to take a castle by surprise, provided always that their commander knows the secret ways." I felt strangely confident, as if my father's spirit guided my steps and my words. Somehow, I knew this was what he intended.

Raven smiled tenderly at me, no trace of mockery on his face. "It will be an honor to celebrate with you if we succeed, to die at your side if we fail." He vanished before I could respond, leaving me to welcome a small group of wild boys and a few girls who rode up the path in a thunder of hooves.

Training and provisioning my new army took a fortnight, as did telling Raven and a few trusted knights all I knew of the ways into the castle. Finally we decided on a three-pronged attack, each entering by a different way. Most of the King's commanders dwelt in the castle under his eyes since he did not trust them. Once the commanders and the King himself were gone, the army would collapse, or so I hoped.

Finally, all was ready and we left under cover of darkness, our army as hidden as it could be. We followed some shepherds through hidden paths in the mountains, avoiding the roads where the King's men patrolled. We rested by day, sleeping in caves and hovels and Raven lay beside me all the while I wondered when he would leave. I could not believe that he would stay. Would he leave after we defeated my father? Or after the coronation? Or simply when it appeared that all hope was lost and the King would win? I found no clues in anything he said to me.

On the final day of our journey, we slept in the caves above the castle. Or I should say the others slept. I tossed and turned, trying to fire my courage with dreams of avenging my father, of taking back the throne that should have been mine. A lifetime of fear was not so easily overcome, however, so I tried instead to think of what I could say to persuade Raven to stay with me. I lay and watched sleeping his face until at last, I could not keep my eyes open any longer and fell into a restless doze.

That night, we gathered ourselves to enter the castle by the secret passages I had known so well. I feared to make a map lest it be discovered and the passages closed to us. Without them, all hope was lost. Instead, I allowed Raven to use his powers to see the passages in my mind, then to pass it on to those of his knights who he trusted most.

I have spoken much of his touch upon my body but how shall I speak of his touch upon my mind? He had told me that he had few such powers in comparison to the older vampires so I did not fear that he might read all my thoughts and hidden desires. Instead, I thought fiercely about the routes we must take to enter the castle and gain the King's apartments. He held my face and looked into my eyes until I thought that my legs would give way beneath me.

I hoped that he would press his lips to my own and tell me all the things that I longed to hear but the border lords were watching. I resigned myself to pain and agony, what I feared might happen if my mind was not my own. Yet when it finally came, his touch was featherlight and cautious, as with one who takes only what he has been given and I loved him for it. That understanding shook me to my core and I was barely able to hold back the words. There would be time later or so I hoped.

Once he gave the routes to his knights, we were ready. He and I were to command one group, his knights the other two. We hoped in this way to overwhelm the guards and commanders and allow a few of us to reach the King. This decided, we began our journey into the castle, moving as quietly as could be done with a hundred men. Raoul we left in charge of our sanctuary and the other servants. He had orders to take them all and flee over the Western Wall if we were defeated. I trembled, thinking of what would be done to us if we failed.

Despite my terrors, we were able to enter the castle and gain the secret passages undiscovered. In the end, it was our decision to separate into three groups that saved us. The King's men found the first group. I'm told that they died valiantly, knights and farmers alike. But the alarm spread through the castle, alerting the guards and they were waiting for us in a force that greatly outnumbered our own when we broke through to the King's chamber.

I had steeled myself for blood and for battle but I had not thought to shield myself for the burning look of contempt and hatred on the face of him I had thought my father. Despite all I could do to command myself, I nearly shrank away, expecting a blow. He laughed, a sound without mirth but strong enough to give me the courage I lacked. I stood before my men then, my sword in my hands, Raven at my side.

He said nothing and I knew that I must speak, must act first. Otherwise the men would never follow me as their king. "Put down your swords and you may follow the King into exile." My voice was steady and I met each man's eyes as if I was a stranger to fear and terror. The King drew his sword in answer and ordered them forward.

"For Kriun!" I yelled and Raven echoed me. I tried to remember all that Raven had tried to teach me and I met the first man's sword with a clash that shook my arms. An arrow from one of the border girls took down a guard and then battle was joined.

Raven was before me in an instant, his sword a blur of light as he dueled against one of the King's commanders. Soon the floor ran slick with blood, both theirs and our own and it became hard to keep our footing. Still, I acquitted myself well, slaying two of the guards and wounding several others. But we were losing and for every one we slew, two more took their places.

It was then, when all hope seemed lost, that our second group arrived. They were greatly reduced in number from battling their way here but still there were enough knights and determined peasants to turn the tide a little our way. That was when the King slew the last of those who stood between us and faced me, hatred burning in his eyes.

I would not let him see that I feared him but my eyes sought Raven without realizing that I did so. That was nearly my undoing. The King swung his blade. It was nearly as long as my body and had it not caught the ceiling in its descent I would have had no time to leap away. Raven had seen this and I could see him assume his demon form, face fixed in a monstrous rage with fangs out of nightmare. Men fell before him like wheat but he was too far away to save me.

I danced away from the King's mighty blade once again before I struck back. I chanted Kriun's name silently to myself to give me the courage to cross my sword with his. I remembered an attack that the border lord had shown me and I slipped beneath his longer blade to strike at his leg. I drew blood and I gave him a wolf cub's smile as I danced away from another weighty blow. We circled as well as we could and he slashed at me suddenly, wounding my arm.

Gripping my sword in my good hand, I shot forward, sending my blade through his already wounded leg. The King bellowed with pain and gave me a blow that sent me flying backwards to crash against the wall. The sword fell from my limp fingers as I fell to the floor and the

King stood swaying above me, raising his blade to end my efforts. I could do nothing but wait and I prepared myself for death.

Then, with a howl of inhuman rage, Raven was between us. His blade caught the King's, knocking it aside before his own sword swept across his opponent's neck. The man who I had thought my father looked almost surprised as his body fell to the floor.

I lay looking up at my preserver, my vampire prince and he looked back at me with his wolf's eyes. Blood ran from his fangs and for a moment, I almost turned away. Then I forced myself to my feet and pulled his face down to mine. I kissed him then, my very heart in my mouth and I whispered, "I love you." But I shuddered as I said it.

His features grew less distorted but his expression was guarded. Several of the commanders surrendered but a few fought on. Raven pushed me gently away and went to finish the battle while I crumpled to my knees next to the King's body. There was nothing more I could do and the pain from my wounded arm soon made the room darken around me.

I lay in my mother's old room, my wounds bandaged when I awoke. Raven did not lie beside me and my heart caught in my throat. Soon the King's own physician came to me and with him a group of those who had served him. I called for those who had followed me and those few of the surviving border lords and peasants who could stand came to wait on me. I made the first lord my chief advisor and told him the rewards I wanted to give those who had fought for me.

Then I asked where the vampire knights were. "Asleep, Majesty. You slept past the dawn." He answered me, a look of slight amusement on his features. I nodded, ignoring the tears that threatened to well up in my eyes. Raven had left no word and though he might walk past the dawn, he had not done it for me. I forced myself to rise and dress and began to go about the business of being a King, though my heart was heavy within me.

Raven slept for several days and I did not see him, busy as I was in planning my coronation, exiling my half-siblings and other kingly tasks.

I missed the feel of his body when I went to my lonely bed at night and I wept until my pillow swam with tears. But I would be a king in fact soon and I could not bring myself to beg him to come to me. Or to love me in return when he did not.

Instead, I pledged my troth to the daughter of one of the border lords who had ridden with us. It was her arrow that had brought down the first of the guards. Thus I cemented the loyalty of the bordermen to me and made my first alliance. But I did not choose a consort because the one who held the first place in my heart had not come to me.

Even after he woke, he came only to the court and not to my chamber, and though my heart broke within me, I did not ask. At last, my heart was numb and I could weep no more. I was crowned King and I rewarded all of those who had placed me on the throne, including the vampires with all that was in my power to offer. Raven sat in council at my right hand but still did not come to my chamber.

The emptiness inside me consumed me but I wed my betrothed and took her to my bed, hoping to sire an heir quickly. When she quickened with child, it was she at last that intervened. I could not have said why she did it but I shall always love her for it. It was she who sent word to Raven and told him that I sent for him in the most urgent of terms.

I started a little to find him in my chamber with a slightly mocking look on his beautiful face. He bowed. "Her Majesty sent me hither to await your commands." I dismissed the waiting servants and petitioners with a gesture, already practiced. "And how do you enjoy being a King, little Beast? I sense that the Queen is already quick with your child. I congratulate you." He bowed, a fleeting look of pain crossing his look.

"Why haven't you come to me, Raven? I thought…I thought after what I said that…"

"Do you think I don't realize that you are afraid of the vampire in me? That you turn away from what I am? I have tasted you only when you hoped to save your father. I thought you would come to my side after the battle, but each night I woke alone." His eyes were the hawk's look that I had seen before but now I could face it without fear. I knew what I must do.

I said nothing but only drew the dagger I wore at my side. With a single motion, I bared my shoulder and held it to the skin near my neck. He met my gaze a moment before he crossed the floor to my side, knocking the blade away. His features distorted, the wolf gleaming from his eyes. Our garments fell away like leaves from a winter's tree and I wrapped my arms around his neck as he sank his fangs into my flesh.

He fed on me, his hands rough on my body as they forced me into readiness for him. I wailed my need, my desire so long suppressed into the flesh of his neck, and he wrapped my legs around his body, holding me up. I bit back a scream as he pierced me, my limbs convulsing as he fed from me and took all that I had to give him. I spilled my seed against him and he laughed to feel me writhe in surrender, making my body beg for what my lips could not, would not.

He pulled away from my throat to look down at me, my blood coating his fangs and his lips. He was a demon in truth and I loved him more than my land, more than my crown. "Little Beast," he growled and thrust against me, cold inside me until I thought I could feel nothing more ever again.

"Beauty," I whispered against the coldness of his lips.

"I love you," he growled in return and joined himself to me as only the best of consorts can do.

# RED SCARE

THE NOTE SAID THAT THE Fat Man knew about Greta and me. It was pinned to my desk with a slick little knife, just the kind scum like his muscle would use. It was a nice touch. I could take a hint. My desk couldn't take too many more, though. A few more calling cards like this one and I'd be sitting behind a pile of matchsticks.

Personally, I didn't give a rat's ass what he knew about me. A few of my friends knew I was really a dame. So did a few of my enemies. Didn't matter much unless I was in the running for Head Gumshoe, which I wasn't. To the world, I was Dash McDermott, private dick, and whether or not I actually had one didn't seem to matter to most of my clients. Of course, that was probably because they usually had other things to worry about.

Now Greta, she was another story. She was a vid star and well on her way to being the next Femme Fatale when Lana Dean retired. A word to the Committee and she'd never work again. The Committee exists primarily to protect us from the Buggies, the Kru'ush Magir, as any right-minded citizen could tell you. Protecting us from ourselves ran a close second.

Of course, nobody outside of the Defense Forces had seen one of the Buggies since the original colonists landed on Falcon. But we all knew that they were out there somewhere, waiting to invade and wipe us all out. Though why they hadn't for the last hundred years or so, no one could say. Still, as the Committee prop goes, "Preparedness is the key."

At least if you believed in bug-eyed monsters. Not me. I believed in staying away from the Committee and going to the vids every Friday like a good Revivalist. Any doubts I had about the Old Earth history they showed, I kept to myself.

Don't get me wrong. There are some great things about living here. Greta, for instance.

Thinking about her made me realize that I'd better meet the Fat Man so I clapped my homburg on my head, folded the knife and stuck it in my pocket. The office door slammed behind me as I went down the dim hallway out into the greenish-yellow sunlight.

A Packard remake cruised by, cybercell motor barely purring as the horn blared and the driver waved at Johnny, the old shoeshine guy on the corner. He waved back, then blinded me with a gold-toothed grin. "How ya doin', Mr. McDermott?"

I grinned back at him as I headed for the streetcar stop. For the thousandth time, I wondered how he paid for that dental job. Authentication like that cost more than I made in a month. He gave me a slow wink but no answers before I turned the corner.

The streetcar that showed up was called "Desire" and it was packed. Pity I just can't resist knives stuck in my desk, not even during rush hour, or I would have caught the next one. When I got off, the Casablanca's awning loomed up ahead. I sauntered down the block, resisting the urge to smooth my lapels just cause Barney the Bruiser stood outside the door watching me. I could feel my fingers ache for the handle of my raygun.

He sneered down at me as I walked up. "Why don'cha try wearing a dress for a change, ya pervert?"

"Hi Barney. Sure, I'll wear a dress for you, honey buns. Why don't you put one on too, and we'll go out for a big night at Sally's. My friends would just die to meet you."

He spat on the asphalt and I bared my teeth at him. "The Fat Boy sent me a calling card. Be a good little toady and tell him I'm here."

"You carrying heat?" A meaty paw reached for me. I stepped back.

"What do you think, sugar? That a delicate flower of womanhood like myself walks the mean streets unprotected? Fatso knows I'm not going to waste him. It'd be bad for my rep. You, on the other hand…" I looked him over speculatively. Even with the raygun on full, he'd make a hell of a pile of ashes.

He stepped back a little, muttering a string of things that I chose not to hear. I watched the big ugly vein in his forehead beat time for a minute before I pushed my way past through the red velvet curtain behind him. The space between my shoulders twitched where his little eyes were burning a hole, but I made myself act casual.

The Fat Man was sitting at his usual table by the bar, facing the door. He looked a little tired in the dim light. Kind of pasty. It cheered me up.

"What do you want, Fat Boy?" I liked messing with his title, especially since he wasn't that big, definitely not Greenstreet material. We just didn't turn out substantial rats like they did back on Earth.

He gave me an evil glare. "You like having a movie star, Mr. McDermott?" He kind of hissed the words, stopping for a long time on the "Mr." His Brit accent needed work.

"I don't think you'll get to take my place if I take a fall, Fatso. Now whaddaya want?" I stepped forward, turning slightly so I could watch Barney coming in the door and the joker standing at the bar behind the Fat Man at the same time. He probably wasn't planning on arranging any accidents for me or he wouldn't have bothered having me show up here, but hey, 'preparedness is the key.'

"Have a seat," he pointed to the chair across from him. I grabbed the one on his right instead and sat close enough that I could fry him before Barney got to me. No point in taking chances.

He pulled a face, but held up his hand to stop Barney where he was, looming a few feet away. "We found your cousin Fortune in an alley down by the Farmer's Market yesterday afternoon." He ran a descriptive finger along his wrinkled throat.

That might have brought a tear to my eye if I hadn't despised Fortune from the bottom of my heart. Aunt Mabel wouldn't be too happy, though. "Yeah? We weren't close. Whaddaya want me for?"

"Some of Fortune's friends think that I had something to do with it."

Fortune had friends? Who knew? "And?" I asked. There had to be something else. Fatso's problems were his own as far as I was concerned.

He followed up with a change of topic. "What do you know about the Kru'ush Magir, McDermott?"

"Not much. You?"

He looked like his fingers just begged to slap me. "This is big stuff. If I didn't have orders... All right. I heard that Fortune made some kind of contact with them. You know where that could lead." His voice dropped so he sounded like a vid villain.

Oh goody. I love listening to a bad Orson Welles' imitation, more than anything in the world. But critiques aside, this was out of my usual league. "Orders" on Falcon only come from the Committee but why did they care about my jackass cousin? I tried to imagine Fortune as the mastermind behind an alien invasion. It sounded kinda ambitious for a two-bit thug. "No, I don't know. Where did that "information" come from, Fatso?"

He leaned forward, looking me in the eye as hard as he could to place his insubstantial weight behind his words. "Reliable sources."

"Right. And I'm Bogart." I stood up. The Fat Man stuck a hand in his jacket. I stuck a hand in mine. Barney started moving, picking up speed as he headed in my direction, only to be stopped again by his boss' upheld hand. He glared at me as the Fat Man put a box on the table in front of me. I opened it to find a glossy goldtone pin, a big star-shaped one, the kind of shimmer that you'd get a femme if you were down on your luck but not flat broke.

"Not my style." I picked it up and flipped it over. The little red lights and the wires told me it wasn't your ordinary shimmer. But then, I never thought it was.

"It's a transmitter, better than any we can make yet. We found it on him. Our sources say it came from off-planet." I looked up at the few beads of sweat lining the fringe of what little hair he had left, then down into his tiny brown eyes. They didn't shift much. Still, I wondered why his boys were close enough to be searching the body before the Defense Forces showed up. That kind of work wasn't usually left up to the hoods, even the official ones like Fatso.

"So what do you want me to do about Fortune's taste in jewelry?"

"In light of your connections..." he steepled his little fingers together like he was thinking hard. I didn't buy it but he kept doing it anyway. "I would like to hire you on behalf of the Committee to investigate this matter. Find out if Fortune really made contact with the Buggies and what his plans were if he succeeded."

I sat back down and gave his proposal some thought. The only thing that Fortune and the Fat Man had in common was a ten-year-old turf war over the scratch trade. Supposedly my cousin was profiting from it and the Committee was out to shut it down but I had my doubts. Today's little game had to be connected to the scratch somehow. I don't know how I knew it, but I did.

The scratch, that lovely liquid silver that you slipped straight into your blood through cuts in your skin, had cost me a couple of friends. And Leandra. I looked at the Fat Man and swallowed both the sudden lump in my throat and a barely controlled desire to pull out my raygun and fry him. But Lee was long gone by now and shooting him wouldn't bring her back. Instead I decided I'd take him for everything he was worth.

"My tab's fifty credits a day. And I get my records changed," I said, almost as an afterthought. It wasn't. Femmes weren't supposed to be gumshoes, but I just wasn't Fatale material, ditto for Romantic Lead. Getting my records changed would transform me into a real gumshoe and keep the Committee off my back for the foreseeable future. Not to mention sparing me some permanent changes on a black market table that I had no desire to make.

He sputtered and jawed about the fate of our world resting in my hands and such for a few minutes. I got forty-five a day in the end and his agreement about the records. Better than I expected so I knew I wasn't expected to survive this job.

I waited till he turned to say something to Barney and I palmed the shimmer. As I left, I passed him back the closed box with his own knife, the one he had so kindly left in my desk, inside it for weight. The shimmer could come in handy, I thought, though for what I didn't know yet. Insurance, maybe.

I wandered back down the street, one baby blue peeled over my shoulder on the lookout for company. I didn't see anyone yet, but they'd be along eventually. I hopped on the next streetcar, then changed cars a couple of times on my way to the Farmer's Market just in case.

For entertainment, I tried to wrap my brain around the idea that my cousin Fortune had contacted bug-eyed monsters from outer space. My right hand toyed with the shimmer in my pocket. What kind of game was the Fat Man playing this time? From what I knew of him, there was no good reason to think that he hadn't sliced Fortune's throat himself. But I kept going anyway; it wasn't like I had anything better to do.

I got off at the Market intending to head for the alleys behind it, back where Fatso said they found Fortune. The legit farmers had their stands in the middle of the Market, piled high with "the fruits of the land," as the Committee liked to call local produce.

I wandered over and got a porkstick. When I turned around, I caught a quick glimpse of a familiar back dodging down one of the alleys and froze. It couldn't be. Scratch junkies didn't last that long.

But I had to find out. My appetite took a quick powder, but I made myself swallow the dry meat anyway before I wound my way through the stands toward the alley. The someone I was chasing was down at the other end, walking away from me.

I nearly lost my nerve when I got a clear eyeball on her feet. They were covered in scales, almost like claws. When I looked further up, I could see something bulging under the shoulders of the blue coat. Wings? For a minute, I wondered what a Buggy really looked like; I'd always had my doubts about the Committee sparktags. Then I started down the alley after her.

That was when she turned around.

It had been four years since I'd seen her last but you don't forget a femme like that. She wore a thick black veil pulled over her face, hanging down from her wide brimmed hat like a storm cloud. From what little I could see of her face, I was grateful for what it spared me. "Hey, Leandra," I spoke softly, forcing the words out.

She cringed when she saw me. I tried not do the same, tried not to remember how pretty she was back when she was my femme. Before she dumped me for Fortune and then him for the scratch. "Hello Dash." Her voice had gone all raspy, but at least she still knew me. How had she managed to change so much and still be alive? Scratch junkies never made it past the dry skin and deeper voice part. After that they just disappeared. My gut said they got iced before they got this far, but I didn't know for sure. Hell, I'd never thought about it much before.

Then I remembered Fortune. "Let's go talk, Lee. There's something I've got to tell you." Better she should hear it from me. I thought she loved Fortune before she got hooked. More than me anyway. I looked away, catching her nod from the corner of my eye. She didn't seem human any more, at least not the way I thought of us. My guts tied themselves in knots while I led the way back to the benches that ringed the outer edge of the Market.

I sat down, shaking all over. I couldn't look at her as she slithered down onto the far edge of the bench, couldn't stand listening to the sounds of things crunching and scraping that weren't the femme I loved anymore. There was a long silence before I could get the words together. "Fortune's dead, Lee." I mumbled. Now, I just wanted to get away, get sick, then drunk, then sick again to wash it out of me.

There was little sob from the other end of the bench. I handed her my handkerchief, and she grabbed it so fast I couldn't see her fingers. The rasp of scales against my fingertips made me pull away anyway, even without seeing them.

"I just saw him two nights ago. He said..." she trailed off, like she couldn't make herself go on.

I pushed, pretending that I wanted to hear more. "What?"

"That he was onto something that might make me better." That'd be pretty big if it was true. Scratch junkies didn't get cured. They cut more and more tiny holes in themselves and rode the wave until the day they died. For a minute, I wished Fortune was still alive so he could pay for this. Sure, he'd tried to stop her, tried to get her off the stuff, but once he failed, he went on sending his boys out to sell the stuff even after he knew what the scratch would do. My hands kept shaking.

She had a different memory of it. "He kept looking for ways to cure me. He didn't want to understand that it was too late. The changes are almost over now. I can feel it," she whispered, voice like scales over stones. I shuddered as she stood up but I kept looking at the ground. In my heart of hearts, I wished she had really died before I'd seen what she looked like now, and I wasn't very proud of that.

"Thanks for telling me. Goodbye, Dash." She took off so fast I wondered if the lumps on her shoulders really were wings, spreading out behind her through slits in the blue coat. I didn't look up to find out. There are some things you just don't want to see.

For the first time, I stopped to wonder if Fortune was a little better than me. He'd stuck around, watching her change into a monster, maybe even trying to fix it. I couldn't even look at her without my guts churning.

I sat there another minute, shivering against the bench, then I dragged myself to my feet and headed for the alleys. There was an old sparktag flickering its broken-bulbed message at the second one I walked past. A Kru'ush Magir blinked crookedly down to light my way, most of the bulbs in its antenna and faceted eyes broken.

Based on what the Fat Man told me, they found Fortune in one of these. I guessed that it was the one with the electriline silhouette of a body on the brick. I figured that this was far as the D. Force boys would go in their investigation. If it wasn't an alien menace or a dead Committee stooge, they didn't pay much attention. Good thing for my racket, anyway, as long as we didn't make enough noise to draw attention to ourselves.

I walked carefully around the crime scene markers and started skirting the disposals that lined the walls. There was nobody else around. I wondered what it was like at night and what the hell Fortune was doing here without muscle.

There was little shining spot under the corner of one disposal. I reached down to pick it up. It turned out to be a string of beads from an earring. More shimmers. Fortune was up to his neck in femmes from the look of it. I wondered for a minute if Leandra had iced him herself, then gave up that thought. It wasn't her. I'd seen her look at him before she'd changed. I kicked the disposal hard, then stuck the beads in my pocket with the other shimmer and poked around some more.

Nothing much turned up. A no-nic cig butt, Randall's Quality, "All of the kicks, none of the risks," like the tag says, showed up on the other side of the alley behind another disposal. Everybody from the Fat Man to Greta smoked them so I decided to leave it there since it wouldn't tell me much. Damn clean alley. Just a little dried blood and an outline to show that it wasn't always this tidy.

I headed out toward the streetcar stop, hunching my shoulders as the wind picked up and. Time to meet Greta and get a drink. Even the little bushes that lined the street looked depressed. The car showed up and I sat and made Greta slowly push Leandra out of my head. It took awhile. Hell, it felt like years.

Greta'd be coming from Studio Row. That was where they made the vids that they sold off planet, not the ones we went to every Friday. The off planet vids were in color and had more skin and blood in them. Big market for that kind of thing in the Leo II worlds. I'd been a walk-on in a few of them, something I did when business was slow. That was how I'd met her. After that, I just got lucky.

I got off the car near Sally's. The more I thought about Leandra, the more I needed a drink. Greta would check here for me when she got off the set anyway. The bug eyes and fuzzy antennae of Kru'ush Magir leered down at me from every corner. I wondered if they really looked like that and I flipped a pebble at one, cracking a bulb. It didn't help any.

The bar was a squat preconstruct wedged in between two warehouses. The plastocon bricks made it look like an Old Earth gas station, minus the windows. Nothing to tell what it was but the little red shoe on the wooden door. Those who needed to know what it meant found the place and the D. Forces left it alone most of the time. I hoped it was one of Sally's good nights. She paid plenty for them.

Vera the bouncer grinned down at me when I came in. "Howya doin', Dash?" I dodged a hearty backslap that would have staggered me and gave her my best fake grin. The one that said "my ex turned into a monster and I can't do anything about it." Her big eyes blinked slowly, mournful now as she gave me her best shot at doggy sympathy without even knowing why.

I headed toward the bar. The place wasn't too crowded yet, and Sally, the queen of my dreams, was tending bar. The rainbow gleam of her dress flashed as the light from the open door caught it, almost blinding me. When I squinted against the glow, I could see from the makeup that we were Judy again tonight. Good. I wasn't up to Bette.

Her long face lit up with a grin until I got closer. "Hey handsome. Oops, deary, I know that look. Business not so good?" I nodded, not ready to talk about Lee. She silently poured me a gin and patted my hand while I downed the drink with the other. It had the acrid aftertaste of old zinc, like the tub out back where it was made.

Sally poured me another, then took off to wait on the boys at the end of the bar, barely wobbling on her new heels as she went. The dim lights danced over the silver glitter that coated them like they were sprinkled with pixie dust. I toasted her with my second glass and stuck a hand in my pocket for the shimmers.

There was something familiar about the earring, but right now I couldn't think what it was. I put it and the pin on the bar in front of me and just looked at them for a while. Maybe the Fat Man iced Fortune. Maybe somebody else did. Maybe Fortune was onto a cure for the scratch. Hell, maybe he was just kidding around. I wouldn't put it past him.

I downed my drink and thought about the Fat Man and Fortune, Fortune and Leandra, Leandra and the scratch. A piece fell into place. It worked if the Buggies were real. Or if Fortune thought they were.

Now I wondered if my cousin had seen who he was doing business with. Were they real Buggies or just muscle in funny costumes courtesy of the Committee? I flipped the pin over and looked at the transmitter on the other side. How the hell did he contact them? Or why pick him, if it was the other way around? My thoughts chased their tails all over the bar but didn't catch them.

Instead I got depressed staring at my reflection in the mirror over the bar. After my third gin, I decided that I didn't look too bad for a guy. Big jaw and smallish blue eyes, solid shoulders, no hips to speak of and breasts tiny enough to bind down almost flat under my Dad's old suits.

I wondered sometimes if he had known what he was doing, bringing me up as a boy. Probably. Even soused, he had been pretty clear about what he wanted. Someone had to follow in his footsteps and it wasn't going to be my sisters. Mom died before she could object so that was that. Most of the time, I could take living this particular lie but every now and then it caught up with me.

Maybe—I hated it when this occurred to me—Lee wouldn't have dumped me if I was a real guy. Maybe I should reconsider the options. I weighed the black market operation against getting my records changed and being even somewhat indebted to the Fat Man.

A couple of hours went by while I wallowed. No Greta. No answers to tonight's thousand credit questions, either. Sally switched me over to juice after my fourth gin. Said I'd just brood if she didn't. Not for the first time,

I thought it was a pity she wasn't my type. I could do with someone taking care of me and Greta wasn't that girl. But then, Lee hadn't been either.

Every time Greta stood me up like this, I figured she'd had it and she was moving on for someone who could do more for her. Like Lee had. I hated that feeling. Maybe she was just working late. That's what she'd tell me when she showed up, no matter what the real story was. So I ate greasy canned meat with Vera, and played some eight ball until I couldn't take it anymore. I blew a kiss to Sally and headed out for home. Damn Greta anyway.

The old dump was only a mile or so away so I decided to walk off my mood. I stuck my hands in my pockets and pulled my hat down against the night wind and snarled every time I thought about femmes, past and present. Even the goons outside the Rialto avoided me, so I knew the tough guy routine was working for me.

It worked so well, I didn't hear them coming behind me. One good shove and I smacked up against the brick wall of the alleyway, hard. "Where's the Buggy, alien lover?" The fist that hit me in the eye made everything go black for a minute. I figured they weren't going to wait for an answer. A few more hits like the first and I was on the ground, curled up in a ball. I was trying to get my fingers inside my jacket for the raygun when the first kick caught me in the ribs.

Then the head. I went down for the count. When I woke up, I was still in the alley and it was a little before dawn. A cold rain drizzled down my nose and it hurt like hell. Probably broken. Goody. Just what I needed. I sat up slowly and the alley walls looped around in a big circle. I closed my eyes, then opened them again a few minutes later. Everything stopped moving.

So did I. I just leaned up against the wall and got wet for a while. When I tried moving again, it all still hurt but nothing was spinning. I dragged myself up on the brick and staggered home, which luckily for me, wasn't that far away. I limped up the steps and into my apartment. Or at least as far as the open door. I stuck a hand in my jacket for my gun. It was gone. Damn. I drew a deep breath and slammed the door open with my foot.

It banged against the wall and Mrs. McCreedy on the other side banged back, but that was about it. I inched inside and hit the lights. They came on and showed the world that I wasn't much of a housekeeper. Even so, I could see the place had been tossed and pretty thoroughly at that. I checked out both rooms and the closet. Nothing and no one.

Every rib howled for a glass of Sally's gin. I needed some answers but I needed to be able to move my right arm without screaming first. The bath came first. It helped but not as much as I thought it should have. Neither did breakfast.

Then I checked my pockets. My raygun wasn't the only thing missing, it turned out. The Fat Man's shimmer was gone, too. It didn't take an Einstein to figure out that it was what they were after. I had a dim memory of the goons yelling something about a "Buggy." What Buggy? And why did they think I was on speaking terms with one?

Somehow, they'd missed the earring. I pulled it out and looked at it. At that moment, I realized that I was starting to believe in the Kru'ush Magir and that was a first. Up until now, I always thought a healthy skepticism about their existence was the best policy. But right now it sure seemed like other people believed in them, at least enough to beat the tar out of me.

I opened my desk drawer and took out some old photos of Lee, more to remind myself of what she looked like before the scratch than anything else. Okay, who am I kidding? I just liked looking at her the way she was. I couldn't help noticing that she didn't favor this kind of shimmer. I stared at them for a few more minutes, then I made myself put them away before I got too down. I tried not to wonder if she still had ears.

I glanced at the photo of Greta on my desk. It took a minute. I took the bag of ice off my nose for a better look. My brain couldn't wrap itself around what I was seeing. I kept looking anyway but it didn't get any better. Maybe every femme in town had shimmers like this and I just hadn't noticed. Maybe Fortune had an ear pierced since I saw him last.

Maybe I was just kidding myself. Maybe I had been for the last three months. I tried to remember if she'd met Fortune when I'd been around but I wasn't getting a picture on that. I thought about how bad she wanted to be Femme Fatale and about how fast she'd come up through the ranks. I'd thought it was talent and looks but now I was starting to wonder. Why would a rising vid star want to go out with me, anyway?

I took the ice off my nose again. The swelling had gone down, but I was going to have a lovely shiner. The part of my brain that wasn't weeping like a baby started planning. If nothing else, I needed to replace my gun so I called my regular guy. He was all out so he recommended someone else. Johnny the shoeshine guy would be glad to oblige me. At least now I knew how he paid for the dental job. By the time I had my piece, the sun was sinking low and the two little moons, Bogie and Lorre, were starting to rise over the horizon.

I wanted to walk but there was no way my ribs were going to let me get away with that. I hopped on a streetcar and headed for the right side of the tracks and Greta's big gray house. My wingtips clicked against the concrete as I walked up the driveway and opened the gate. Looking up at the place, I could see a light on in her room.

My new raygun made a comforting lump against the few ribs that didn't hurt. I wondered how I was going to ask her about Fortune. Then I wondered about the Fat Man. There was no way he wasn't in on this. Why else would he bring me into it? I knew Fortune, I knew about the scratch and I knew…Lee. Lee who'd changed more than any scratch junky I'd ever seen and lived longer.

I decided I'd go ask. Greta If I was right, She had to be working for the Fat Man. Nothing else made sense. I wondered if he was up there in her room waiting for me, with Barney and some of his other thugs. I made myself head up the drive breathing in the stink of a setup every step of the way.

When I got to the front door, I had a little surprise. It was open. I was inside with my raygun out within two breaths. The hall was dark, and something crunched underfoot. My pulse started a quick dance tempo.

I put my back to the wall and stepped lightly around the corner into the parlor. From here, I could see the bedroom light shining down the stairs.

I crept along watching the shadows. Nothing moved. Sidling up to the stairs, I started climbing, one foot after the other, not a thought in my head. Just fear, pure and simple. The bedroom was a wreck, drawers dumped, jewelry and facepaint everywhere, but that was it. The body I thought I'd see wasn't there but someone had sure packed in a hurry. My heartbeat went from a foxtrot to a waltz. All right, maybe a tango. But if she wasn't here, where was she?

I looked around some more. A gleam on the floor caught my eye. I shoved the blanket aside and found the Fat Man's shimmer, the one that the boys in the alley had taken off me. What the hell was it doing here?

All of a sudden, I wasn't sure I wanted to know. I stuck the pin in my pocket and listened to my gut. I decided to believe that Greta was safe with the Fat Man. Then I decided to leave by the fire escape and worry about it all from a few blocks away.

The beam that caught my hand on the railing wasn't set for low burn. My skin blistered as I yanked it back and rolled forward down the metal stairs, grabbed the railing at the bottom with my good hand, and jumped over it into the bushes. The shrubs were crisped behind me as I scrambled along the side of the house, aiming for the shadows and the trees out front.

I doubled around to the front of the house and the firepower got turned off. There was no good way to outrun them from here so I hunkered down to wait and listen to my hand and my ribs scream. The handlights they carried flashed on the leaves in front of me so I stayed low. My good thumb found the high setting on my raygun, and clicked it on. A brief whisper told me that they were coming. I clutched the gun and tried not to think about much of anything.

Right about then, my new friends got to the front of the house. There were four of them, led by my old pal Barney. I almost expected one of the others to be Johnny the shoeshine guy. It was that kind of night. But no, the rest were just high-class muscle.

If I got out of here, Fatso and I were going to chat. When I got out of here. Something twitched in my pocket and I pulled out the shimmer with my bad hand, gritting my teeth against the scrape of wool on burned skin. The little lights were flashing at me. I swallowed a curse and tried not to think about whether or not I'd signaled for backup and who might be coming to provide it.

Barney, that clever boy, seemed to think I might have headed out into the trees, never mind that they would have seen me cutting across the lawn. He and two of the goons headed over to the gate. Number four stayed about ten steps in front of me. Time to make my move. I slipped the shimmer back into my pocket. Nothing I could do about it now. I angled around a bush for a clear shot and hit him on heavy stun. Me and my soft heart.

I made it as far as the backyard when I heard a kind of crackling sound off to my right, between me and the bad guys. The blast of scorching air hit me hard, and the yells from behind me told me I wasn't the only one. A blast of raygun fire hit the hot spot and the air fired back with a reddish gold flame, not blue-white like our guns. My backup had arrived.

I started shaking but I kept moving. If I stayed, either the thugs or whatever was in that hot spot were going to get me. Just then I didn't need to know for sure whether the Kru'ush Magir looked like a sparktag or not.

A doorway shot open in the air. Another red gold flame flashed out and I could hear a scream at the other end of the lawn. I stopped moving and held my hands up. That was when she walked out, big leathery wings flowing behind her like something out of an Old Earth hell. This time, she didn't bother with a veil and her feet looked the same as the ones on her pals standing behind her. She glided over the grass until she came closer than I liked.

"Hello, Dash." I could hear her hiss around the "s."

I looked up into those big brown eyes under the thick ridges of her new face. "Hi, Lee." She didn't look much like a sparktag. It made it all worse, somehow; it would have been easier if she looked more like a

Buggy. It would have made her more of an enemy. I made myself ask the obvious question. "So, are you going to tell me what all this is about?"

"You already know, don't you Dash?"

"Humor me."

"The first Committee needed something to keep itself in power after the Plague hit and things were falling apart. They thought up the Kru'ush Magir. But after a while, an imaginary enemy wasn't good enough. People were starting to ask too many questions about how no one ever saw one and our Founding Committee members couldn't have that."

"So they thought up the scratch and just rounded up the junkies when they started to change. That's why only the Defense boys ever saw one. And why they could never seem to shut down the trade." I added, lowering my arms. She didn't seem likely to shoot me just now.

"Yesss. Fortune figured it out and helped some of us hide until we got stronger and completed the change. He tried to distract the Fat Man while we broke into the D. Force's stock and stole what we needed to expose them. That's what got him killed." She looked almost weepy. "It's not over yet, Dash. Things have changed and we have you and your little Greta to thank for it. If she hadn't iced Fortune and you hadn't led them right to me at the market yesterday, we might have stayed in the shadows. But my friends had to come for me. No more hiding for us after that."

I must have looked surprised. Those cold brown eyes took me in for a minute. "Yes, honey. Greta. You always suspected she'd do anything to be Femme Fatale and you were right."

"So where is she now?" I tried not to sound too anxious, or too used.

She made a movement that looked like a shrug. "She got what wanted, at least for now. She's probably back at Committee Headquarters making her report." It was like a blow to the gut. Why me? I wasn't a bad guy, not for a femme anyway.

Her raspy voice picked up again. "For the moment, I've got more important things to worry about. We'll take over distribution of the scratch ourselves and decide who joins us from now on. When this war is over, we'll run this world." She looked as if she was waiting to see if I wanted to join the winning side but my face must have spoken for itself. She extended a claw in my general vicinity.

I reached into my pocket without a word and handed over the shimmer, being careful not to touch her scales. She took it, then grabbed my burned hand and flipped it over. Without a word, she ran a long, slightly forked tongue over it. I jerked away, feeling sick, but my skin lost its angry red glow and the blisters disappeared.

She looked me over for a minute and I knew I'd been given up as a loss. Ouch. "Goodbye, Dash." She turned to walk back to her buddies. There were more of them then I had noticed at first. Not quite an army, but a definite start.

A sudden raygun blast broke up our little party and she knocked me flying out of its range. My head hit a rock in the grass. I'll never know if she looked back before she disappeared.

When I came to awhile later, my head hurt like hell and goon ashes were blowing across the grass. I knew had to get the hell away from here before anyone showed up to ask questions. The war would catch up with me sooner or later anyway whether I wanted it to or not. None of us would be able to stay out of it if we stayed on Falcon, not if I knew the Committee. Dragging myself to my feet, I wobbled toward the back gate that I had started for in the beginning.

Once outside on the street, I aimed for Sally's and just kept on walking. I looked at the ground so I didn't have to see the D. Force's version of the Buggies staring down at me. The Fat Man and Greta could wait until tomorrow; I knew where to find them.

If I got lucky tonight, maybe I'd meet a new femme at the bar, a nice ordinary one. Maybe we could get together before the war came home. That'd be nice. A guy like me likes to have a femme to think about when she's at the front. I shivered and walked faster.

# A Day at the Inn, A Night at the Palace

Morning hit me like a kick from my horse. I thought about summoning a shriek of despair as I opened my eyes, but it was clear that it would hurt too much. Besides, somewhere nearby someone else was groaning enough for both of us.

First I wondered why I let Raven get me into this, whatever this was, even without knowing how my cousin was involved. Then I squinted against the light pouring in through what appeared to be wooden shutters and took a slow, cautious look around. The room looked familiar, in a many tankards later, I-wish-I-was-still asleep sort of way. There were tables, benches and the smell of stale beer and overworked swordswoman. Ah, that I recognized.

But there was something else too. A flowery scent of clean, well-dressed highborn lady hung in the air in a perfume cloud. That was… unusual, given the kind of women I usually woke up with. All the more so as my foggy mind had recognized the room I was lying in. Highborn ladies did not come to an inn like The Sodden Rat, and that in itself was most wise of them.

I widened my squint and looked around. Raven was nowhere to be seen. But on my swordarm side, buried amidst a mound of pink silk, I could see another familiar face. What in the Seven Hells was Her Highness Princess Miaqi-Tan Sera doing here?

We had had a brief audience with Her Highness two nights ago. She had summoned us to a secret meeting to discuss the possibility of her assuming her father's throne upon his death. There was one minor inconvenience, that being the older brother who stood between her and the throne. This was the problem that we were supposed to correct on her behalf.

We had turned the job down, with Raven summoning his most flowery and careful phrasing. It wasn't so much that we loved the idea of spendthrift, drunken and cruel Prince Herali on the throne as it was that we didn't think Miaqi could succeed in seizing her father's throne. "She lacks the requisite force of mind to slaughter her family and hold the throne once the deed was done," Raven had said thoughtfully when we were out of earshot. "Though I admire her enthusiasm."

I had agreed, with some regret. I was curious to see what would happen. But I had no great enthusiasm for turning assassin. Raven and I were mercenaries, soldiers, occasionally thieves out of necessity, but that was the limit of our skills. In any case, meddling in the affairs of the Sunborn generally caused one to wind up dead sooner rather than later. I had no desire to see the Lady's caves before my time either.

And yet, here she was again. Only this time, we were lying on the floor of the main room of the Rat and I had no memory of how either of us had gotten there. Or where Raven was. I dragged myself onto my hands and knees and crawled over to her. "Your Highness," I began carefully. "Your Highness, are you all right?"

One amber eye opened and gazed at me with a startling amount of recognition. It was oddly flattering. Normally, women noticed Raven and not me. At least at first. "Highness?" she croaked. "Nice to hear you giving me the respect I deserve, little cousin."

"Cousin?" I sat up and stared down at her. Raven and I came from minor nobility in the outlying provinces, but I was quite certain that we were not related to any of the court Sunborn. Perhaps it was some sort of affectionate term? Or a joke? I wished Raven was here. He was much better with delirious women than I was.

I tried again. "Princess Miaqi? Are you able to move?"

That seemed to revive her. Both amber eyes shot open and she sat up straight, an expression of pure horror twisting her normally pretty face. Her beringed fingers went to her round breasts, then swept downward over the lush curve of her hips beneath the silk of her dress. Something about that exploration seemed unexpected. "Seven Hells! What's happened to me?" She stared at me, wild-eyed.

"I'm not sure, Highness. I am surprised as you are to find myself here at your side." I pulled myself slowly to my feet. "I don't suppose you know where my cousin Raven is?"

"Where I am? I'm in front of you!"

It was worse than I thought. Princess Miaqi's quest for the throne had led to madness. Very sudden madness. Now what was I supposed to do? I was a fighter, not a nursemaid. "Perhaps I could fetch you some ale, Princess? Help you to sit up?"

"It's me, Maeve. Seven Hells, can't you tell that it's me?" Princess Miaqi's delicate tapered fingers buried themselves in her long black hair. I found that I wanted to do the same, consequences be damned.

*No, Maeve, no. Do not entertain fantasies about the beautiful but unfortunate and clearly deranged Sunborn. Those lead to dungeons and beheadings.* "Why don't you let me help you up to a bench?" I stood, still swaying a bit myself and tried to sound soothing.

Princess Miaqi lurched upward at the same time, one thin arm flailing out to catch herself on a nearby table. "Listen, Maeve, cousin, do you remember when we left Tacred? Do you remember what I said when you told me you could never marry me? Do you remember that I said we should come here and pledge our swords to the King?"

Yes, he'd said that. And he'd said that he felt the same way about marrying me. We'd stolen my brother's swords and run away that night.

Now, it was my turn to look astonished. I hadn't left Raven alone with the Princess so he couldn't have told her about us. True, the scandal of our supposed elopement, then subsequent failure to marry, had been quite notorious for a time. In Tacred, which was the size of a farmer's field. That alone should have kept the news well away from Miaqi's ears. "Go on," I said at last.

"We ran away with me dressed in your girl's clothes because I was more believable as a maiden than you were. No one knows that except for me and you, right?" She was staring at me with a pleading expression in those golden eyes now. And she was right, I'd never told anyone else that story and guessed that Raven had not either, which left one other possibility…

"Raven?" I could hear the uncertainty in my voice. "Why you look like Princess Miaqi?" Maybe it was just a glamour. Of late, my cousin was always looking for the chance to hone what magical skills he possessed. He must have been practicing and something went wrong. That was it. I leaned against a table and waited for a reasonable explanation.

"I don't *look* like Princess Miaqi! I *am* Princess Miaqi!" Miaqi wailed and buried her face in her hands.

This was going to end well.

And if it was true, we were in horrible, horrible trouble. I groaned and tried again to think through the haze that still filled my brain. We'd set out from Tacred to do great deeds but somehow it hadn't worked out that way. A few days ago, I'd have said that we both needed a change, to do something besides sell our swords. But this was more of a change than I had in mind. A lot more.

"Should I call you 'Raven' then?" One amber eye glared at me between parted fingers. "Right. Raven, it is. Do you remember what happened?" I gestured toward the princess' curvy form. The round high globe of her breasts, the gentle sweep of her rounded hips, the…yes, we were in horrible, horrible trouble.

The Rat's potboy wandered in from the kitchen, rubbed his eyes and blinked. Then stood there open-mouthed. You would think he had never seen a Sunborn princess up close and personal before.

Even in my less than alert state, it didn't take much time to realize that if the Princess was here, she was missing from the Palace. And from there. I could work out who was most likely to be blamed for how she got here. We needed somewhere to talk in private. Now.

"My cousin's just created an illusion, lad. Nothing to stare at, though he's well worth a second look." I tossed him a copper. "Hold your tongue and there's another in it for you. Now, who's upstairs?"

He stumbled through a list of cutthroats and scum who I wouldn't consider waking up with Raven-as-Princess in tow until he got to a familiar name. Roderick the Many-Handed was a Palace Guard now. But before he got respectable, he had been a mercenary and we had all fought together in the ill-fated invasion of the neighboring kingdom of Serest.

Hopefully, he'd remember enough of the good old days to hold his tongue for a few hours while I figured out what to do next. Or maybe he'd have some useful advice. In any case, I didn't have a better idea.

I grabbed Miaqi's arm and towed her toward the stairs. "Upstairs, Prin—er, Raven. Let's go visit an old friend."

"What are you doing? You can't mean…" Miaqi ran out of breath as I herded her up the stairs. Apparently, the Princess wasn't in full fighting trim, which would make my life easier for the moment. I shoved her down the hallway as gently as I could, listening for the tell tale signs of Roderick's snore at each dilapidated doorway.

"What are you doing, Maeve? Don't you remember what happened the last time Roderick and I met?" I did remember, but I thought we had bigger problems now. Miaqi, all right, *Raven*, looked as if she wanted to bolt back down the stairs. Fortunately, I was still holding her arm. It wasn't like Roderick would skewer Raven on sight regardless of which body he was in. I hoped.

I knocked on the door that sounded like the best possibility. "Rod? You in there?" No answer. I knocked again, this time hearing the ominous silence that indicates that an opponent is now waiting with a drawn sword on the other side of a closed door to see what you'll do next. I shoved the Princess out of the way and kicked the door hard.

It slammed open, then just as quickly slammed shut. A distinctly unRoderick feminine squeal wafted forth. He'd be extra pleased to see me and the Princess if he had company. I tried not to dwell on that problem as I yanked my sword free of its scabbard and waited for what I knew would follow. The door shot open again and there was clash of blades as Roderick's sword met mine.

I parried his thrusts twice before he recognized me. "Maeve? What are you doing here with…Your Highness?" His sword dropped to a more discrete position. Roderick the Many-Handed was quite impressively naked. "Did you kidnap—"

"Who're they?" His companion joined him in the doorway, wearing a torn shift that might have once been white. She had long red hair and big brown eyes and was looking at me with great interest.

I looked back with equal interest, but settled for a small bow of acknowledgment. "Corporal Maeve Tacredi, known as 'Maeve the Red,' last of the Prince's of Surest's Company, at your service." From behind me, I could hear Raven snicker. Like it wasn't a version of the same speech that he tried on every barmaid we met.

"Ginn." Her gaze swept me over again, this time with a bit more warmth. I wondered if she was seeing my body, broader and stronger than that of most men. Or just the ugly scar that ran the length of my cheek, souvenir of a duel fought years ago. I shrugged the thought off and looked at Rod.

He growled something that had clearly started out as an oath before it got bitten off. "Maeve, why is Her Highness Princess Miaqi-Tan Sera standing in the hallway behind you?"

It was a reasonable question. If only I had a reasonable answer. "Let an old swordsister in, Roderick. I need to get her out of sight for the moment. I'll explain once we're inside."

Rod actually blushed. But he stepped back. I took the opportunity to grab the Princess' arm and push her forward into the room, only a moment later realizing that I was still having trouble thinking of her as Raven. Ginn handed Rod his trousers and shut the door. I admired her presence of mind, among other things. It was a very thin shift.

Raven poked me sharply in the back. "Now what?"

It was an excellent question. Rod turned away and was pulling his trousers on but his companion was still watching us. Raven sighed and walked over to the bed, sitting on its edge with an audible thump. "Let's get this over with." There was a pause. "I am not who I appear to be."

Roderick turned around and ran a hand through his thinning black hair. None of us were getting any younger. My own years were weighing on me like plate armor today. Still, I held up a hand to stop any further discussion and tilted my head toward the girl. The fewer who knew what had happened to Miaqi, the better. Rod clearly understood my meaning but shrugged.

Ginn looked from him to me and gave me an impish grin. "Oh no, I'm not leaving unless you throw me out. And then I'll make so much noise the Guards will show up to see what's going on. I want to hear this." She looked at Raven expectantly.

Raven buried her face in her hands and groaned. "What's one more? So a little while ago, we woke up downstairs on the floor—"

Ginn made a disgusted sound and I noticed that Rod was now standing at something approaching parade attention, sword at his side. The fact that he still didn't have his shirt on made it less impressive than it might have been. It lasted right up until Raven told the rest of the story, "Last night, I was Raven Foesbane and this morning, I'm Princess Miaqi Tan-Sera."

If I hadn't been waiting for Rod to make his move, things might have ended badly. Well, they were still likely to end that way but at least

I bought us more time. My blade caught his mid swing and I ducked under the whoosh of the blade in his other hand. He wasn't called "Many-Handed" for nothing. "Rod!" I shouted to get his attention.

All of which was focused on Raven/Miaqi. I was just an obstacle, at least until I kicked him sharply in the leg. "Ow!" Roderick glared at me.

"Stop it," I said firmly. "We need to figure out why this happened and how to turn him back. Then you can fight him."

"That's easy," Ginn spoke up. We all looked at her with varying degrees of disbelief. "It is. I mean the why this happened part. Everyone knows the Sunborn are fighting each other for the throne. What better disguise for the Princess than a new body?" She shrugged. "Her brother won't know what hit him."

Raven/Miaqi stared at me. "Then when I get my body back, I'll be—"

"The assassin who killed the heir to the throne?" I offered.

"And on the block," Rod helpfully finished my thought with a slash across his throat. He looked a lot more cheerful now. It was nice to see that Raven's charm was holding up, regardless of what form he took.

The look the Princess gave me was pure Raven. "We've got to stop her."

"Well, she'll want her old body back sooner or later." Ginn shrugged. We all looked at her again, this time with a lot less disbelief. "She can't take the throne as someone else, after all. She's got to be the Princess again."

"Which means we were put here for safe keeping. But if I wanted to make sure my body was available to switch back to when I wanted it, I'd also make sure that someone was keeping an eye on it." I stared suspiciously at Roderick.

He picked up his uniform shirt and shrugged. "You came to me, remember?"

"Alright." There was nothing I could do about it right now anyway. "The question is how do we stop her?" I looked, not at Raven like I usually did, but at Ginn. She gave me another appraising glance that nearly made me blush.

"We have to get into the palace," Raven said in flutelike tones. He stood up and began to pace back and forth, long pink gown tripping him up in the tiny room. Rod and I backed up and the girl went to sit on the bed. We all watched the Princess who was not a Princess walk with Raven's strides. It was getting easier to believe that Raven was in there, somewhere.

"What makes you think that's where she'll be?" I asked, just because no one else had. I looked around to see if anyone else was wondering.

Rod was clearly intrigued and annoyed at himself for it. Soon he would be annoyed at Raven again and I wasn't looking forward to that.

It did make me wonder if we could keep Raven in Miaqi's body for awhile longer, long enough so that every fighter, thief and mercenary in the city who he'd ever cheated out of their winnings or whose mistress he'd bedded forgot who he was. But we'd both die of old age before that happened. I sighed and resigned myself to storming the Sunborn's palace instead, though to what end I couldn't say.

"I know that she'll be there because her brother is there. The King is dying. The whole kingdom knows that. What better time and place to remove her rival?" Raven dragged his pink train out of the way and swore. "I need new clothes!"

"Done," Ginn shimmied out of her shift and handed it over. "I'll trade."

"They say," Rod added, clearly distracted by all of it, "that the mage Keranin is her lover..." He trailed off.

I looked at Ginn and it was my turn to look appraising. Rod had excellent taste. And it was clear that Raven was too stunned to take much notice, which told me all I needed to know. If he was too distracted to notice a pretty woman, then I'd need to do more of the planning than usual. In general, strategy was his strong point, fighting was mine. But perhaps it was time for a change.

More of a change.

I scowled out the window, then back at Ginn. And like magic, and much as I was enjoying the view, I had an idea. If we could pass as palace servants, we might be able to figure out where Miaqi was and what she and this mage Keranin had done to steal Raven's body. Servants know everything. "I think we can get into the palace unnoticed if we can disguise you, Raven. Especially if we have some help." I stared meaningfully at Rod, who scowled back.

"Why should I risk my commission to help Raven? I like him better the way he is now." Rod leered suggestively and Raven flushed crimson, eyes flashing.

Ginn went over to help Raven out of the dress, if by "help," one mean "remove with a speed and enthusiasm that stopped just short of tearing" the delicate silk. A few moments later, Raven was wearing the dirty shift and Ginn looked like a cross between a scullery maid and a princess. I liked the transition enough to wink at her. She handed Raven a grubby dress to put over the shift.

"Is that good enough to pass for one of the lower palace servants?" I asked Rod, gesturing at the dress. We'd have to steal better clothes somewhere along the way but this might be enough to get us inside.

"Yes," Ginn said decisively. She held out her hand for the Princess' jewelry.

"No," said Rod, with equal surety.

"Well? Which one is it?" I wanted a mug of ale. More importantly, I wanted the gold to buy myself enough ale to forget that any of this had ever happened. I wasn't likely to get either of those things any time soon and the knowledge was making me impatient and angry. The next step after that involved demonstrating how I'd earned the "Red" part of my name. I took a deep breath and tried not to explode.

"It's enough to get you into the kitchens. That's where my sister works as a pit and ash girl. If you want to get close to the Sunborn upstairs, you need a uniform so you'll have to steal those." Ginn was sweeping back and forth in the pink silk, twisting around to admire her posterior.

I admired it too while I wondered how good her information was. The pit and ash cleaners were the lowest of the kitchen servants, not worth wasting a uniform on. And there wouldn't be a lot of them, unlike say, maids, so it would be harder to pass without notice either in the kitchens or outside them.

That sent me off into wondering what difference it made if we were noticed or not when we didn't know where we were going to do in the palace, once we got there. The tromp of boots on cobblestones outside the window interrupted my reverie. I glanced outside and down at a squad of Guards who were marching up to the Rat's door. There was only reason that I could think of for them to be there.

Raven's eyes rolled like a frightened horse's and Ginn stripped off the silk gown. She stuffed it up the chimney of the crumbling fireplace with a skill that suggested long practice with hiding things from the Guards. Then she hid a necklace and some rings in the straw, slipped under the blanket and beckoned to Rod. "Rub soot on her face and just walk out like you woke up with your lightskirt. Go to the palace kitchen and look for Elan. That's my sister; tell her I said to help you if she can," she said as if she'd done this before too. Which, perhaps, she had.

Then she winked at me. I thought about winking back, but it seemed like too much of a promise. I might not be back this way. Though I surprised myself by how much I wanted to be sure that I did.

Instead I grabbed some grime from the fireplace and rubbed it on Raven's face. He pulled me out of the room as Ginn kissed Rod with evident enthusiasm. A sharp pang went through me at the sight, but this was not the time to linger.

Raven was messing up his hair and biting his lip when I looked his way. He reached out and seized my arm just as the first of the Guards marched up the stairs. A high-pitched giggle filled the air. "Oh, you're so strong! Buy a girl an ale and some bread now. It's the least you can do after wearing me out like that." It took me a moment to realize that the voice was coming from Raven. He fluttered Miaqi's lashes at me and simpered as he molded his body to my side as much as my leather armor would permit.

It was…distracting. And disturbing. Miaqi was lovely, certainly, but I hadn't really wanted to bed her when she was in possession of her own body. The fact that I was even somewhat tempted now with my cousin in residence didn't bear too much scrutiny.

But the Guard captain was in front of us, oversized face set in a near permanent scowl. "State your names and your purpose here."

Raven simpered and fluttered even more. Then thrust his bosom out further than even I thought possible and said, "I'm Venna and I'm a serving wench at the Boar. This is the mighty warrior Maeve the Red. Surely you've heard of her! As for our purpose, well, Captain, I'm sure you can guess." More giggles. I looked stern and solemn, or at least I thought that's what I was doing, which meant I probably looked like a large, slightly confused horse.

The Captain peered at me. "Maeve the Red, eh? I thought you'd be taller."

My hand went to the hilt of my sword and he stepped back. "Are we done, Captain? I have an appointment to keep." I went for a slightly menacing tone in case the sword hilt wasn't enough of a hint. He nodded, face a bit paler, and we walked down the hallway and marched down the stairs as the Guards began banging on doors. I heard mutters of "Where in the Hells is she?" from behind us and bit back a grin.

Then I remembered that I was still wearing my armor and carrying a sword. Precisely the sort of thing that kitchen pit and ash cleaners didn't wear, as far as I knew. "I need to hide my sword and armor," I muttered to Raven as we walked through yet more Guards. He giggled vacantly, which I took for agreement, then began steering me slightly away from the palace which we could see looming over the marketplace. I wondered where we were going.

A few steps and a couple of alleys later and I no longer had that question. Now it was my turn to stare at Raven as if he had lost all his senses. "No. I'll never see it any of it again and you know how I feel about this sword."

Raven's expression on Miaqi's face was jarring, to say the least. "Maeve, I want my body back. I want it now. We can't get into the palace if you're dressed like that. This is just until we come back."

"What makes you think we're coming back?" I growled. Magic always made me nervous. You never knew when your opponent might turn into a snake or an ogre or fly away. Or turn you into something. I had a squad leader once who got turned into a puddle of horse piss by a battle mage. It was very upsetting. Not to mention messy. But I was digressing because I definitely didn't want to leave my armor and sword with…

"I knew you'd be back." The woman on the doorstep might have been Ginn's mother, if I hadn't known better. "You just can't stay away, can you?" She noticed Raven. "And you brought a new friend. Interesting."

"Mirna. I hadn't thought to find myself with you again so soon. This is a happy accident. Allow me to present my cousin, Kira, who's come to visit from Tacred. Like a little sister she is to me." I hugged Raven in an aggressively friendly manner that aped that of my own brothers and hoped it would be enough to draw attention from her.

It seemed to be. Mirna dismissed Raven as insignificant. "And you want something. What is it now, Maeve? My best years weren't enough for you?"

"It was two moons between campaigns three seasons ago, Mirna. You kicked me out because your husband was coming back, the way I remember it. But I have missed you," I tried to ape one of Raven's expressions. He poked me hard in the back by way of a hint to hurry up. "May we come in?"

It took longer than either Raven or I wanted, but then, Mirna was right. I had missed a few things about her. And those things took time. Even so, before nightfall we were on our way to the palace kitchens. Mirna saw us out with a smile and some of her husband's clothes, which fit me well enough to let me pass for a pit cleaner if no one looked too closely.

They didn't. I had become too used to being Maeve the Red, known for being able to kill a man before he had drawn three breaths. I was feared, sometimes even desired, but always noticed. Now I wasn't and I didn't like it much.

Raven, on the other hand, sashayed down the street flirting with every passing man as if the Sunborn's Guards weren't looking for him. He was, I reflected as I glared at him, behaving exactly like the sort of girl he flirted with and bedded in every tavern and market stall in every town we ever traveled through. I suppose dignity was too much to expect.

On the other hand, no one would suspect that he was Princess Miaqi, at least not until we got close enough to the palace for someone to recognize his face. I wondered if the mage and the Princess really were lovers. If Miaqi was recognized, perhaps we could get captured and brought to the mage that much faster. Or killed sooner. I decided not to mention this notion to Raven.

The palace was at the very center of the city, perched on the highest hill and surrounded by the houses of rich merchants and nobles. Hired household swords watched us carefully from doorsteps and guard posts. Servants in livery sneered at us as we walked steadily upward toward the rear gate of the palace. Even I was thoroughly ashamed of us by the time we got there.

"You look like a very believable pit and ash man, cousin." Raven muttered from the corner of his very pink lips. We had joined the end of a lengthy procession that was wending its way under the stone walls and through the portcullis.

"That's what will keep my head on my shoulders for the moment, cousin. See if you can do the same."

Certainly the guards seemed to believe we were who we said we were when we reached the gates. Their hands roved so freely over Raven that I thought we would end by fighting our way in, but he clenched his jaw and forced out a smile and a few giggles. I wondered if he'd learn something from this; his hands were certainly free enough with women when he was in his own body. I looked forward to living long enough to ask.

Eventually, we were allowed to pass and make our way through the endless courtyards and corridors of the palace to its kitchens. Raven poked me hard every time he thought I didn't look enough like a servant. I poked him back every time I could get away with it and we were both sore by the time we reached the kitchen door. There a red-faced bellowing cook greeted us, "You! Why are you late?"

Raven started to reply, only to get shoved toward the fireplace by the cook's meaty paw. My turn came next. "Turn the spit, you fool! Can't you see the meat is starting to burn?"

Now that he mentioned it, I could see it. I took my place at one side of the vast pit and began turning as Raven started shoveling ash. Apparently, our disguises had worked, at least for the cook. The woman shoveling ashes next to Raven looked puzzled though. "Ginn sent us," Raven hissed, presumably taking a guess based on the girl's red hair.

"Did she now?" We both got a crooked grin. "She must not like you much. You'll be at this all night."

"We can't stay!" Now I was hissing. "We have to find the King's mage."

"Well, he won't be passing through here," she laughed, as if the notion was entertaining.

"That's why we need to get to him," Raven repeated patiently. "Where are his rooms?"

"What do you want with him anyway? Turn you into a puddle of horse-piss if you anger him, or so it's said." There was more shoveling while I shuddered and kept turning the meat. And there was a shower of curses from the cook, the junior cooks and some others I couldn't identify. We were quiet for a while.

Finally Raven spoke up again. "Have you ever heard anything about him being able to shift into other bodies? Do the servants speak of such things?"

She raised an eyebrow. "The 'servants'? Unlike, say, your gracious lord and lady selves?" She took in our clothes at a glance. "But you aren't what you seem to be, then, are you? Are you here to assassinate him?"

I intervened, seeing as my cousin appeared about to agree, "No. He stole...something of ours. We need to steal it back." It was as good a description of our current circumstances as I could muster on the spot. Raven gave me a begrudging nod that tilted Miaqi's tresses into the firelight and made our new friend jump and narrow her eyes.

"Right. I wonder what it was that he took. And if I should curtsey and scrape or perhaps speak to the Guards." Elan kept looking at Raven who tried his most charming and innocent smile on her. It didn't work as well on Miaqi's features. She frowned suspiciously.

"Please help us," I said finally. "All we want is to take back what was ours, then leave the palace. Nothing more than that. We won't get you into trouble," As I said it, I finally began to wonder just how we were going to get Raven's true form back. It wasn't like the mage was simply going to wave a hand and switch bodies with the princess, after all. Not without persuasion in some form. I wondered if Raven had thought that part through. I knew I hadn't.

"That seems like quite a bit." But she shrugged and stopped frowning. "But it's your doom. Through that doorway, up the first two flights of stairs, three corridors west, if you can get past the corridor guards and the footmen and maids. Then I think you can get to the stairs to the wizard's tower." She bent back over the ashes with a tired grace.

Raven jerked his head at the cooks and gave me a meaningful look. I wasn't sure what it was supposed to tell me, but I thought I could guess. Shoving Elan aside from the fire and tossing a flaming log across the floor to create a distraction was the work of moments and singed fingers.

A chorus of yells and much scrambling from cooks and kitchen servants and we were through the door at the far end of the kitchen. The corridor was full of yet more servants and we hung our heads and tried to look as if we were on an errand of some sort.

From the stories that the bards tell, you'd think it was easy to get your hands on a disguise in a palace full of people. What they seem to forget is that palaces are indeed full of people. No convenient dark corridors, everyone with an errand to run or a place to guard. It makes it quite difficult to knock a couple of servants or guards out and steal their uniforms.

But since we are who we are, we eventually made our way to the upper floors in ill-fitting livery, hoping that the mage's rooms were obvious and easy to find. Or at least, I was hoping. Raven was wearing a maid's uniform and the oddest expression on his face. He remembered to duck his head and look away whenever we passed a guard or servants, but he was clearly distracted.

The other thing that those ballads of daring rescues and so forth fail to note is just how very long it takes to get from the lower levels of a palace to the upper ones. It felt like a forced march through the northern mountains after a while: down endless corridors, up steep staircases that went from wood to stone as we climbed higher. Eventually, I stopped one of the maids to ask where we were, over Raven's whispered objections.

The nervous looking maid told me enough that I was able to lead us up another corridor to the bottom of yet another winding flight of stairs. This one led, inevitably, to the one of the towers. "Towers," Raven murmured. "Why does it always have to be towers?"

He had a point. Wizards and mages usually took the high ground. Presumably because it made it easier to see you coming, but I guessed there was more to it than that. But it wasn't as if I knew any personally and could ask them. Except Raven, and he wasn't a real wizard.

Or was he? That thought made me take a long look at my cousin. It was partially because he was much more fun to look at this way than he normally was, but also because for the first time I wondered what kind of wizard he would make. If he could harness what powers that he had. Up until now, I hadn't seen him do much.

He must have been thinking something along the same lines since he held his hand over the stairs and closed his eyes like he was expecting something to happen. I noticed a ring on his finger that I hadn't seen there before. He must have hidden it inside his clothes but I couldn't think why he would have done that. He moved Miaqi's lips silently while I tried to look as if this what we were supposed to be doing. Fortunately, the armies of servants and guards who filled the lower corridors seemed to be giving this one a wide berth.

A very, very pale green glow lit Raven's fingertips for an instant. Then it faded and he slumped against the tower wall. The questions poured from my kips in a flood of nervous chatter, "When did you learn to do that? What's it supposed to do? I thought we were going to head up there and hold the wizard at sword's point until he changes you back. You know, what we usually do."

He opened Miaqi's eyes in a catlike glare. "We don't have any swords right now, Maeve," he said in a dangerously reasonable voice. "What we do have is some pretty bad disguises, our wits and my magic. What's upstairs," he pointed upward, "is a mage who can change me into this." He gestured at Miaqi's curves. "We need something more. I'm trying to see if I can find out something about him before we go up there."

"Actually, what's waiting for you upstairs is the least of your worries right now." Raven's voice came from behind us, echoing against the walls. I spun around, reaching for a sword that wasn't there. Then I struck out as hard as I could with my fist. Princess Miaqi Tan-sera stepped aside, laughing.

Of course, she did have a sword and it was held in Raven's hand as if it had always been there. She pointed it at Raven and gestured upwards, the look in her eyes unmistakable. Apparently, she'd found that ruthless edge that she had lacked before. How fortunate for us. We started up the steps ahead of her, her blade a fingers-breadth from Raven's throat.

My head whirled with strategies, each formulated, then dismissed almost as quickly as they arrived. If I fought Miaqi on the stairs, I might win, even without a sword. But then how would we get Raven back into his own body? I kept climbing and tried not to think too hard about what would happen if we couldn't get out of this.

When we got to the top of the stairs, Miaqi poked me in the back with the point of the sword, which I now recognized as Raven's second best. From the look on his face, he had already noticed. "Open the door." Her tone, combined with Raven's customarily arrogant-sounding voice, was enough to make my blood heat.

But that made no difference. We still didn't have a plan. So I improvised.

I opened the door and stepped inside fast, hoping to find a weapon or at least a good vantage point for an attack. It might have worked if she hadn't thrown Raven in after me, knocking to my knees when he landed on top of me.

"That's quite the entrance." The voice came from somewhere above me, but I was having trouble hearing over Raven's cursing, not to mention seeing through the mane of Miaqi's hair that now covered my eyes.

Raven tumbled off my back and I looked up into the thin face and mildly surprised expression of a much younger man than I was expecting. In fact, he looked too young to have a beard. Certainly too young to be a King's mage, though I could see dried herbs and the requisite mysterious bowls on the tables around the room behind him.

Miaqi stepped forward, after shutting and bolting the door behind her. "Apparently this fool and his companion decided to save us the trouble of finding them when it is time to change me back." She sneered at Raven, who scrambled to his feet, a snarl twisting his pretty face. I caught his arm before he lunged at her.

"Why not change back now?" I asked in my most reasonable voice. "Seeing as we're all here."

Miaqi laughed. It was Raven's laugh, but she managed to make her own. I didn't like it much. Surprisingly enough, neither did her wizard. I could see Keranin frown from the edge of my eye as I watched the Princess. Perhaps that could be useful.

"And why would I want to do that? My brother still lives. You're a woman, you know how it is to be overlooked, your talents disregarded." She gave me a burning stare, then glanced at the wizard as if for confirmation. "I will change back when I'm done with him, not a moment sooner."

Raven gave her a look of pure incredulity, then looked at me if to see whether or not I'd deny it. Considering that our families had nearly forced us to wed because they thought it would make me give up the sword, expecting me to deny Miaqi's words was rather foolish of him.

In general, no, I wasn't overlooked. But then I was taller than most men and was one of the most feared swordswomen in the Eight Realms. That didn't stop some of our brethren from assuming that Raven was more deadly with a blade than I and testing me until I drew blood. I could only imagine what it would be like to be passed over for the throne by a brutal and incompetent sot simply because he was my brother and therefore innately worthy of the throne.

Though I wasn't entirely sure yet that she would be an improvement, I ignored Raven and nodded cautiously at the Princess. There was no harm in pretending that I could be won over. Perhaps I could. She did, after all, have both sword and mage on her side.

Speaking of which, I wondered how the mage felt about Miaqi's quest for the throne. Right now, he was looking at her with an odd expression on his face. I studied both his face and the emotions flickering across it. He was fine-boned, with dark brown skin that suggested an origin in the western mountains of the far kingdoms. Beneath the gold and blue robe that he wore, he was slender, not much taller than Miaqi herself. There was also something familiar in the way that he moved.

Apparently it dawned on Raven at the same time. "You're not what you appear to be, either," my cousin said, stepping closer to the mage with narrowed eyes. The mage stepped back, his fingers beginning to glow.

"Enough!" Miaqi barked.

I stepped between them, then cursed the impulse that made me do it. Under other circumstances, it might have been fun to watch my cousin get his comeuppance at the hands of a beautiful princess and her female mage. But not if he got turned into a puddle of horse piss in the process. So there I was, in the middle of it all, but still without an idea of what to do next.

I tried diplomacy. "All right. We've all got our secrets. What if we help you defeat your brother? Then you switch bodies back and ascend the throne as yourself. My cousin and I forget all this ever happened and join the campaign on the Southern border." It was a safe thing to say; there was always a campaign on the Southern border.

"When M—Her Highness ascends the throne, there will be no more war on the Southern border," the mage's voice was clear and high, and not surprisingly like a girl's. The mage and the princess exchanged a look and the latter stood up a bit straighter.

Well, now we knew how the mage felt about Miaqi's quest for the throne. Raven and I exchanged a glance of our own. A Sunborn ruler with a peaceful agenda was something new and potentially troublesome. But Raven didn't look worried. In fact, he gave me a tiny wink. Evidently, he thought he had a plan. I looked from him to the mage. Her face appeared to be bright with hope and love, all of it directed at the Princess.

*Idealists.* I nearly shook my head. Still, I couldn't help myself from trying to imagine what the kingdom would look like if there were no campaign on the Southern border. Or elsewhere. What would I do if I didn't live by my sword? It was a troubling, but not unappealing thought.

Unbidden, the Rat and a certain red-haired serving girl came to mind. Perhaps I did know what I might do, were there no more campaigns. Then again, perhaps idealism was contagious. I shook my head. Time enough to worry about that when we got Raven back to being Raven.

My cousin tapped my foot impatiently with his. He was telling the Princess and her mage that he had a plan to get Miaqi on the throne, perhaps even without actually killing her brother. It involved kidnapping and magic and changing the Prince into someone else. I stopped listening halfway through when it became clear that it was too elaborate to pull off without an army, which we didn't have.

I could see that the Princess thinking something similar. Every time the plan took another twist, she frowned and I couldn't see any confusion or puzzlement on what would normally have been Raven's face. I liked her better for her pragmatism but I wondered whether she could come up with something that was more effective.

I also wondered how long it would take for the Prince to realize that his sister was up to something and simply kill us all out of hand. It would be the most efficient thing to do. It would be what I would do in his shoes. I decided it was time to ask if anyone else had the same thought. "What will the Prince be doing while we're running around the palace switching bodies and so forth? He's not a complete idiot. His advisors will know you're up to something," this last said to the Princess and the mage.

"And my father is dying. Whatever we do, we do now before it's too late." Miaqi set Raven's lips in a thin line. Determination sat well on his features. I hadn't seen it for quite some time. There had been a time, right after we arrived in the Sunborn's city that both of us had ideals, had dreams of serving a great and noble prince and doing legendary deeds. It turned out to be harder than we thought. Too many campaigns had come and gone since then for those dreams to survive intact. Still, I was finding a spark of my former self tonight.

"How did you change them?" I asked the mage, gesturing at Raven and the Princess. "Is it something you could do from a distance?"

She looked at Miaqi as if for permission or something like it. The Princess said nothing. I couldn't blame them. Once we knew what we needed, we could take it from them. Raven swore angrily and stepped up to the table, fingers glowing pale green once more. Evidently that had been his plan.

I grabbed his shoulder and shook him a little, and the glow faded.

"Wait." I looked at the mage again. She gave me an intent stare back, her lips thin with anger, or perhaps her version of determination. Raven's arm quivered beneath my hand, drawing my attention back to him. "We'll need something different." I could feel his fury building, even in the wrong body.

"I was unaware that you had a choice in the matter," Princess Miaqi Tan-sera nearly growled the words. "We need to end this tonight. To do that, we need to find my brother."

"And how will you be making sure we're the ones who are blamed for the deed?" Raven said softly, an edge to his tone.

I read guilt in the mage's face and posture and some of my newfound enthusiasm ebbed away. She glanced up and murmured, "You would have done the same."

It wouldn't have occurred to me, so no, I wouldn't have, but this didn't seem the time to mention it. I was beginning to hear noises outside the tower. Noises that sounded suspiciously like armed men moving in the courtyard, being as quiet as one can in chainmail. "Is there another way out of here besides the stairs? I think we'll have company soon." Again, the mage and the princess exchanged glances, then the mage beckoned us forward.

"Over here." She pulled back a tapestry and gestured to what seemed to be blank stone. Raven swore under his breath as it was made clear that we needed to turn away so that we wouldn't know how to open the tower's secret entrance. Then both mage and princess busied themselves finding a latch of some sort.  From the corner of my eye, I saw Raven's hand dart to something on one of the tables then vanish into his clothes. I did some small amount of pilfering of my own, palming a bag with a slight metal jingle to it.

Then a door behind one of the tapestries slid open. We followed the mage into the secret stairwell while Miaqi followed on our heels, pulling everything shut behind her. "So," I asked quietly as we made our way down the stair, "the first plan was to attack and assassinate your brother while you are still in Raven's body, then switch back to your own body and blame the assassination on the real Raven. What's the second idea?" I hoped my tone made it clear that the first one was no longer the plan.

Raven cleared his throat. "Why don't we kill your brother, switch our bodies back and we'll get out of your hair instead? Pay us off and we'll disappear to the Northern Kingdoms or the Islands of the Southern Sea or some other place that is far, far away."

He did have excellent focus; it was the plan that made the most sense. Although Miaqi's first plan was ruthlessly efficient, repetition should make this second proposal familiar enough that it would seem most logical. If we had time to convince her.

That was the moment when the mage turned to face us from the first landing. "It would make sense, sister dear. If I hadn't taken matters into my own hands and forced that fool mage of yours to make a different switch, it might have worked."

We all stared at him. He'd been so convincing as the mage. Miaqi went very pale. Life had been so much simpler back when we just fought battles for money and stole things. I wanted simple again, any kind of simple. I was also closer to the mage than anyone else. I swung my fist hard at her jaw as the sound of feet on the stairs below us echoed through the stone corridors. I connected and the mage or the prince or whoever I just hit reeled back with an oath. I could see fingers start to glow again and I lunged forward, Raven at my heels.

I wondered what he was going to do until I realized the glowing fingers were his. Miaqi was right behind him, Raven's sword in her hand. The prince snarled and yanked a dagger from his robes as I hit him again.

This time, I really noticed the ring on the mage's fingers and realized that it matched the one Raven was wearing. Raven must have been thinking the same thing and grabbed for it. When his glowing fingertips met the green stone, there was a flash of light. Miaqi touched it an instant later and the three of them lit up like a Festival night fire.

I fell back, tripped and rolled down the stairs to the next landing and hit the wall hard. Which is why I missed exactly what happened next. When I could crawl back to the steps and look up, a green cloud was settling like swamp miss. Then it disappeared. I couldn't see any of them, but I could hear the prince's men running up the stairs, moving faster to respond to whatever they thought would be waiting for them.

There was no other sound. I scrambled to my feet and ran up the stairs, trying not to fall over. The walls swam around me. Raven, Princess Miaqi and the prince all lay still on the stone floor when I reached the landing. For a moment, I thought they were dead. I checked my cousin first.

Or at least what I thought was my cousin. I placed one hand on her breast and leaned down to see if I could feel her breathing. The smack that struck my cheek made my head ring even more. Princess Miaqi glared up at me out of her own eyes. "Unhand me." Her snarl was impressive.

I yanked my hand back and stood up. That left two possibilities for where Raven was now. I reached for Raven's body, more cautiously this time. I managed to avoid the flailing arms as he woke up from his magical slumber. Then I grabbed him by the throat to get his attention. "What did you say to me the night we left Tacred, cousin?"

Raven stared at me, wide-eyed. It wasn't his voice that answered. "I said that we shouldn't be forced to marry each other. That we could take our swords and go to the Sunborn court and find glory and riches there." The mage's voice filled the landing, sounding weary and annoyed. "And we have to go, Maeve. They're almost here."

Miaqi grabbed the sword and held it to Raven's throat. "I think you assassinated my brother," she said, steel in her voice.

I grabbed Raven's new arm and we ran up the stairs the way we had come, though not without a backwards glance at his former body. The Prince only screamed once before his armsmen arrived. We kept running. Princess Miaqi would convince them that she had avenged her brother's death; it would be a simple matter to find her mage, then have her switch herself into someone else's body, at least from the Princess' standpoint. The body of Prince Kerali could be given a Sunborn's funeral and Princess Miaqi would be Queen Miaqi.

Whatever happened next, our part was done. I looked at my cousin's new body and wondered how long it would take to get used to him…her this way. At least she could pass for a young man if you didn't know what to look for. But nothing at all like my muscular cousin with his scarred face and his dark eyes that made women melt.

My hand felt the bag of coins in my belt, the ones I had stolen before we left. I thought about red hair and second chances.

We found the hidden door in the tower and Raven turned and smiled at me with her new mouth as I found the catch and the door opened. It was a very disturbing smile. It made me think of towers and horse piss and people who thought nothing of taking over your body for their own purposes.

She held out his hand and I looked down at the ring. It still had a pale green glow. "Do you like that body, Maeve? I'm thinking we could make some changes."

I wondered if Roderick could help me get into the King's Guard. Boring guard work would be just the thing. I could use my wages to save for an inn or something like it. I backed away from this stranger who might or might not be my cousin. In the moment I knew exactly what I wanted and it didn't involve fighting more battles or changing into someone else. "I like this body just fine, Raven."

We looked at each other for a long moment, and it seemed like he might be Raven again. Or at least a version of him, though transformed in more ways than one. "Now that I know how to do it, cousin, it's fairly simple. When the rings touched out there, I understood it all." Her eyes glowed, then she shrugged and walked to the tower window. "I'll miss you. I'll come and visit, little cousin. But for now, I have a lot to learn."

She stared outside for a long moment until her whole body began to glow around the edges, then just as suddenly she was gone. I dashed over to see a raven nearly tumble out of the sky before it righted itself and began flying unsteadily away from the tower.

I watched her go, then looked around for more gold, taking all that I could find. Enough, perhaps, to buy the Rat and charm a clever woman who might warm my bed for a long time to come. When I listened at the secret door, the stairs below were silent. I slipped down them and out of the palace, bound for a familiar inn and a second chance.

# VADIJA

I HAVE HEARD IT SAID THAT even Vadija the Merry could not lift the sorrows from Laith. In all the tales the sadness swam sluggishly through the streets of the city like the giant carp in the slow moving River Omphere or the mist clouds from the Kaleva Mountains. Each inhabitant carried the city's misery balanced precariously on their packs or on their bare shoulders as they walked the gray avenues, one foot dragging up to collapse down in front of the other.

So it was said. Said with a kind of pride, at that. But I didn't believe it. I had heard that the city wasn't a happy place, mind you. But I knew that Vadija had a merry and glorious laugh, a laugh that changed things. They said it was like a clarion call to arms, if you were a soldier, and liked being one. Or the wind whipping through the Forest of Anma Bekash, if you were a hunter. Once, Puar the money-lender even said to me "Ah, Sira, her laugh is like a rain of gold coins poured down a chimney and ringing on the stones below." From her, this was the highest of praise.

I thought I heard Vadija laugh once myself before I heard her name. The sound rode down on the wind and sang around the chimney of my farm, making the little bells on the door ring and the dogs howl with the shock of it. Swirling and roaring, it swept around me until I came near to howling myself. I didn't know what it was then, but I left that day. There was nothing to hold me once I heard it. Her laugh is like that.

But even she couldn't change Laith of the Sorrows, or so they told me as I followed the news of her laughter from my distant valley and days of unending work. Always she went a little before me and I had to make my own way. But I kept walking for I had no laugh of my own in those days. I thought she might tell me how she found hers.

In the beginning, I washed and cleaned at the inns and little farms to keep bread in my pack and a roof over my head. I told tales to the children back then, for they were the only ones who heard them. When I could, I sat and listened to the rare talespinner who would venture so far from the cities of the coast, letting the words wash over me and wondering always where they had found such things.

It was then I first heard Vadija's name and learned that it was her laughter that drew me from my home. But though I listened until I could repeat the tales, I had no thought to become a talespinner myself, not at first. Certainly I knew I could not be one because everyone said that I was not the way a talespinner should be. After all, talespinners are long and lean where I am soft and round, dark where I am golden, mysterious where I am open and speak what I mean. So it was said. But sometimes when I thought those things, I remembered Vadija's laugh.

Then all things seemed possible.

As I traveled, I began to see words growing in the hedges and drifting on the breeze. It terrified me at first, for I knew no one else who could see them. I tried to ignore them, turning away from the small whispers of sound and the touch of dreams.

But soon I could see them even while I slept. They led me through the dreamlands and my waking days until I could stand it no more and I reached out to one, touching it. Then another. I called them to me and they came. I was no longer afraid.

With the words I began to weave the webs that drew in those who listened. One night, a circle at the fire followed me up the Princess of

Velena's rainbow stairs. I made the steps glisten with color and shine with the firelight's glow in the eyes of those who heard until I could see them myself. The next night, another circle swam behind me with Gregoth of the Sea, gasping at the vengeance that he wrecked on those who slew his people, and at the sudden tang of salt in the air.

After that, I began to tell stories at the inns and wayside traveler's rests. These were tales about strange lands and mighty warriors, like those I told my little ones before the wasting fever carried them off. Lord Death took them, just as he had taken their father before them, and I could do nothing but watch. Until I heard Vadija, I wished that he had taken me, too.

I found my tales hard to tell at first, but the words kept flowing around me and I went with them until I could no more stop telling stories than I could stop following Vadija. After a while, I even made up new tales. Kingdoms fell, lovers were reunited, evil was conquered: such was the stuff of the stories that I told. I began to feel joy in the telling of what could be and what should not, and soon I had a small laugh of my own.

But my tales about Vadija were best of all, at least to me, and they came to me often when I walked or when I washed and tended. I told them to the women and children and those who were worn from their day's work. In those stories, she laughed and armies crumbled. Tyrants flew away on the wind. Always her laugh changed things for the best. So I said and so I believed though I had done nothing but follow her trail, never once laying eyes on her.

Still, I talked to many on the road who had heard her laugh. Some of them even claimed to have seen her. She was young or old, lean or fat, beautiful beyond a winter's frost on lacy tree branches, or ugly and grim like the burning lava in the mountains on the southern edge of the world, depending on who told me the story.

I had my own idea, held close within me with the tales that I told no one else. I knew that she must be a big, queenly woman with strong arms and a great soft belly, bigger even than my own. For how else could she have the power to laugh such a laugh that changed those who heard it? But I didn't know so I looked for her to see for myself. Before I heard her, I never could have wanted such a thing

After a time, people began to know my name and my tales kept my belly round though I walked leagues each day, following the trail she left behind her. Finally, her path turned toward Laith of the Sorrows, a city out of legend, and there I went also.

It was midday when I arrived and stood before the walls. I paused and trembled outside the gates long before I was willing to follow her inside.

There were many tales of how Laith gained its sorrows. In some, they sacrificed their children to one of the Old Gods to save themselves from siege. In others, they betrayed their king and brought his curse down upon them. At the end of each story, they were left gray and solemn, bereft of joy and music for season turn to season turn from my grandmere's time onward. I remembered each story as I paused between the cold metal gates before stepping forward. They closed with a bang to swallow me as I set foot on the flagstones of Laith.

Once inside, I could see no more of the lands outside for Laith's sorrows are sealed in by the high walls. There were no inns and no other places where people could gather to hear my tales so instead I walked through the city looking for Vadija.

As I searched, the gray walls to each side and the gray paving stones beneath my feet sent icy fingers through me and I shivered, warm though my cloak was. The sun's dim light barely lit my way as those who lived in this place shouldered past me, unseeing, and my heart grew colder and colder.

When I had wandered some time down the long avenues where not a single flower bloomed, I could feel the wings of the city's sorrows settling around my shoulders. "Why, why did she come here?" I wailed in a whisper, fearing to speak aloud and draw the misery closer. I could see no one who could be her in the dismal faces that passed me but I knew she must be here somewhere. There was nowhere else for her to go unless she flew over the mountains that circled the city on three sides. Besides, a voice whispered inside me, how could she deny such pain? Or such a challenge? How I longed then to have her power!

I tried to ignore my thoughts and listened hard for her laugh, but there was nothing. No chime of bells or dogs barking or normal city sounds. I could hear only the creak of passing wagons the color of twilight and the soft, whispered exchanges between the few merchants and those who bought from them. The words were so soft that none fell to the cold hard ground, so light that no tales could grow from them.

The weight of despair settled heavier and heavier upon my shoulders until I had to sit or fall to my knees. I sank onto a cold step, cursing Vadija for coming here and myself for following her. My tales began to fade when I did this, gliding away like water with no basin left to hold it. How long I sat this way I do not know, for the hours pass strangely in Laith of the Sorrows. Soon there was no joy left in me and I began to forget Vadija's laugh and the world beyond the city walls.

Still I sat and drifted until I gazed at nothing but the gray stones beneath my feet. After a great while, I knew that someone stood before me, but by then I had not even the strength to look up. "Outlander, you must leave this place," the voice whispered down at me like a breeze. I knew that what it said was right but I could not lift my head to go. A gnarled hand clasped my shoulder hard but it was nothing compared to the despair that held me and I scarcely felt it.

The hand reached down for my own and tugged upward until I was dragged unwillingly to my feet. Bony fingers reached under my chin and forced my eyes up to meet those of an old, old woman, her face gray and drained like the others I had seen. But her eyes were different. In their black depths, I could see a tale growing, a story of gray and cold, but a story nonetheless.

"Tell me what you seek, Outlander," her voice licked at my hearing like a small wind, like a sigh.

I tried to remember and all that came to me was my dream of Vadija, and I saw her as I imagined that she must be. She did not laugh, not here in this twilight place, and she shrank in size with the loss. I shrank with her, folding in around the vision, bright garments dimming. She was little more than I had been before I left the farm, and the sight pained me. "I was looking for Vadija," I whispered back to the woman, tears rolling down my cheeks.

"I thought you might be," the dark eyes twinkled slightly and I found that I could lift my head on my own, without the support of her hand. I still had no words, no tales to tell until she spoke again, "Tell me about her, talespinner."

I wondered how she could see the words to know me for what I was until I looked and saw those that had fallen to the gray stones around me. Many were fading away, but a small few still glowed brightly against the dim light and the cold. "Vadija..." I stumbled over her name but I whispered on, coaxing the few remaining words back to me, remembering a tale that I had told no one else. "Vadija came once to a valley far from here. There, I heard I her laugh for the first and only time." The woman's sparkling eyes were closed for a moment.

"What did the valley look like, talespinner?"

I told her what I could still remember of my home and my family. Sometimes the words came to me and sometimes I made new ones as I told her the tale of how I had come to seek Vadija. With each turning of the tale's web, I could feel the city's sorrow loosen its grip upon us both. She wore the ghost of a smile and I stood on my own, my voice more than a whisper, growing in strength. There was a wind now that night had fallen, and though it was a cold one, I welcomed it and the words that it brought.

She asked me many questions as we stood shivering in that wind and twice the merchant on whose steps we sat came forth to drive us away, but was terrified by the strangeness of that which she did not know and retreated inside.

With each answer and each word, I grew warmer until I slipped my cloak from my shoulders. It was then that I saw the little blossom growing in a crack between the gray stones, drawing itself up from where my tears had fallen. It was but one against all that gray expanse, but it was enough.

I pointed to it and laughed. It was just a little laugh but I saw the woman's eyes grow wide at hearing it and she smiled a little. I laughed again for the small joys of seeing her smile and the tiny flower struggling against the sad city. The wind caught the sound this time and sent it upward to dash against the gray stone walls and the closed windows of Laith. The stone sent my laugh back, flinging it between the wind and the stone until I saw the chink of windows and doors opening as those who lived in the city looked out to see what was wrong.

The bits and pieces of my laugh danced around them on the wind and they drew back, many of them, retreating into the gray insides of their chilled homes. Only one, a young man with dead eyes, came out to stand beside the woman. His glance fell upon the flower and upon the words that lay on the stone and he blinked slowly, carefully, as though trying to understand what they meant. I wondered that one with eyes so dead could see the words, but perhaps he did not.

He reached out to the flower at my feet and pulled it up. Its delicate beauty vanished in a moment and he held a gray blossom in his palm. His face opened somewhat in astonishment, then closed as he laid the flower back at my feet. Without a word, he turned and walked back into his house, and his door and all the others that remained open shut against the small remains of my laugh and the tiny petals of the gray flower.

I met the eyes of the old woman, and found their gentle spark fading. "He does not need your gift yet," she whispered softly, but I did not understand. I tried to force a laugh, but it would not come. The cold crept up my limbs, tendrils reaching once again from the stones beneath my feet to root me to the spot. My spirit cried out for Vadija, but still I heard nothing until at last, I grew angry with cold and loss.

I threw my head back and I howled her name out upon the wind that carried no more words. Once more, it dashed my voice upon the walls and flung it at the city gates at the far end of the street. Wearily, they swung open, but I could see no one standing outside, waiting to be swallowed by the city.

Quickly, I grabbed the old woman's hands and marched down the street pulling her unresisting behind me. If Vadija would not come to me, then I would wait for her at the city gates until she emerged. So said the voice of my anger as it buzzed and crackled around my ears. How dared she do this to me, dragging me from hearth and home to this place? The despair that I had left with the telling of my tale began to return, but I fought it until we reached the gates.

Here, the woman stopped and would go no further. "I can't leave."

The whisper made me pause in my headlong rush to leave the city behind me. "Why not?" I demanded as I bathed my eyes in view of the lands beyond the city gate.

"Because I built this place, I and all the others. It is part of us and we of it. I must stay and help those who want to leave weave tales of their own. There is nothing for me there," she gestured at the lands outside. In my anger and my astonishment, I threw back my head and I laughed, a harsh noise in that quiet place.

She flinched away from the brittle hardness of the sound that dashed like ice on the wind, tinkling against the stone walls and shattering. For a moment, I was tall and lean and mysterious, as it was said a talespinner should be. My laugh rose until bitter tears flowed down my cheeks and I sought outside for the words that would break the stone walls, for I wanted to succeed in my anger where Vadija had not in her merriment.

"Please don't." I barely heard her speak, but it was enough. I stopped laughing and looked at her. Then I was short and round, though not as merry and frank as I had been since I began to follow Vadija. The old woman stood before me, thin shoulders bowed with the weight of the city's grief, but still with a little light in her eyes for those who could see it. Now I began to understand. I knew where Vadija came from. With a small shove, the woman pushed me outside the city gates and backed away from them as they began to close once more, sealing her in.

The lands beyond called me, their words caressing my face and pulling me back to them, but I stood instead for a time looking upon the walls of Laith of the Sorrows. As I stood my laugh grew strong within me, filling me with tales, and I could feel myself grow with them until I was rounder and taller than I had been before I came to here.

I thought about my children and my husband and the man with the dead eyes and I wept then, the tears pouring down my cheeks in a steady stream until a small creek flowed away from my feet. Tiny flowers sprang up against the walls of the city and I laughed once more, even in my sorrow, and I grew no smaller.

Long I sat and thought about what had been and what could be until I looked to the lands beyond the city. I thought of a funny story that Puar the moneylender had told me, a simple tale unworthy of a talespinner, but with a light of its own. I thought too of the old woman with her listening eyes and of what she had asked. After a while, I knew that I didn't need to see Vadija anymore. I went away then without loosening my merriment against the grim walls.

My laugh went on before me on the wind, whipping away to ring around the chimneys of small farms and knocking on the doors of tyrants. But always it went ahead, never behind to the city that I left. For it was said that even Vadija the Merry could not lift the sorrows from Laith. So it was said and so it would be.

❧❧❧

# BIOGRAPHY

CATHERINE LUNDOFF IS A TRANSPLANTED Brooklynite who lives in scenic Minnesota with her wife, bookbinder and conservator Jana Pullman, and their cats, the latter of whom are ostensibly Egyptian in origin. In former lives, she was an archaeologist and a bookstore owner, though not at the same time. These days, she does arcane things with computer software at large companies and hangs out at science fiction conventions.

Her recent works include short stories in *The Mammoth Book of the Adventures of Professor Moriarty*, *The Mammoth Book of Jack the Ripper Stories, Respectable Horror* and *Tales of the Unanticipated*, and essays in *Nightmare Magazine: Queers Destroy Horror Special Issue* and *SF Signal*. Her books include *Silver Moon* and *A Day at the Inn, a Night at the Palace and Other Stories* and the Goldie Award-winning collections *Crave* and *Night's Kiss*. She has also co-edited or edited two anthologies: *Hellebore and Rue: Tales of Queer Women and Magic* (with JoSelle Vanderhooft) and the Spectrum Award-winning anthology *Haunted Hearths and Sapphic Shades: Lesbian Ghost Stories*. She sometimes teaches writing classes at The Loft Literary Center in Minneapolis and elsewhere.

Website
**www.catherinelundoff.com**

# ABOUT QUEEN OF SWORDS PRESS

Queen of Swords is a new independent small press specializing in swashbuckling tales of derring-do, bold new adventures in time and space, mysterious stories of the occult and arcane and fantastical tales of people and lands far and near.

Visit us online at **www.queenofswordspress.com** and sign up for our mailing list to get notified about upcoming releases and offers. Or follow us on Facebook at the Queen of Swords Press page so you don't miss any press news.

If you have a moment, the author would appreciate you taking the time to leave a review for this book at Goodreads, your blog, or on the site you purchased it from.

Thank you for your assistance and your support of our authors.

www.ingramcontent.com/pod-product-compliance
Lightning Source LLC
Chambersburg PA
CBHW070500120726
47910CB00003B/1074